THE DIST TRAVELLED

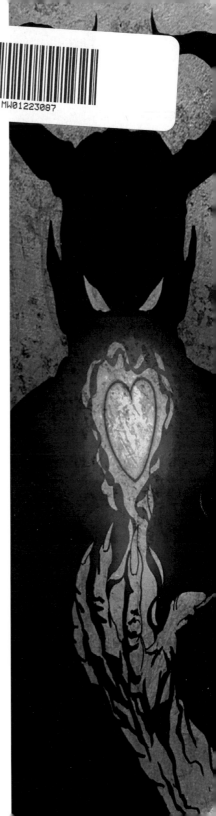

THE DISTANCE TRAVELLED
by Brett Alexander Savory
has been published in an edition
of 400 copies
offered for sale
in the following manner:

Three hundred signed & numbered,
limited edition trade paperbacks.

One hundred signed & numbered,
limited edition hardcovers.

NUMBER: _____

BRETT ALEXANDER SAVORY

THE DISTANCE TRAVELLED

A NOVEL BY

BRETT ALEXANDER SAVORY

THE DISTANCE TRAVELLED

NECRO PUBLICATIONS
2006

first hardcover edition
THE DISTANCE TRAVELLED

The Distance Travelled © 2006 by Brett Alexander Savory

cover art © 2006 Homeros Gilani

interior art © 2006 Travis Anthony Soumis

this edition March 2006 © Necro Publications

book design & typesetting:
David G. Barnett
faT caT Design
PO BOX 540298
Orlando, FL 32854-0298

assistant editors:
Amanda Baird
John Everson
Jeff Funk
C. Dennis Moore

a Necro Publication
PO Box 540298
Orlando, FL 32854-0298

hardcover
ISBN: 1-889186-61-9

trade paperback
ISBN: 1-889186-62-7

Printed by
Publishers' Graphics
Carol Stream, IL

Dedication

to my wife, Sandra Kasturi
best of all possible monkeys

Acknowledgments

Jason Taniguchi, creator of Yoniga—not to mention Satan's therapist
My agent, Steve Calcutt of the Anubis Literary Agency
Robbie and Billy, my brothers in Diablo Red
Bob Boyczuk, King of NHL '06
Weedman and Bunny
China Tom Miéville
Mum and Don
Pa and Sis
Eyean
Kel
et
al

When the pig comes crashing through my kitchen window, I'm not sure what to think.

I mean, dig: There I am just hanging out, eating some Boo Berry, waiting for the afternoon rack session (hoping that Stanson and Jonesy are on duty 'cause they usually give me a break—Barnes and Salinger always stretch me till they hear ligaments tear and sockets pop), when lo, what's this flying through my window? A big, fat, porcine letter bomb.

I jump out of my chair and run over to the window to try to get a look at the bastards who launched it, but by the time I get there, all that remain are the shattered window—bits still dropping off, tinkling in the post-apigalyptic silence—flames belching from the Lake of Sorrow (I have a villa on the waterfront), and smoking brimstone as far as the eye can see.

The pig scrambles to its feet and dashes into my living room, squealing all the way. I decide to abandon my Boo Berry in favour of trying to catch its dirty pig ass, and so stomp along after it. That's when my talking thermometer goes off:

"The indoor temperature is four billion, one million, six hundred and fifty-two thousand, four hundred and twenty-one point seven degrees Celsius. The outdoor temperature is four billion, nine million, seven hundred and sixty-three thousand, five hundred and seventy-six point eight degrees Celsius."

Great. A heat wave and I have to chase this pig around my house. *And* I've a racking to attend in forty-five minutes.

THE DISTANCE TRAVELLED

"Come here, ya little porker!" I shout, trudging into the living room, glancing about for his little pigtail as he perhaps shuffles behind the TV or tries to squeeze under the coffee table. Nothing.

I have to seal up this window soon, or I'll bake. The A/C units down here are pretty powerful, but they can only take so much. I glance around again, feeling the heat from the window more with each second.

"Ah, forget it," I grumble, and head for the basement to see what I have to seal the pig point-of-entry.

By the time I get back upstairs with the sheet metal, the pig is on his last spoonful of Boo Berry.

Cheeky little fucker.

«« — »»

So.

Sheet metal in hand and pig in the oven (little bugger put up a good fight—tried poking one of my eyes out with that spoon), I'm determined to deter further piggings, so on the sheet metal, I paint a big pig's head in a circle with a diagonal line crossing through it, the words

NO PIGS!

in big, black letters underneath it.

Once outside, even with my protective clothes on, I feel the heat of the lake punch me like a fist.

The Lake of Sorrows belches up a great gout of lava and fire, and I have to duck and cover from the shower as it rains down on my house. Luckily none of it falls through the new hole. I have to get that metal up before I lose my whole place, like I've already lost a window and a perfectly delicious bowl of Boo Berry.

Up goes the sheet metal. I drill small holes through the brick, then grab the cordless screwdriver and in go one, two thick screws. Great. Marvellous. I put the third screw on the end of the driver…

And hear an engine.

Louder…louder, still.

I hear hooting and hollering as the vehicle comes into view— a dune buggy. The driver points and laughs at me. His buddies spot me and join in the fun. As they get closer, the driver squints, reading the writing on the sheet metal. He bursts into more raucous laughter and floors the buggy. A guy in back stands up,

reveals one arm holding a short rope. Lifting his arm higher reveals the pig attached to the rope. It looks terrified and squeals above their laughter.

With a grunt, the guy swings the pig around his head several times, lasso-style—cowboys from Hell.

I hold up my hands and scream, "No pigs!" But it's too late. I duck. The pig crashes through the unscrewed bottom half of the sheet metal, and I hear it snorting all the way across my kitchen floor, then thudding against the wall and scrambling off to hide.

"Cock*suckers!*" I roar, and throw my screwdriver at them. It whistles over their heads and melts into the lake. I quickly reach down and grab my drill, pull back and let fly. Still plugged in, extension cord in tow (yes, Hell has electricity; the Amish were right), the cord reaches its limit and snaps from the outlet. It whips back and collides with the forehead of the still-standing pig-thrower in the back seat. His laughter stops and he grunts as his body tumbles backward out of the car. He lands in a cloud of dust near the shore of the lake.

The dune buggy speeds off around the corner, laughter from the remaining pig hooligans drifting back to their unfortunate comrade.

13

Grinning madly, I cross the street and grab the pig-tossing bastard by the back of his leather jacket. Yeah, these guys are real cool. No protective outerwear for them. They're mean mother-fuckers, tossing farm animals through people's windows, then driving away, laughing in their cute little dune buggy.

"Come on, shithead, you're going to find that pig you just threw in my house. And now that my screwdriver's gone, you're going to hammer these last two screws in with your face."

He groans, mutters some obscenity at me.

I drag him to my 'window' through the dirt and lava, drop him, kick him hard in the gut so he can't run away, bend and yank out the sheet metal from the inside of the house, straighten it as best I can, kick the bastard again, and pull him to his feet.

With one hand, I place a screw into the third hole I'd drilled; with the other, I pound PigBoy's forehead into it.

"You like that?" I ask him.

No reply.

Soon enough, the screw is driven all the way in, and we're onto the fourth and final one in no time. Blood cascades down the boy's face and, for the last few knocks of the final screw, he's unconscious.

Should I leave him out here to bake? Maybe just toss him in the lake and watch him dissolve?

THE DISTANCE TRAVELLED

No, he still has to find the pig that's loose in my house—no doubt munching on my Wheaties by now—and besides, I have some questions for him. For example, where are they getting these pigs from? They must be coming from Upside (Hell contains precisely zero animals), but how? And if there *is* this opening to the natural world, why are people only grabbing pigs?

I drag PigBoy into my house, put the coffeepot on, and wait for him to wake up.

his is how I got here:

Driving on a country road. Nothing but farmland for miles and miles. Gravel spluttering and popping in my wheel wells. Hot day. Not hot as Hell, because I now know how hot Hell can get, but still pretty brutal.

Zoning. Just staring ahead at the heat-shimmering trees to either side of me. Not even sleepy, just caught in that nowhere-land of hazy days and even hazier thoughts.

In my peripheral, a flash of orange and white.

Then a crunch, and the car lifts on the right side, like I'd just barrelled over a speed bump.

My heart slams in my chest. Sweat pops out on my forehead. I cram on the brakes. A plume of dirt rises behind me. The car stops.

In the rearview mirror, a woman—partially obscured by the cloud of dust I've created—runs to the edge of the road. She kneels. Screams once.

I open the door, get out of the car, walk toward the kneeling woman and her scream. The dust clears more with every step I take, and I see what she is kneeling over.

White shorts. Orange shirt. Splashes of dark red across them.

It is a young girl. She does not move.

The woman screams again, this time much longer. I can't tell if I'm breathing anymore. I just stand there in the road and blink quickly, maybe waiting to wake up.

THE DISTANCE TRAVELLED

I hear a screen door slam, then gravel crunching, look up, see a man with a shotgun. Wet eyes. Determination in his step. He stops in front of me, plants his feet. Two giant oaks rooted in the ground. He takes one deep breath, raises the barrel.

I wonder if he was perhaps at the window, watching his daughter and wife play outside, maybe thinking about how good his life is, how lucky a man he is to have this wonderful family.

Life is like this, I think, my heart settling, slowing. *For both of us, friend. It steals things when we're not looking.*

And then I am incapable of thinking anything at all, because my face has been blasted through the back of my skull.

When I open my eyes—these eyes that should no longer open, in my skull that should no longer be anything but splinters—I am in a house. Not a house I've ever been in before. Someone else's house.

But now mine.

Now and forever.

It's hot. Hot as Hell.

I immediately start sweating.

3

My talking thermometer tells me it's getting even hotter out. The sheet metal helps, but it's still getting mighty toasty in my kitchen.

PigBoy slumps in a chair in my kitchen and mutters things every once in awhile. Things about sex, chocolate, staples, and bunnies. I don't want to know.

I sip from my mug and think about how I'd like to bash this kid's head against my wall again.

You know, they should really have some sort of rehab program down here. I mean, how do they expect Hell to ever improve when they just leave us all to our own devices? No wonder folks have taken to throwing farm animals through innocent folks' windows. That's the level of frustration we have down here.

PigBoy comes around slowly, asks where he is. I kick out a foot and topple him from his chair, onto my kitchen floor.

"Rise and shine, chump. You're going to talk to me, and you're not going to give me any bullshit about how you can't remember stuff because I bashed your cranium against a brick wall."

I look down at myself and notice I've spilled coffee on my 'Remember, kids, Satan loves you!' T-shirt. I hear squealing and things getting knocked over in my living room. Not a good day, all told. Not a good day at all. I'm really starting to get mad.

I stand up and walk over to the kid, put a foot on his throat, watch his face turn all the colours of the spectrum. "Now, I don't know who else you've 'pigged,' but this time you chose the wrong house.

"I have a rack session at three that I don't plan to be late for, so you're going to answer some questions, then, before I leave, you're going to catch that pig you threw in here, got it?"

He twitches a little. Good enough.

I release my foot from his throat and he gasps for air, goes backward through his colour scheme.

I sip my coffee again, return to my chair, and watch PigBoy get slowly to his feet, wavering a little. Blood is caked on his hair and face. He has beady little weasel eyes, black as soot, and blond, matted hair. Angular features contrast with his pug nose.

Yet something about him makes me soften my anger toward him. Maybe it's the way he fidgets with the zipper on his leather coat, like the proverbial little boy caught with his hand in the cookie jar.

I furrow my brow and open my mouth to speak. That's when the second pig-of-the-day trundles out of the living room, apparently having had enough fun for now smashing up everything.

The kid—not even looking in the pig's direction, eyes still stuck to his zipper—draws a pistol from his belt and fires. The pig squeals once, falls on its side, dead.

PigBoy looks back to me. "Okay, so what are your questions?"

I have to give it to him. The kid has style.

«« — »»

We pop the second pig in my oven—a tight fit, to be sure, but we manage. I let him clean his face, but the gash in his forehead is nasty and keeps reopening whenever he wrinkles his brow or makes any sort of expression involving the top half of his face. I give him a wet cloth to keep on hand for soaking up the blood.

"So why pigs?" I ask.

"Dunno," says PigBoy. "That's what falls out of the hole, so that's what we throw." He sips his java, grimaces. "Irish Cream?"

"Yes," I say.

"Thought so." He puts the cup down and fiddles some more with his zipper.

Ignoring the slight to my choice of coffee, I push on. "So you just grabbed some and started chucking them through peoples' kitchen windows?"

"Yup. Got any cookies?"

"No."

PigBoy flares his nostrils, but keeps quiet.

"How many did you get?"

The pigs crackle in the oven. The kitchen smells good.

"A bunch. Been back a few times to reload."

I nod, gulp the rest of my java, eye the pot.

"Any idea where they learned to eat with proper kitchen utensils, PigBoy?"

He looks up from his zipper. "Huh?"

"Yeah, the first one you threw finished off my last bowl of Boo Berry before I caught it."

He blinks. "Rough, man. That sucks."

I nod again. I chalk the pig's manners (and the fact that it didn't just immediately flash-fry to crispy bacon) up to *Star Trek* logic—you know, when the writers can't think of a decent explanation for something that makes no real sense:

But Captain, where did the pig learn to eat with a spoon?

It must have been his transference from Upside to Hell, Spock.

Ah, of course, the Transference Anomaly.

More crackling and popping of flesh and fats from the oven.

"Smells damn fine," says PigBoy, inhaling deeply.

"So why didn't you shoot me instead of the pig?" I ask.

"You want me to shoot you?"

"Well, not particularly. But you could have and gotten away."

The thought is sobering. He *could* very easily have just popped me, slowed me down at least a few seconds, and taken off. I'm such an idiot. Why didn't I frisk him?

I rise from my seat, grab the coffeepot, tip the dregs into my mug, lift it to my face, close my eyes, inhale deeply. The steam clears my mind. I sip and swallow, allowing the liquid to funnel through my mouth, slide across my teeth, slither down my throat. I don't care what anyone says, Irish Cream rules.

"No idea why I corked the pig and not you," he says. "Just didn't occur to me, I guess."

"What's your name?" I ask.

"Doesn't matter," he says, "I like what you call me better, anyhow."

I nod. Fair enough.

Two-thirty-five. Almost time for my rack session.

"You know who's on rack duty today?" I ask.

"No idea," PigBoy answers.

"Damn," I whisper.

Better not be Barnes and Salinger, that's all I know. Stanson

19

and Jonesy are as gentle as they can be about the whole business, but Barnes and Salinger are just downright nasty. Like being tortured isn't already uncomfortable enough, they have to call you names and shove you onto the rack and all sorts of other crap that just makes the whole experience intolerable.

Looking at PigBoy, smelling the pigs in my oven, and imagining the joy of spending the day at my natural height of 6' 2", I decide right then and there that I'm playing hooky. Fuck Barnes and fuck Salinger and fuck The Big Red Fella, too. It's time to eat some pig, then pop over to this mysterious hole to Upside to see what's what.

20

otta fuel up my El Camino, though, first. Yeah, I
know—cool-ass car, no doubt. But before you
attribute it to my great taste, I have to come clean
and say that the house's previous occupant left it
here. Where did said occupant go, and why did he
leave behind such a badass set of wheels? Your guess is as good
as mine…but after being here for as long as I have, your guess,
I'm sure, is likely more forgiving than mine.

Fuel, then. Perhaps here in Hell we melt down corpses for
fuel, eh? Or maybe we just tap the blood from folks' veins and
cruise around on that? If only it were so fanciful. No, we just go
to the gas station, like folks do Upside.

Pigs in our bellies, the fires of the Sorrow licking and lapping
at our tires as we speed along the hard-packed dirt shore, PigBoy
and I don't speak, but listen instead to the she-bop sounds of a
Cyndi Lauper cover band coming from the tape deck. PigBoy
taps his foot to the beat, staring straight ahead. I drum my fingers
on the steering wheel. Just two badass motherfuckers from Hell
cruising in a Camino, grooving to cheesy '80s pop rock.

It doesn't get much better than this.

As you might expect, the gas stations are located a good distance from the ever-erupting lake, so I take the side road that
branches off from the lakeshore (the sign stuck into the dirt reads:
GUS & TOM'S GAS—COME FETCH IT), and follow it around
a bend where the station hides behind a massive outcropping of

rock. Sometimes the pumps are working, sometimes not, so at one point Gus decided to put up a second sign (which he'd stolen from the motel down the road) that told you whether or not they were working.

I pull the Camino up to the pumps and cut the engine. The VACANCY sign glows red, barely visible against the backdrop of natural red expanse. The best way to tell if it's on is just to look for the preceding NO. If it's not lit, you're in luck.

PigBoy continues tapping his foot when the engine flutters off and the music cuts out. I glance at him, then at his foot. He stops, fiddles with his zipper.

I get out of the car, shrug out of my protective gear, reach in, and chuck it in the back seat. Out here, away from the lake, it's not so bad. And besides, if PigBoy can endure it, so can I.

I look around for Gus but see nothing, no movement inside the station.

"Gus!" I bellow, and hear the lake far to my back belch up another great gout of steam and lava, the faint sprinkle as its offspring hits the dirt shore. "Gus, get out here; I haven't got all day!"

Nothing.

Where could he be? Surely those crumbling bones of his couldn't take him far enough away to get out of earshot.

"GUS!!"

I see him stand up in the window of the station. He must've been lying on the ratty old couch, which is right next to his rusty old desk. Not many positive adjectives can be employed to describe things associated with Gus, I'm afraid.

He shuffles to the door and tries to open it with all the prowess of a little kid just big enough to reach the handle. He keeps losing his grip, the bell hanging above chiming with every abortive attempt.

Finally, he manages to sustain a grip on it and he shuffles through. Now it's time for the Great Journey—the two-minute marathon across to the pumps. I decide to sit in the car and have a smoke.

"PigBoy, you smoke?"

"Yup," he says, watching Gus through the passenger-side window, proffering his pack to me. "He always move that slow?"

"Actually," I say, pushing in the Camino's lighter, taking the topmost cigarette from PigBoy's pack, "he's moving rather quickly today. Sometimes he falls down. That's when you can go home, cook and eat your lunch, and come back before he gets here."

The lighter pops out.

And by now, you'll be wondering where the Tom of "Gus and Tom's Gas" is. Tom is Gus's business partner—more of a silent partner, really, though not because he doesn't do anything around the station, but mainly 'cause Tom doesn't talk much. Where Gus'll about jaw your ear off, old Tom China would just as soon stare at a passing snake and blow spit bubbles at it than string more than five words together into a coherent thought. Tom'll be around here somewhere, maybe fixing Jimmy Johnson's monster truck, or young Miss Appleton's decrepit '73 Mustang. Our Tom may not be the brightest bulb in the box, but he certainly knows a fine-looking woman when he sees one.

Gus—now almost halfway to the pumps (surely a record)—stumbles, nearly falls, and rights himself once again. His overalls are black. Folks around here speculate that there aren't even any actual threads anymore under all the oil and grease.

A fella can't look at old Gus for too long. I won't go into detail, but try to imagine a corpse mid-way between fresh death and clean, white bones—that's Gus. When he 'walks,' it looks like he's held together by nothing more substantial than Scotch tape.

"So how did you and your buddies find this little hole into Upside, anyway?" I ask PigBoy, exhaling smoke.

23

PigBoy's little piggy nose twitches. "Do you mind not blowing smoke in my face?"

"Huh?" I'd gotten the cigarette from *him*, remember.

"Yeah, that death you're sucking into yourself—that shit. Keep it away from me."

"You don't smoke?" I ask, confused.

"Would I ask you to keep it away from me if I did?"

I blink a few times, shake my head, decide to let it rest. "Okay, whatever."

"Thank you."

Gus is nearly to us now, but I have a good half-minute or so left to kill, I figure. "So, how'd ya find the hole?"

"This guy named Dante found it."

"*The* Dante?"

"No, just *a* Dante. Do I look like the kinda guy Aligheri would hang out with? Come on."

He has a point.

"Okay, so this Dante dude found the hole. How'd he do it?"

"By accident. We—"

Gus suddenly thrusts his head in the passenger-side window, his raspy, dead-leaf voice cutting PigBoy off. "You tryin' ta git us all killed!?" he barks at me.

THE DISTANCE TRAVELLED

Enter: Gus Henry Vaughan, dilapidated proprietor of the local pumps.

"What's your problem, Gus? Calm down," I say, flicking some ash out my window.

"'Calm down,' he says! You know where you are, boy?" Gus bellows, glaring at the smoke in my hand, sloppy eyes wet and glassy. "Yer at a GAS STATION, that's where!" His jaw cracks on the last word and nearly falls off. He snicks it back into place and rattles his head around to settle it straight.

PigBoy looks at me with smug satisfaction.

Fucking non-smokers.

"Fine," I say, butting the cigarette out in the car's ashtray. "Happy, you old bitch?"

Gus closes his eyes and nods off. Falls completely asleep.

"GUS!" I shout.

"Huh!?" He wakes up with a start and bashes his noggin off the inside of the roof. This time his jaw *does* fall off, right into PigBoy's lap.

"Shit!" PigBoy yelps, squirming in the seat. "Pick it up! Get it offa me!"

24

Gus reaches down and picks up his jaw; maggots fall off the edge of the passenger seat, squiggle on the floor. In a panic, PigBoy leans back quickly and brushes the rest of the vermin onto the others, stomps them to mush.

"Gas?" Gus asks, after securing his jaw back into place.

"Yep," I say. "Fill 'er up." PigBoy keeps stomping at the maggots.

"Yeah, you're real tough, Piggy."

He stops driving his foot into the floor, looks at me, back still arched against the seat. "Fuck you." He slides down the seat and fiddles with his zipper again. I try to engage him in conversation, asking him to finish his story about Dante and the hole to Upside, but he keeps silent, won't even look at me anymore.

So sensitive. My, my.

Then it suddenly hits me.

"You know what?" I say. "I'm already sick of your shit and I've barely known you an hour. First, you whine that I'm blowing smoke in your face from a cigarette that *you* gave me. Then you bitch about Gus's maggoty jawbone like it's *his* fault he's rotting and can't stay awake for more than twenty minutes at a stretch, and that he's so old his body parts sometimes trail after him like strung-up cans on a wedding car. You throw a smelly pig through my window and act like it's nothing—not even a proper apology from your sorry ass when I *could* very well have just tossed you into the lake. You *do* realize where we are, right? Hell. Aitch Ee Double Hockey Sticks. You don't get here by being a goddamn whiner."

His eyes are locked to mine, lips pressed tight to each other, hermetically sealed.

Outside, Gus finishes pumping the gas, switches the NO portion of the motel sign on—we got the last full tank. He leans in the passenger-side window again, this time holding his jaw on with one hand and glaring at PigBoy. "Here, look, ya happy, young'n?" he wheezes. "I'ma holdin' myself together fer ya. Gods forbid I might leave a piece o' myself behind in yer lovely automobile! What would the ladies think, eh!?" He chuckles, coughs up something black and squirming, spits it out into his hand, examines it, pops it back into his mouth, and swallows.

PigBoy doesn't even acknowledge his presence. His eyes are intent on mine. I decide to call him out.

"You're from Upside, aren't you?"

Silence.

"You gonna pay me, ya cheap bastards?" Gus asks, oblivious to the tension in the car.

"Answer me, PigBoy."

A beat, then his eyes finally drop. "My name's Aaron."

"Uh-huh."

Back to fiddling with his zipper, but this time he talks as well. "I came after them," he said, his voice cracking.

I dip into my wallet, extract a Canadian fifty. The Canadian dollar is Hell's official currency. Rumour has it The Big Red Fella adopted it simply because it was 'pretty.'

I've come to form the opinion over the years that the reason no one ever sees The Big Red Fella is that if anyone ever did, they'd see that he was just a big, red-skinned freak, and we'd all band together to kick his fruity little ass. So he stays hidden, giving his oh-so-dark commands from the security of whatever pink, frilly throne he has deemed worthy to squeeze his fat, fiery butt into.

Gus snatches the red bill from my fingers and stands up, bashing his head once again. Pulling out properly and straightening up with enough spine cracking to constitute a twenty-one-gun salute, he turns around muttering curses about the sad state of Hell to let such a long-standing member as himself be left to such decrepitude of mind and body.

Poor old Gus. You have to feel sorry for him.

"Gus!" I shout after him, trying to think of something nice to say to leave the exchange on a better foot.

He turns around. "Yuh?"

"Where's old Tom? Haven't seen him in a while." I'm smiling so hard it hurts. Gus is a good guy...not to mention the co-owner of the only gas station in my area. "Sure would like to shoot the shit with him—been too long."

Gus just stares at me.

"You *want* to talk to Tom? You actually *want* to? What's gotten into you, boy? You hit yer head?"

"Nah, I just wanna, uh..." My voice cracks and trails off. "Just wanna...see what he's up to, you know?"

Gus squints, genuinely concerned. He looks like he's trying to work out whether I'm fucking with him or not. As a general rule, most folks turn around and walk the opposite way when Tom comes out for one of his rare visits with the customers. But I don't mind him much. He's big, yeah, and scary as all get-out when he gets mad, and maybe he doesn't talk about things the way most people do, sure, but what the fuck, you know? He's got an eye for the ladies, and that's a subject I can wax on about for hours.

26

I think Tom and I were about the most desperate men in Hell—until he started seeing his little Mustang Sally, Miss Appleton. Up to then, though, neither of us had been on a date in more years than I care to recall. Me because I'm intensely impatient, incredibly overbearing, stubborn as molasses, and one *mean* motherfuck of a drunk. Tom because he's a ten-foot-tall demonic HellRat.

We all have our crosses to bear.

"Well, alright, I guess," Gus eventually says, tentatively. A couple of small bones fall off him and drop to the dirt while he stands in indecision. "I'll go see if he's around."

As Gus staggers away, I turn back to PigBoy. Tears glisten on his eyelids.

"Listen, Aaron—"

"Please call me PigBoy. I told you I like that name better," he says to his zipper quietly. He looks up at me. "Okay?"

"Alright, man, whatever you want."

He nods and bends his head down again.

"What, exactly, did you come down here for? Were they your pigs they stole or something?" I ask.

He looks up, hitches a sob, looks out the window behind me, watches the far-off lake erupt and rain lava down. I know by the look in his eye that this is about something more than just pigs.

"They took my sister," he says, and closes his eyes.

«« — »»

"Can I have one of those smokes?" PigBoy says.

I knock the pack against the dashboard, pluck one free, hand it to him. "Don't inhale too deeply the first time, alright?"

He nods, gives me this 'fuck you, I know what I'm doing' look, lights up, pulls on the cigarette like he's sucking back his last breath of oxygen, then heaves forward in the seat, spluttering and hacking.

I grin, say, "Told you, tough guy. Maybe next time—"

And then there's a giant rat's head next to my window. "Hey, Stu. See me?" it says in a low, gravelly voice.

"Tom China," I say. "As I live and breathe. Or, well, as I *used* to live and breathe. Whatever. Fucking Tom China."

The enormous head withdraws and all I see are his cranium-sized kneecaps, and a bit of his five-foot-long legs. I try opening the car door, big smile on my face. I'm happy to see old Tom, but the big oaf won't move his 500-pound carcass out of my way so I can step out of the car.

"Tom," I say, pushing the car door gently against his kneecaps, give him a couple soft nudges. "Dude, I can't get out. Step back a little…"

Tom doesn't budge.

27

After a couple more gentle nudges, I resort to a good, solid crack against Tom's kneecaps, and he finally lumbers back one full step.

Getting out, closing my door, and looking up, it seems like Tom's gotten even taller since the last time I saw him. It must be obvious that I'm thinking this 'cause Tom peers down at me with his beady little eyes, says, "Eleven feet now."

"Goddamn," I say. I'd forgotten.

Tom's disease.

"Don't look sad," he says. "Time is fun. Have it."

"You still feeling okay, Tom? No pain?"

Tom blinks his small black eyes at me, tries to smile big, but all he can manage is a lopsided grin that slips off his face as soon as the words are out. "No pain, Stu. No pain."

Yeah, sure, I think, but decide to let it go. Big Tom doesn't need me bringing him down today.

"So you seen Miss Appleton lately, Tommy?" I ask, all sunshine and puffy white clouds.

Tom visibly brightens. He shuffles a little from foot to foot, and if I didn't know better, I'd say the big galoot is blushing.

The Distance Travelled

"Car," he says, and giggles a little—a strange sound coming from an eleven-foot monster. "Car and car and car and…girl," he says, chuckles to himself, and punches me lightly in the shoulder.

"What a ladies man!" I shout, then reach up and punch big Tom in the ribs.

"Laaaadiiies!" Tom shouts, and we both set to giggling, poking and wrestling each other through the laughter.

"Ladies, indeed, Tommy. Ladies, indeed," I say, and we sober up some, exchange what I think of as a meaningful look, and Tom turns around and lumbers back through the gas station's front door.

I watch him go, wondering how much time he's got left.

Human beings down here don't die. Not easily anyway. Not unless our heads have been crushed to so much pulp, or our bodies split into several quivering pieces. We're suckers for that 'everlasting pain and eternal damnation' spiel. If we're still basically in one piece, we heal. But for Tom and the few other HellRats that still live here, they're homegrown, and they can die of things like disease or old age, like we do Upside.

The diseases might be different, but it's the same result.

I open my car door, get in slowly, close it, look over at PigBoy.

"Big fucker," he says, and fiddles with his zipper.

"Yeah. Big fucker," I say.

I turn the key in the ignition.

5

e drive farther on, away from the lake, eruptions from that direction becoming ever more distant until soon they're inaudible. Turns out PigBoy memorized the path back to the hole to Upside after the pig thieves took him in as one of their own.

"So where did you tell them you were from?" I ask, incredulous. I mean, these kids aren't rocket scientists, I know, but surely they can tell a dead Hell-dweller from an Upsider.

"Oh, they know I'm from Upside, but they don't care. I got them pigs to throw; that's all they care about."

"So they knew you were from the farm, right?"

"Nah, they just know I'm an Upsider. I told them I was stealing pigs myself from that very same farm for kicks, so I might as well steal some for them, too. Told 'em I fell through the hole during a midnight raid, and that's how I wound up down here. They told me they wanted the pigs to throw through people's windows. Don't ask me why. I said it sounded like fun, and that I was just a weaseling little thief from Upside, anyway, so could I join them, since I'd nothing to keep me there, anyway.

"They said they'd take me in if I supplied them with more pigs to throw. I agreed and that was that."

"Weird as shit, man."

PigBoy nods.

"I mean, what's the deal with this porcine pastime, anyway?

What's so cool about smashing folks' windows in with farm animals?"

"From what I understand," PigBoy continues, tossing his pack of smokes to me, "—here, you have them; I was just using them as a prop, anyway, to make me look 'cool'—Dante was driving back from a thumb-screwing, happened to look up the rock face where the hole is, and noticed a pig fall out of mid-air, topple into the flame pit below. He went to check it out, climbed all the way up these rock-hewn stairs and waited for another one to plop out. About two hours later, just when he thought he must have imagined it, one did, and it, too, toppled into the flame pit. So he reached his hand up into the place where he'd seen the pigs fall from and got nipped by another pig. Figuring this was the source, he went to get his buddies. Shortly after that, I fell down the hole.

"See, I'd seen this huge guy make off with my sister after she got off the school bus that day. She was walking toward the house, just like always, the bus rumbling away in the distance, when a dude darted out from the side of the barn and snatched her up. I ran out of the house, down our back porch steps, and to the barn where I'd seen him take her. I was poking around in the grain sacks and hay, a big, heavy log in my hands, ready to beat the bastard senseless, when I fell through the hole. Dante and his buddies found me unconscious on the rock ledge.

"When I woke up, I saw that none of these guys were big enough to be the guy that grabbed my sister, so I told them my little fib, they boosted me back up into the hole, I shoved some more pigs down, and we went a-piggin'."

"Jesus," I say. "Must be rich kids to throw away good meat like that. The only place you'd catch me throwing pigs—or any other edible animal, for that matter—is down my throat and into my belly."

"Yeah, they're rich," says PigBoy, watching the various torture blocks go by on either side of the car—hangings, brandings, stake burnings, rack sessions, eviscerations, decapitations, the whole nine yards. "One of them—Dante—is Barnes' kid. Barnes is the big fucker who stole my sister."

Now, Barnes, as you know, is not a particularly well-liked rack sessionist. He's probably the most sadistic one down here— more so than The Big Red Fella, I've heard. Not only is he one of the meanest buggers, he's also one of the most influential. Hell has its social classes, too, and they're not at all unlike Upside's.

And, of course, there's his buddy, Salinger. Oh so mysterious Salinger, with his single name. He makes a point of telling everyone he tortures that he has no first name. Like that makes him more evil or something.

Some of us call him Sally, just to piss him off.

As we drive past the torture blocks—windows down, hot wind blowing our hair—screams whip by as knives slice the meat off arms, legs, torsos; heat sears flesh; fire crisps hair, blisters bodies. I glance quickly to one side before whipping my eyes back around to the road—I've never developed the stomach for watching it, like so many do—and in that quick look, I lock eyes with the one guy I don't want to see today. The one guy I have an appointment with this afternoon. The one fucking guy I've *just* been talking about.

Now, I'm familiar with the expression "speak of the devil," but it's incredibly corny for that to apply down here, of all places. So I drive on, try to pretend I didn't see him.

Over the screams for mercy, the whines, the mewls, the roaring wall of sound that scars intense human suffering into the air itself, I hear the little shit's voice. Hear it like he's right in the car with me: *"StuAAAART!!"*

Salinger. His voice is high-pitched, sort of wheezy, and heavy with a London accent.

I sigh. Long and deep.

I know if I don't stop, when my next rack session rolls around he's going to stretch me till I break apart. And yeah, okay, I know, Upsiders don't have much of a frame of reference for that kind of pain, so let me tell you that it hurts like bloody hell.

I dig into the brakes with both feet. Red dust plumes behind me. The car stops. I hear Salinger's voice again. I turn my head in that direction, and there he is, about fifty feet back. He's got one hand in the air, waving at me, the other crammed inside someone's stomach, rooting around like he's lost his watch.

"Oy!" he roars over the wall of suffering. "Three o'clock, Stuart! Three. O. Fucking. Clock! Where d'you think you're goin', eh!?"

PigBoy turns toward me. "Stuart? Your name's *Stuart?*"

"My name's Stu," I say, a bristly little brush of defiance. "Just...Stu. Got it?"

PigBoy smirks and nods, turns around, looks out the windshield. "Well, whatever. We don't have time for this. You wanna see where those pigs are coming through, or don't you?"

"Yeah, I wanna see, but dude, if I don't go for my session now, Salinger'll flay me next time...slowly...and with, like, a fucking potato peeler or something. You never know what that sick bitch'll get up to." I shiver at the thought of it.

The Distance Travelled

I turn around in my seat, wave my hand and try to smile a little, so that Salinger can see I'm complying. He turns back to his work, digs around some more inside the twitching body on the rack beside him.

I put the car in reverse, start backing up. Some of the torture blocks are so close to the red-dirt road, you can smell the sweat of the victims. As I roll by one poor sod being hacked at with a cleaver, a spurt of blood splashes the side of my face. I decide it's time to roll up my window.

PigBoy shakes his head, pulls the gun from his waistband, holds it up for me to see. "Fine, then, we'll just straighten out this Salinger fuck and be on our way." He cocks the weapon.

"Put that thing away, you idiot!"

I put the brakes on again, crunching dirt. Salinger turns his bald head at the noise, squints to see what's going on.

"All shooting Salinger will do is piss him off. This isn't Upside," I say, eyeing the rearview mirror. "You can't just pull out a gun and blow people away down here. They won't die easily, dumbass. They might stumble and fall, and maybe even say 'ouch,' if you're lucky, but look around you—these people die in more and more horrific ways every day of their afterlives. And Salinger? Fucking *Salinger??* Gimme a break. You'd need a bloody tank—a really big, heavy bugger of a tank, with giant razor blades on its treads to even slow him down. He's like a cockroach—a thin, wiry, bald, merciless fucking war-machine cockroach. Okay? So just put the gun away."

PigBoy blinks at me, lowers his gun slowly, pops it into his waistband.

I pull the Camino off to the side of the road, kill the engine. I open my door, drop one foot out onto the flat, cracked ground that marks the beginning of the sprawling expanse of my neighbourhood torture blocks.

«« — »»

"Stuart!" Salinger bellows as PigBoy and I approach. He is up to his elbows in intestines. The reason he's yelling even though we're now standing only a few feet away is that the poor bugger whose intestines he's rummaging about in is screaming his face off. "You little shit, you weren't going to show, were you?"

Salinger is smiling so wide, it looks like his skull's about to crack.

"'Course I was," I mumble, look down the road in the direction I'd been heading. "I was just going to get some…uh…some, you know…" I wave ineffectually in the general direction of absolutely nothing.

"Yeah, yeah, whatever, Stuart. Save your breath. You'll need it for screaming soon enough. Who's your buddy?"

I glance over. "PigBoy," I say. "Fucker threw a pig at me."

Salinger stops what he's doing for a moment. The torturee resigns himself to whining and moaning quietly in the interim. Salinger fixes me in the eye, says, "You deserve to have pigs thrown at you." And then he goes back to work. The screeching resumes.

PigBoy goes back to zipper fiddling; I shift from foot to foot, watching Salinger yank out a spleen, a liver, and some other organs I can't readily identify.

"Uh, Salinger? Can we hurry this up a bit? PigBoy and I have some important business to attend to, you know?"

There's only one thing I hate more than pain, and that's *waiting* for pain.

Salinger pulls his hands out of the guy on the rack, leaving a giant hole gaping in his gut. He wipes his hands and arms off with a crisp, white towel. The stark red on the pristine white is for effect, I'm sure.

"Gotta go, have ya?" he says, and winks at the moaning tor-turee. The guy doesn't wink back. "Well, what's so bloody important that you thought you'd try to skip out on your appoint-ment, eh?"

33

Wiping. Smiling. Waiting.

I look at PigBoy, try to gauge his reaction. Is our destination something I shouldn't share with the friendly neighbourhood psycho—especially a psycho with strong ties to Barnes?

PigBoy notices my meaningful glance, but returns it with nothing I can read. So I just plunge on.

"Seems someone stole this guy's sister," I say. "Someone from down here."

To our left, another torturer grins impishly and impales a naked old man on a spear. The old man slides drearily down the wooden shaft, not returning any of the torturer's enthusiasm.

"From down here?" Salinger says, raises a bushy black eye-brow. "But there's no way *up* there, Stu. Can't steal what you can't get to."

"There's a hole," PigBoy says. "It's invisible, but it's there." He looks down at his boots. "I know, 'cause I came through it."

Salinger's eyes spark. He steps closer to PigBoy, sniffs the air. Steps closer still, takes a bigger sniff at him. "Ahhhh," he says. "An Upsider, eh? I haven't smelled Upside meat in so, so long...."

PigBoy wrinkles his nose at Salinger's proximity, the smell of blood and human suffering coming off him in waves. He goes for the gun in his waistband.

"Hold on now, whoa..." I reach over to ease his hand back into the waistband, as Salinger, eyes closed, lost in the scent of living flesh, sways from side to side, oblivious. I mouth the word 'no' to PigBoy.

"Fucking 'ell, that's nice," Salinger whispers.

PigBoy endures this olfactory probe, tight-lipped.

After a few more moments of deep inhalation, Salinger finally steps back a pace, opens his eyes slowly. "So," he says, his voice huskier than before. "This hole, then. Where is it?"

There's a shift in Salinger's demeanor and, quite suddenly, he loses the glaze in his eyes, and the glint returns. Sharp. Honed attention. And even though I don't know where the hole is, I know this is where the information has to stop.

"Can't tell you, Sally. Top secret," I say, then smile the way he smiles—all lips, no teeth—and he doesn't take to that too kindly at all.

34

A wiry arm whips out and snakes around my throat, choking me. Since I don't need to breathe, it's not my breath I'm worried about—it's my vocal cords. Oxygen I can do without; speech is essential to talking my way out of shit like this.

"Wait! I can explain!" is what I try to say, but Salinger's grip is so tight, all that comes out is a faint wisp of air.

Salinger squeezes harder.

PigBoy sees his opportunity. He pulls out his gun, holds it tight against the temple of Salinger's shiny dome. "Let him go, motherfucker."

Salinger is seething, barely hears PigBoy. His eyes flick quickly to the gun. "Or what?"

PigBoy cocks the gun, moves the snout to point into the well of one of Salinger's eye sockets. "Or I'll blow this eyeball through the back of your head."

"Yeah? Well, go ahead, mate," Salinger says. "I'll hunt you down with the other eye and rip you into very, very small pieces. Only my *head* will heal pretty quick; your *body* won't."

I gasp something else unintelligible. Cartilage cracks in my throat as Salinger tightens his grip. Leaning in even closer, he says, "Don't you ever call me Sally. *Ever.* Do you understand?"

I nod twice quickly. More snapping in my neck.

"Now," he says, "I'm going to release you because I want to

release you. Not because this shitty little twerp beside you thinks he's Charles fucking Bronson."

His hands fall away from my throat. My own hands replace them, massaging gently. I won't be able to speak with any strength for at least an hour, maybe two.

"Thanks," I whisper.

PigBoy eases the gun back into his waistband.

"Get on the rack, my Stuart," Salinger says, his tone telling me he's through playing around. "You'll tell me where the hole is once I get you on here." He pats the rack.

His skull-splitting smile is absent.

«« —»»

On the rack. And the pain is unthinkable.

I can't see what, but Salinger's got something metal and solid stuffed in my chest, and he's rocking back and forth on my ribs with his full weight.

Snap. Scream.

Snap. Scream.

This is the way things go.

I guess PigBoy has never seen anything like this, because he just stares at the hole in my chest and blinks very quickly.

My hoarse cries join the chorus. It gives me comfort. To know others are suffering at the same time gives me a certain sense of camaraderie.

Over the din, I hear the sound of an engine. It's a sound I recognize.

Salinger cracks another rib with the metal thing. Some drool from his bottom lip slops inside my gaping chest wound.

"Aw, for chrissakes, Salinger, control yourself," I whisper. He ignores me and keeps crushing my bones.

The sound of the engine gets closer.

PigBoy steps forward, looking like he has something terribly important to impart. "Okay, okay, quit that shit," he says, shaking his head from side to side. "I can't stand to look at it any longer. Stop it and I'll tell you where the damn hole is. I can take you right to it."

Salinger whistles, pulls the metal thing out of me, shakes off some organ or other onto the ground.

They itch a little when they grow back, but otherwise you barely notice.

"Oh, the hero has come to save the day," Salinger says. "Even though it doesn't need saving." He turns away from PigBoy,

35

flicks a switch on the metal thing, a bone saw pops out of one end, and he goes back into me, bits of my skeleton flying up into his face. I try to remember exactly where I left off in my screaming.

The engine gets closer still.

"Hey!" PigBoy shouts, taking another step closer, now risking getting blood flecks on his nice leather jacket. "I said I'd take you right *to* the fucking thing! Quit sawing!"

I appreciate what the kid's trying to do, but he's going about it all wrong. If I didn't have a crushed trachea and a bone saw ripping my guts apart, I'd tell him so.

I turn my head the little bit that I can, and I finally see the source of the engine noise—it's that fucking dune buggy. And it's carrying the same shitheads who pig-bombed my house. Save one, actually—said absent shithead currently becoming very ticked at being ignored. He reaches into his waistband, grabs his gun, and points it at Salinger's head. Again.

I roll my eyes and swallow gobs of arterial blood.

Salinger looks up from his work. "Oh, that again, eh? I meant what I said, you little prick. You pull that trigger and I'll—"

36

The roar of the passing dune buggy drowns the rest out, but it doesn't matter, because Salinger wouldn't have said much more after that, anyway. PigBoy fires two rounds into Salinger's head—one rips through his left eye, blowing shards of bone and a large glop of blood out the side of his skull, splattering my face; the other screams through his neck and lodges in my right shoulder.

At the same time that Salinger falls to the ground, bleeding and cursing, the cocksuckers in the dune buggy start chucking pigs into the crowd. Big ones, small ones, fat ones, skinny ones. Brown ones, pink ones, black ones. Pigs with only three legs, with only one eye, with three balls, with no balls. Anything capable of being turned into ham is coming out of the back of that dune buggy. The squealing turns the near-solid wall of background agony noises into a cacophonous brick shithouse.

PigBoy holsters his weapon, runs over to me, and unties the straps that hold me to the rack, starting with the wrists.

On the ground, right beside us, Salinger tries to stand up, holding the side of his head with one hand, his shredded neck with the other. "Fucking…" he croaks, before PigBoy kicks his legs out from under him.

More straps snap—chest, legs, head—and I'm free.

Free to pitch forward onto a fat pink pig as it scurries by, snuffling and wheezing. The grunting animal drags me about five

feet before I roll off its back and bounce my face off the hard, cracked ground. More pigs trundle over me. Errant hooves sink into my chest cavity. I bellow as loudly as my ruined throat will allow.

Another buggy drives by, hot on the heels of the first one. More leather-jacketed hooligans cackling laughter and tossing ham grenades at everyone.

PigBoy wades through the confusion toward me, picks me up by one arm, slings the arm over his shoulder, grabs my belt with the other hand, and hauls me up.

We hobble to the edge of the road, as a cloud of dust blooms, marking the passage of the pig posse. It balloons up into the air, spreads thin to the sides, and then they're gone.

PigBoy twists his head around, looks for Salinger. No sign of him. Which is somehow worse than knowing he's in a red rage and currently stomping through several layers of pig ass to crush our skulls together. I feel what's left of my stomach sink.

"I've lost a lot of blood," I croak to PigBoy. "I'll need to rest up somewhere for a while. Gotta heal…"

"Where to, then?" he says, straining to hold me up. I'm a limp, bloody rag. Dead weight—my feet barely shuffling along enough to keep us moving in stumbling steps.

There's only one place I can even think of to go. "Gus and Tom's," I say.

The kid says nothing, just drags me to the Camino, loads me into the passenger's side, keeping an eye out for dune buggies.

Gravel flies as we peel away from the chaos.

e pull into Gus and Tom's gas station. The angle we approach from lets me see around to the side of the garage in back. I see old Tom bent over, working under the hood of Miss Appleton's Mustang. It's on several layers of wooden blocks to raise it somewhere near Tom's height. It doesn't look quite as decrepit as the last time I saw it. Tom may not be that quick on the draw, but goddamn if he can't fix cars.

No sign of Gus. Must be inside the station, lying on the couch.

"Round back," I say to PigBoy. "Just get us hidden."

We drive around the back of the building.

Tom China's a giant grease spot. He hears our tires crunching, turns to see what's making the noise.

PigBoy stops the car, gets out, comes around to my side to help me out.

Tom always smiles when he works, but when he sees us, his smile drops clean off his face. "Fellas!" is all he says.

PigBoy, slathered in my blood, walks a few feet, his arm around my waist in support. Then he falls to his knees, bringing me with him. Safely behind the station, he rolls away from me onto his back, stares at the flat red of the underworld's ceiling.

I stay up on my knees for a moment, my eyes shut tight against the pain, then I follow PigBoy's example, careening to the opposite side. My head lands on one of Tom's shoes. I crack an eyelid, look straight up, and there's Tom, just staring down at me, mouth flopping around at the bottom of his face, trying to form words, but only coming up with fishy gurgling noises.

Eventually, something in his oversized cranium shifts into gear, and his foot pulls away from under my head. His footsteps crunch farther and farther away, until I hear—through a bubbling aural haze—the screen door at the front of the gas station open quickly, close loudly. Heated voices float back to me on the crisp air. My brain faintly registers explosions from the Lake of Sorrow.

Gazing straight up, where Tom's head used to be, I see a lazy cloud floating around far above me. It is the only cloud in sight.

Gears grind somewhere in the back of my skull.

A black umbrella suddenly blots the cloud out, then a grey-haired, distinguished-looking gentleman in a crisp, black suit leans over me, squinting hard. "See that cloud there?" he says, points a finger up into his umbrella. "Been following that cloud for as long as I can remember. You'd think it would have taken me somewhere interesting, wouldn't you? I certainly thought so. But it hasn't. Just the same old places I've been before."

The man smiles wide, leans a little closer to me. "So why do I keep following it, right? Right?" He leans back a bit, points again into his umbrella, winks at me. "Because I'm convinced that I haven't yet been everywhere it has to go. That's why."

The man steps politely over my bleeding carcass, carries on behind the gas station slowly, occasionally checking the position of the cloud, making sure to stay just under it at all times.

Gears grind in my skull again, this time fainter, and I realize the sound isn't coming from inside my head, but from the cloud as it drifts away.

Footsteps again. This time, two sets—one hurried and plodding, the other slow and shuffling.

"Fellas!" Tom bellows again, and then Gus's rotting decay is thrust full into my face.

"What the goddamn hell happened to you two!?" Gus barks at me. His breath is the smell of several dead bodies stacked on top of one another in a damp cave.

"Back up, Gus," I croak and turn my face away from him. "Jesus…"

"Don't you gimme Jesus, ya dumb son of a bitch. Ya think I want whatever done this to ya to come here and do the same to me?"

"Didn't follow us," I manage to splutter out.

"Oh, really. And just how d'ya figure that?" Gus turns his

head, looks behind him at the Camino's tire tracks. "Blind, is he?"

"Very funny, Gus. Now…you think you might be able to…" I lift myself partially off the ground with one hand, slip in the sticky blood that slicks both my arms, and plop right back down where I started. "…help me get inside so I can heal up a bit?"

Gus just glares down at me through his weathered, sunken eye sockets.

"Or," I say, "would you rather I just lay out here…where anyone who might come looking can see me?"

A beat passes before strong arms burrow under my mangled body, lift me up, and carry me to Gus's couch inside the gas station. Through blood-crusted eyelids, I look outside the grimy window next to me, spot the lazy cloud high up near Hell's ceiling. I drift into black listening to the cloud grind and whir, leading its solitary follower around in familiar, comfortable circles.

43

hen I wake up, everyone's huddled around me, staring. PigBoy, Gus, Tom, and even the lovely Miss Appleton, all sitting on metal chairs with cheap vinyl coverings. I blink several times, sit up slowly, using the edge of the dirty window beside me for support.

"What?" I ask when I'm sitting upright.

No one speaks.

"Whatwhatwhat, what the fuck are you all looking at?"

Finally, Gus says, "Well, shit, boy, you been out for nearly fifteen hours."

"Fifteen…"

It seems ridiculous. I'm a fast healer. Once, after a decidedly nasty night out crop touring—I mouthed off a little too much to some other guys out touring and got my ass beat hard for my troubles—I came back in such bad shape, I couldn't stand, and my flesh was completely black and blue. Barely a square inch of white skin left when I took off my clothes to shower. I passed out from the pain when my head hit the pillow, and woke up my regular eight hours later feeling completely fine. Refreshed even.

But this…this is something else. Salinger seriously fucked me up.

"Yeah," Miss Appleton says, her voice sultry, like her windpipe is made of smoked hickory. "We thought maybe you were going to die. You know—forever."

Tight black dress. Dark auburn hair, long, wavy. Sharp fea-

The Distance Travelled

tures. Full lips. Really, *really* red. A total '40s film noir dame. I have no trouble understanding old Tom's obsession with her.

"Well, I appreciate the concern, I really do, but I'm fine now. Bit more brutalized than I'd figured, I guess, but everything seems to have grown back and healed over, just like always. Take a lot more than fucking Salinger to take me out for the long haul."

I smile. No one smiles with me.

Down here, there's one thing no one much likes to talk about, and that's the definitive *end*. At some point—and no one's quite been able to put their finger on exactly when—people finally just disappear. Dramatically, in a puff of smoke. Some think it's God releasing those who have served their sentence. Others, who don't believe in God, think your energy just sort of peters out. You don't get transferred into another Hell-bound body; you don't go back to Upside for another go-round; you don't do anything. You simply cease to exist. All that you ever were or ever could have been—truly and completely extinguished.

People would rather continue in any form at all—tortured Hell-dweller, slug, dung beetle, whatever—than just suddenly cease to be.

"Anyway," I say, clearing my throat, patting my newly healed midsection, trying to lighten the mood. "Any Irish Cream kicking around?"

Gus waves my question away with an impatient hand. "Salinger did this? What the hell'd ya do to get that mean bag of shit so riled up?"

I shrug. "He asked a question I didn't want to answer." I glance at PigBoy, but his eyes are down on his zipper. Fiddle, fiddle.

"Uh-huh," Gus says, unimpressed with my sidestepping. I'm usually not evasive about anything with Gus—Gus is just good old Gus—but this whole pig-throwing situation and some punk from Upside suddenly dropping in to find his kidnapped sister has put me a bit out of sorts. "So what's this kid's deal? What's he doing with you?"

After some prodding, PigBoy opens up and tells everyone his story, all the way up to our most recent adventure.

"Damn," Gus says once PigBoy's done. "Kid saved your bacon, sounds like to me, Stu. Least you can do is try to help him find his sister."

"Yeah, well, I was already thinking about it when we ran into Salinger at his torture block. Bastard spotted me and I figured I'd just get it over with now, rather than endure whatever sick shit he might come up with before my next appointment as punishment for ducking him. It went from bad to worse after that.

"Look, can someone throw me on some coffee? I need a serious java fix."

Without a word—and that's another reason I like him as much as I do—Tom gets up from his chair, ducks his head down, and clomps off to the coffeepot in the next room.

With Tom out of the room, I lean in to Gus, whisper, "How's he doing?"

Gus looks at the floor. "Few weeks, maybe more, maybe less. Hard to tell." He lifts his head. "But who knows? Maybe he'll just completely recover..." he says, letting that last trail off, his eyes finding his shoes again.

I nod. Everyone's quiet.

In the next room, Tom's big hands go through the motions of making a pot of coffee, and I wonder if there's anything after this for HellRats. Do they go somewhere else? I wonder about the Absolute End. Maybe that's their fate.

You'd think when you died, you'd get all the answers, but that's not how it is at all.

For someone like Tom, though, there has to be something. Something better.

Gus shakes his head quickly, slaps his hands on his bony thighs, looks up at me. "Enough of this gloomy crap. We all think about it too much already. Onward and upward. Where'd ya say ya was headed when ya run into Salinger? Some hole where pigs drop out? I still ain't quite clear on that part of PigBoy's story."

47

"Yeah, the hole. Pigs drop out. Morons in dune buggies grab 'em, tie ropes around their necks, chuck 'em through folks' windows. Only rich kids could get that bored," I say.

Gus looks out the window. "So why d'ya think Salinger didn't follow you? I'da thought you'd need a small army to fend that mean bugger off."

PigBoy and I exchange a glance. We both shrug, shake our heads slowly, searching for something, anything to explain it.

"No idea, Gus," I say. "Only thing I can think is that we actually did some decent damage to him, slowed him down enough that he had to stay put and heal."

"So what's yer plan now?" Gus asks.

I think about this for a minute. Gus is right; I do owe the kid something. "Drink my coffee," I say. "Find the hole. Try to piece together where PigBoy's sister is. Rescue her. Come back here, drink some more coffee. Go home, go to bed."

"Just like that, huh?"

"Hey," I say, "you asked me what my plan was. Whether it all happens like that isn't up to me. Isn't up to you, either. But ya gotta go into weird shit like this with a certain mindset, you know?"

Tom lumbers back in holding a black coffee mug. He can't get his big sausage fingers inside the mug handle, so he carries it by its sides. Written in red and orange on the side of the mug is "Hell's Kitchen—Really, *really* hot food!"

"That place still open?" I ask no one in particular, taking the steaming mug from Tom's dinner-plate hand.

"Far as I know," Gus says.

"Definitely still open," says Miss Appleton. "I sang there last weekend."

"You sing?" I ask. "What sort of stuff?"

"Torch songs. Death metal. Whatever the patrons want to hear."

"You do death? Let's hear some."

"It's not very ladylike. I'm sure you don't want to hear it." Miss Appleton turns a bit red, shoots a quick glance over at Tom, who shuffles his feet and looks away, the ghost of a smile on his big fat rodent face.

I'll bet old Tom's heard her growl. The lucky dog.

"Food any good?" I say.

"Good as it gets," Miss Appleton says, relieved that the subject has changed.

"So what's your first name, anyway? Tommy here never did tell me."

"That's because," Miss Appleton says, smirking, "I haven't told Tom." She raises an eyebrow.

Fair enough.

"Fine," I say. "I'll just call you Apple till you tell me what it really is." I return the raised eyebrow, and she's back to smirking again.

I blow on my coffee, send ripples across its black surface, take a sip. Coffee clears my thinking paths, seems to order the general swirl of thoughts in my head. I take another couple of sips and it does its trick. With my body relatively restored, my simple plan becomes more focussed. I itch to get going.

"So," I say. "Who's coming with us?"

Gus and Tom look at each other, exchange a glance that only good friends can, and nod at the same time. "Folks," Gus says, "can pump their own damn gas. No idea how much longer these old bones o' mine are gonna stay knitted together, and I wanna do something important before I'm booted out of the game."

Tom grins and says, "Game is truth, Stu. Time for the good time."

48

"Damn straight, old Tom," I say, wondering exactly which wires in Tom's giant brain are crossed. "And you, pretty little Apple? You comin' or stayin'?"

"Think I'll sit this one out, drive my newly repaired car around, pick up boys. You know. Girl stuff." She winks at me, smiles at Tom.

Tom looks momentarily crestfallen, then realizes she's just playing, and immediately brightens. "No fooling Tom," he says, and points at Apple and me. "No way. Sharp as sticks!" Tom laughs hard.

I smile, and wish hard that there were something I could do to stop him from growing.

Then an image pops into my mind. A cloud. The sound of the cloud grinding, floating away. Cloud Guy, who said he followed it because he hasn't yet been everywhere it's going.

"Oh, say." I snap my fingers, glad to've remembered. "What's the deal with Cloud Guy? You know, dude in the black suit with the umbrella that follows that cloud around."

Frowns, blank stares. PigBoy fiddling.

Apple says, "Cloud Guy? Who's Cloud Guy?"

"Never heard of 'im," says Gus.

"You didn't see him walking away from me out back?"

Silence.

49

Gus: "You say he follows a cloud?"

Me: "Yeah, a cloud. First time I've ever seen a cloud down here, too."

Gus: "That's 'cause there ain't no other clouds down here."

Me: "None?"

Gus: "None."

Me: "Just the one?"

Gus: "Just the one."

Tom: "One is none until there's one." Old Tom smiles wide, like he just cured cancer.

"Goddamn," I say. "So it just sort of floats around all by itself? What sort of weather system generates *one* fucking cloud?"

"It's mechanical," says Gus.

That grinding sound. Gears.

"Yeah," Gus continues. "The Big Red Fella supposedly made it eons ago. One little cloud supposed to produce rain for the whole underworld. Funny joke. Ha, ha. I've heard it drops a pretty mean shower when it finally opens up. Never seen it in action, myself."

"Have any of you seen it?" I ask.

'Nope's all around. I frown, drop my head, look down at the floor. Pop my head back up, turn to Gus. "And you've never seen the guy that follows it around? No legends about him? No myths in any of those old, dusty books in your library?"

Gus shakes his head slowly from side to side.

"Huh," I say, scratching my chin. "Well, fuck it. There's work to do.

"PigBoy, let's go find your sister."

8

W e leave Apple to hold the fort, call the fuel truck to refill the pumps, and keep her ear to the ground, maybe chat some fellas up to see if there's any word on all this pig-throwing and kidnapping business.

PigBoy brings the Camino around to the front of the station. We pile into it. Gus takes a full minute to creak himself up and into the bed of the car. Tom tromps up into the bed, nearly crushing my suspension, flops himself next to Gus, props his back against the rear window. At least with Tom so snug against him, Gus won't have to worry about breaking any of his brittle, rotted bones if we get into an accident.

We peel out of the gas station, throw on some cheesy '80s pop music, and sing along—even old Gus, his ancient vocal cords still strong enough to carry over the rushing wind. Tom, however, just makes shit up as he goes. But he stays in time and can carry a tune better—and sure as hell louder—than the rest of us combined, so who are we to bitch?

Though it's a serious matter we're facing, there's a sense of adventure in the car that feels fresh. This gives us purpose, something to *do* in a place where any sort of fun is, by this realm's very nature, hard to come by.

"Turn left at the next intersection," PigBoy mutters. "It's just over that rise." He points a grubby finger toward a gigantic rock face, probably about 200 feet high. Etched into its side are shimmering steps of granite—shimmering from the reflective glow of the flames that lick and lap from various torture pits scattered through this section of the underworld. The steps lead up to a small ledge.

"That's where they throw people off into the main pit," says PigBoy. "I've seen them do it. And I've also seen what's *in* the pit."

Crunching gravel, I pull the Camino up to the scree reaching up the side of the rock. I cut the engine and turn to PigBoy. "There's something *in* the pit? In the flames?" I glance over at the raging wall of fire and can't imagine what sort of beast could survive in it.

"Yeah. But with any luck we won't see it. I think it only comes up to the surface when it's summoned, and I think that only happens when they have someone to throw in. As long as you don't freak out and lose your cool, that shouldn't be the case."

Hey, hang on now. Hold the phone.

This Upsider's telling me more about the place I'd been relegated to for over thirty years than I know myself...not to mention being cocky about it, too. "How long you been here, kid?"

"'Bout a week." He unclips his seatbelt, smirks at me, opens his door, steps out onto the crunchy, steaming surface, and slams the door shut.

52

When I get out of the car and that wall of heat slams into me, I fully realize just how ineffectual any air conditioner could ever be against the sheer blazing heat of this place. I'm already sweating like mad and wishing for my protective outdoor gear, but PigBoy doesn't even seem to notice.

Gus and Tom climb slowly out of the Camino's bed—Gus because he's older than Moses, Tom because having five-foot-long legs comes with its own set of troubles. After a couple minutes of struggling, turning side to side, trying to use his arms to push his bulk up to his legs, Tom muttering, "Not movin', nope. Can't get it on. Can't get 'er goin'," we realize PigBoy and I will have to each take an arm and yank the big bugger out.

When we finally yank his ass out of the Camino's bed, Tom stands up to his full height, winces, wiggles his rodent whiskers at us and says, "Not again. Too hard. Gotta not. Please gotta not."

I pat his ribs. "Gotcha, big Tom. But for now, this'll have to do. These old Elkys weren't particularly built with comfort in mind. We'll try to figure some other way to cart you around."

Tom smiles. "Cartings for big Tom. Sounds mighty Jim. Need to get home soon. Heart is missing Apple." He smiles wide. "She sure is the eye of mine."

"We'll get you on back to your sweet little lady as soon as possible, okay? Just gotta check out this hole, see if we can't get a clue about all this crap."

Tom nods, wraps his head-sized, meaty paws around the straps of his overalls—Tom's way of indicating that he's ready to get on with things.

I turn around, move beside PigBoy, look up at the stairs and the ledge. "Lemme ask you something," I say, turning toward him. "How is it you're here for a week and you've completely acclimatized to the temperature when I've been here for thirty years and am currently baking my balls off?"

He looks at me and taps his temple, smiling. "It's all up here, *mi compadre*. Power of the mind."

I grunt and follow him as he makes his way to the bottom step.

"You guys're gonna *climb* those steps?"

I turn around, look at Gus. Put my hands out, open-palmed. "You have a better idea?"

"Sure do. Don't go up 'em at all—climbing or otherwise. What in tarnation you wanna go up there for anyway? I mean, aren't we supposed to be looking for the kid's sister? I'm willin' to bet my crappy old decayin' bones that the fellas what took her aren't hangin' around the scene of the crime."

53

"Actually, Gus, criminals *do* return to the scenes of their crimes. It's a documented fact. It's quite common. Didn't you ever return to the scene of any of your crimes?"

Gus goes stiff, looks at me hard. "Don't wanna talk about none of what I did Upside, boy. I don't wanna talk about it and you don't wanna hear it, so let's just leave it be."

"Alright, alright, ease off," I say, put a hand up, then turn to address Tom and PigBoy. "I figure the best idea right now is to wait here, see if they come back—they're gonna need a pig refill eventually if they plan to continue their porcine kitchen bombings. Some of us should stay down here, hidden behind some rocks or something, then jump out and stop them if they come. Ambush 'em. We could be here for a good while, though, so it probably shouldn't be Gus, since Gus has a habit of—"

I look over at him. He's nodded off.

"—nodding off in the middle of things, no matter how important," I finish, poke my index finger into his brittle ribcage. He snorts, eyes popping open. "I'm listenin', I'm listenin'. Get on with it already!"

I crane my neck to look at the sheerness of the steps leading up to the ledge. "Then again, I don't think you can make it up those steps, Gus. Nimble as you are." I wink at him. "So how about this: PigBoy and I will go up there, see what's what, while you and Tom stay down here with your eyes peeled. Sound good?"

Tom slaps Gus on the back, nearly breaking him in half. "Good as it gets!" he says. Gus just grumbles and leans back, trying to snap the ridges of his spine back into place.

"Right, so it's settled. Hide behind that jumble of rocks next to the road, fellas." I point to a small outcropping near where I parked the Camino. "Gus, make sure Tom stays down. He gets too excited, he'll blow the whole deal. And Tom, make sure Gus stays awake, okay?"

"No sleep till bedtime!" Tom barks.

Good enough for me.

"Let's go, Piggy." I clap him on the back, feeling comfortable being in charge.

"Uh…Stu, don't you wanna hide the car?" PigBoy says.

I'm a couple of steps ahead of him. I stop, turn around, feeling my leadership slipping away in tiny increments. "Yeah, of course," I say, switching the angle of my steps so I'm heading toward the car, trying to act like that's where I'd been going in the first place.

54

I jump in the driver's seat, start it up, pull it behind the rock outcropping, and cut the engine. By the time I step back out and into the crushing heat, Tom and Gus have made their way over, too. They sit quietly, like an old married couple, on either side of the car's hood, passing between them a small bag of peanuts Gus must have grabbed on the way out of the gas station. Gus chews and creaks his bones around, trying to get comfortable; Tom chews and settles deeper into the giant indent he left when he first sat down.

"You're hammering that out when we get back to the station, Tommy, ya big lug!" I holler as I stride toward PigBoy, who's waiting for me at the bottom of the scree. Tom doesn't hear me— just passes the bag of peanuts to his friend and waits for something to happen.

PigBoy and I climb upward, each step more slippery than the last. He continues explaining his mind-over-matter theory. I barely catch most of it for trying to prevent myself from falling off the narrow staircase and into the pit. He, of course, just carries on like it's no big deal, sometimes hopping up two and three steps at a time. *Ah, youth,* I think. But then youth doesn't really have much to do with it. Here I am, veteran Hell-dweller— already *dead,* for chrissakes—and I'm petrified of falling off into the awaiting flame-pit…and whatever lurks inside. And here's Upside Kid, still alive, probably twenty years old, jumping around and actually *flirting* with death. True death. *I* would just endure the torments of the flames and the Hell-thing in its pit, then get carted back to my house and wait for the next fresh set of torments, but he—*he* would truly die, losing all chance of seeing Upside again.

Slipping on some loose rock and nearly tumbling to my pseudo-death, I tune in again to his mind-over-matter theory.

"…ya know? I mean, look, are you telling me you weren't programmed to believe that 'Hell is hot' and that's why you feel the heat?"

The kid somehow manages to stay five full steps ahead of me at all times. I'm drenched in sweat, yet he's completely bone-dry.

But he's right—mind over matter is exactly why I'm sweating my ass off and he's not. This place has been tailor-made to suit the Hell-bound's expectations. On some level, perhaps through a collective subconscious, we know where we're going before we die, know it instinctively, like an animal knows when it's about to die and so crawls off to find a quiet place in which to do it. And with that knowledge comes the trappings, how we perceive Hell, what we expect from it. No doubt a lot of this place only became what it is because we created it in our collective mind's eye's image.

55

Smart kid. But none of it stops me from sweating eighty percent of my body's water content out onto these steaming granite steps.

Finally reaching the ledge of the rock, PigBoy shoves his hands in his pockets, closes his eyes, looks to be gathering himself. The ledge is about twenty feet long and four feet wide. Not much room for error.

I join him a few seconds later, leaning over, hands on my knees, sweaty hair stuck in strands to my face.

The hole must be just above us somewhere, part of the seamless rock-ceiling overhead. "So where is it?" I croak.

Since I don't breathe, I'm not out of breath, but my throat still gets dry, and I still sweat like an ice-cold can of cola on a blistering summer day, same as I did Upside.

"Should be right around—" PigBoy reaches his hand above him and feels along the smooth, black rock "—here somewhere."

Suddenly his hand is sucked up through the rock. Sounds pour out from the place where his hand disappeared—squealing, hooves tromping, snuffling. The smell is absolutely horrendous—it's that barn/hay/animal-shit smell. Pungent as fuck.

"Ah!" PigBoy yelps, yanks his arm back down. It's covered in shit and has a big gash in it. Blood wells up and dribbles to his feet. He hisses and holds the injured hand under his arm.

I feel a rumbling from below.

PigBoy and I lock horrified stares. The Flame Pit Thing. Maybe it caught scent of the blood.

"Uh, Piggy?" I say, heart triphammering, gaze glued to the flames below. "I *seriously* suggest we get the hell outta here—right now." I moisten my throat a little to finish off. "I think we're done looking for clues now. We can't find your sister if we're charbroiled."

PigBoy grimaces in pain, nods, clenches his teeth.

Then there's an ear-piercing squeal and two fat pigs suddenly drop out of the hole above us. One of them bounces off the ledge, falls into the pit; the other gains its balance, scuttles toward me where I stand on the top step of the staircase.

"Oh, shit," I say, eyes bugging, "Get away, you little—!"

It bolts between my legs with a grunt, forcing them open. I lose my balance, pinwheel my arms, feel my body falling sideways toward the pit, the flames, and whatever nasty Hell-thing is waiting below.

56

A comic-book-perfect "Aiiiiiiieeeeeeeeeeee!!!!" tears through my windpipe before PigBoy whips out an arm and snags me, hauling me vertical again, reeling me in. I cling to the wall, right cheek glued to its smooth surface, whimpering a little. The pig trundles down the rock-hewn stairs, tripping over bits of rubble, getting smaller and smaller, till it's nothing but a tiny pink dot.

It's hard to tell from this high up, but it looks like Gus and Tom throw peanuts at it as it runs past the Camino.

Another rumble from below and the flames lick higher.

I get a hold of myself and grab PigBoy's wrist. "Let's bolt. That fucking thing's gonna surface real soon and I don't wanna be here when it does." I turn to take the first step but PigBoy stands his ground, shaking his wrist free of my grip. I look back. "What!? What's your problem now? Let's *vamoose!*"

"No time," he says. "The thing has smelled two things: my blood and the pig's bacon. It's gonna want the source of one or the other, so we have to make sure it gets the bacon. If we don't, and we only get halfway down those slippery steps when the thing surfaces…well, put a fucking fork in us—we're done."

He thrusts his good hand up into the hole and looks to be fishing around. He yelps a few more times, then yanks down hard.

This time it's my turn to save him. A runty little pig comes through the hole, thrashing this way and that. I grab PigBoy in a full body hug, stabilizing him against the pig's frenzied movements.

Then, apparently tired of merely rumbling, the beast below shoots up out of the pit, turning the air around us white-hot. I instinctively shut my eyes, awaiting my painful transformation to charcoal. I feel PigBoy lean to one side for leverage, then the fading squeals and grunts of the pig as he tosses it over the edge. I can't open my eyes. The heat is incredible, and I know if I open them, they'll be burned right out of my skull. I'll get them back, of course, for future torment, but the prospect of feeling them crisped in my head is not one that particularly appeals to me.

So I wait. For annihilation. For complete disintegration.

The wall of heat retreats; comparatively cool air replaces it. But I still can't open my eyes.

PigBoy chuckles.

"Hey, tough guy," he says, breaking my vice-like grip on him and standing back, "it's gone. You can open your eyes now."

I crack a lid, see PigBoy's smug grin.

"You kept your eyes open, didn't you?" I ask, an unmistakable edge to my voice. "You probably stared it down, too."

His grin doesn't falter. "It was the pig that saved us, just the pig. Let's get back down to Gus and Tom—if Dante and his boys *do* come back, it'll be a lot easier to stop them with four of us blocking the road," he says. "And who knows how long this hole's gonna be here. I gotta find my sister and get back."

Still pissed—feeling like I need to say something to wrestle control back from him, feeling completely impotent in the face of his matter-of-fact solutions to everything—I glance up at the ceiling where the pigs had come out. Perhaps a second too long.

And PigBoy knows exactly what I'm thinking.

He smirks, lifts his eyes to the same spot in the ceiling. "Yeah, you could probably go right up that hole—I could boost you through, no problem—and you'd never have to look back. Could probably be your ticket outta here. More likely than not, in fact. Say the word, and I'll hoist you through."

I'm thinking about it, wondering if it would work, wondering if it could really be so easy to escape eternal damnation. But who am I fooling? I was vague and completely imprecise about my reasons for wanting to come up here in the first place. There was no reason to come up onto this ledge at all. We could both be behind those rocks down there right now, sharing peanuts with Gus and Tom, waiting for Dante and his dune buggy full of hooligans. But we're here instead…and I think PigBoy knew all along.

"You had to come," he says. "I knew you would. The moment I told you about the hole, I knew—even if you didn't—that you'd need to come here first before you'd do anything to help me.

"You needed the choice."

He takes a step back, gets down on one knee, locks the fingers from both hands together in front of him, making a boost for me. "Come on, then," he says, and just stares at me, expressionless. "I can get Tom and Gus to help me find my sister. No sweat."

I glance up to the ceiling only a few feet above our heads, then back down to his cupped hands. One quick step forward and I'm free.

I look back to Gus and Tom sitting on the hood of my car. They'll be fine. Gus'll take care of Tom until...well, until he doesn't need taking care of anymore. What else is here for me? No one. Nothing.

Except PigBoy and his stolen sister.

But PigBoy's not giving me any puppy-dog eyes, not trying to convince me to stay using any sentimental bullshit. He's just waiting to lift me clean out of here, up into a new life. Or whatever kind of life the living dead might be able to muster Upside, anyway.

Better than this, though. Got to be better than this.

So why am I hesitating? What the fuck is wrong with me? I should have been up and gone the second he had his fingers locked together. Just up and away like—

Gears.

I hear those goddamn gears again.

I whip my head around, and approaching slowly from behind is the cloud. The single mechanical cloud I saw lying on my back behind Gus and Tom's place when I wasn't much more than a raw, pulpy mess of pain. It's just chugging like a soft train toward me.

"Hey," I say, turning around, away from PigBoy and his offer of freedom, hardly aware that I'm speaking, "it's the cloud...."

The cloud gets closer, louder. It's about fifteen feet across and maybe twenty long. Puffy and white. If I reach my arm out, I'll touch it with my hand. But I don't. I just watch it drift by. When it gets far enough past me that I can see behind it, I see its gears working away. Its rusted insides look like a combination of clock cogs and some bizarre pulley system, with a propeller sticking out the back. There's a crumbling exhaust pipe poking out of one side, too. The part of the cloud all around the tailpipe is dark brown, streaked with grime and smoke.

It puffs and chugs by me, turns in a slightly different direction, and carries on, the gears clunking softer and softer until I barely hear them.

Remembering my similar experience from before, I glance down to look for Cloud Guy, scan the red rocks below for a sign of his black umbrella. But there are no rocks beneath where the cloud is, just the raging inferno of the flame pit, along with the occasional rumbling from deep inside its guts.

My eyes adjust to the red-orange glare of the immense fire…and I spot it—a black umbrella bobbing about in the flames, directly underneath where the cloud is floating.

PigBoy walks over to me, puts a hand on my shoulder. "You alright? We should go back down now. No telling when that flame-pit thing's gonna pop up again for more grub, now that he's had a sample—spoon-fed to him, no less." He waits a beat, takes his hand from my shoulder. "So you're not abandoning me, then?"

I try to turn my head to answer him, to tell him yes, I'm going to stay, I'm going to help him find his sister, but I can't move. My eyes just follow the little black umbrella until it's no longer hovering in zillion-degree flame, but is now weaving in and out of piles of red rubble.

"That's insane," I whisper, my eyes stinging from staring unblinking for so long.

"What's insane?" PigBoy asks, following my gaze.

59

"That," I say, and point at the umbrella. "He just walked right through the pit, through the flames."

"Who did?" says PigBoy.

Finally able to rip my eyes away from Cloud Guy, I turn to look at PigBoy. I see in his face that he's genuinely confused, that he honestly doesn't see anything down there.

"Yeah," I whisper, after a few seconds.

"Yeah what?"

"Yeah, I'll help you." I look him square in the face. "But I think you already knew that."

We're halfway down the slippery stairs—twice I grab onto PigBoy before falling off the staircase—when above the crackling and popping and rumbling of the flames, I hear that familiar dune buggy engine. The buggy is a tiny speck far up the road, followed by a small cloud of red dust.

I glance down at Gus and Tom still hiding behind the big out-cropping of rock, sharing peanuts on my Camino's hood.

I nudge PigBoy, nod my head in the buggy's direction. He gets my drift, scrambles past me. "Hurry up!" he whispers on his way by.

Yeah, 'cause I'm just dawdling here. Thought I'd break out a picnic basket and relax in the super-extreme melt-your-face-off heat just for the fuck of it.

Stumbling down the steps as fast as I can, I reach the bottom a full minute after PigBoy. Looking toward the outcropping, I see that he's already sharing hood space with Gus and Tom. He motions with his hands and points in the direction of the dune buggy. He passes something to Gus, but I can't make out what it is. By the time I make it to where they are, ready to do some quick thinking to come up with a plan, they just tell me to hush and get down, the plan already having been discussed and agreed upon.

When did I get old? When did I lose my edge? I'm sitting here on the hood of my Camino, feeling depressed, feeling out of the loop. Feeling forgotten. I mean, I'm glad the situation is under control—I just wish I were the one controlling it.

The buggy's engine grows louder. I look over at Tom, hunched down near the front of the car, his beady little rat eyes intent on a section of the road before us. I have a quick moment of panic as a thought crosses my mind. That *can't* be what their plan is. It's ridiculous, ludicrous. It'll never work. It—

The buggy's growl is right inside my head when Tom suddenly leaps out from behind the rock and into the road.

Gravel spits up and flies in every direction as the buggy slams on its brakes. Tom waves his giant arms and screeches like a banshee. Gus and I pop our heads above the rock to watch, cringing, expecting to see Tom get splattered all over the front of the buggy, but it skids to a sideways halt several inches in front of him.

No one says a word. Red dust plumes, obscuring Tom completely. When the dust passes him, settling back into the road, Tom has his arms down, a light film of the dust coating his overalls. He coughs once.

"Oy!" barks the driver of the dune buggy. "What's this about then, eh? Get the fuck out the road, ya bleedin' behemoth!" Some words I catch clearly, others I just guess at as they're lost in an Ozzy Osbourne multi-word slur.

Tom just stands there, shifting his weight from foot to foot.

The passenger stands up in the buggy, leather-clad head to toe. "This here's *our* place." Slow Texas drawl, cold syrup over flapjacks. "Whadda y'all think yer doin'?"

"Yeah," says the driver, "and what's with the fucking ambush?"

PigBoy steps out in front with Tom, pats the big fella on the lower back. "Good job, Tom."

I walk out, too—more because I want to be included than anything else. Gus stays behind, munches on peanuts. I don't blame him one bit, either. If I were that old and rotted, I wouldn't give people the time of day, never mind stand in front of a dune buggy loaded with hostile, angst-ridden young Hell punks.

The two guys in the back of the buggy jump out onto the road. One is tall and lanky. Stringy hair. Misfits T-shirt. Grinning skull. Real dopey looking. The other is also tall, but built like a Volvo. Stocky, uncrushable. He's wearing khakis and a casual red button-up shirt. Brown leather belt. Very suave.

Volvo speaks, the intense menace of German engineering: "Well, what have we here. Aaron. Goddamn. Shouldn't you be a sack of bones bobbing around in the Lake of Sorrows right about now?"

PigBoy nods. "Yeah, well I'm not, am I? No thanks to you. Racing off, leaving me for dead." PigBoy spits on the ground in front of the buggy. "Fuckers."

The driver tilts his head to one side, narrows his eyes to slits. He jumps down from the buggy, crunches red dirt under his heels as he approaches us. His eyes never leave PigBoy's face.

He's wearing a skintight black T-shirt, which in bold, block white lettering reads: NO, I'M JUST *A* DANTE.

Stopping a few feet away from PigBoy, he spreads his hands out in front of him, says, "Look, mate, we don't owe each other anything, yeah? You got us some pigs to throw, we threw 'em. Now we've come back for more. But see, you've outlived your usefulness since pigs aren't too smart and will probably just keep dropping through that hole until they're all gone. We don't need you to fetch 'em. We was just trying to make you feel...you know...wanted or something, yeah?" He turns around, gives his boys a sly grin. "We actually had a bet going about how long you'd last down here. Tender Upside flesh like yours..."

"Dante, you fucking—"

"Fucking what, eh?" And in the space of a second, Dante's face is an inch away from PigBoy's.

63

Beside me, Tom growls low in his throat.

"Fucking what?" Dante says again. "Come on, you little bitch. Say it. Say what you wanna say."

PigBoy's hands shake. He clenches them into fists at his sides. Shit is about to get ugly. I feel it like a thin shard of glass sliding into my belly.

"Where's my sister?" PigBoy whispers. Tom takes a step closer to Dante.

Without taking his eyes off PigBoy's face, Dante says, "Call your boy off, Aaron. Tell him to take a step back or you'll never see your sister in one piece again. I know where she is. Now call him the fuck off."

Tom's growl gets louder. Sweat slicks my palms.

"Call. Him. *Off.*"

I glance over at Tom. He's looking right at me. He seems to be waiting for any kind of signal to mash all four of these boys to red pulp.

PigBoy says, "Leave it alone, Tom. Just stay where you are."

Tom takes another step closer.

Dante raises an eyebrow. "They'll kill her if I don't come back. That what you want, you spineless little shit? You want your sister dead? Tell your boy to take one more step. Go ahead. Tell him."

"Stay back," PigBoy says, raising his voice. "Tom. Stay back."

But Tom's not listening. His little black eyes are still locked on me. That's when I realize it: I am in control. This is up to me. What goes down right now is my call.

I open my mouth to speak. Tom takes it as the signal to start shredding. He moves forward, hands the size of frying pans opening to crush Dante's skull.

"Tom, stop," I say.

One of Tom's hands hovers just over Dante's head. He looks back at me. "*Don't* stop," he says. "I see it. I see it. His head in my hand. I see it."

"I know, Tom. But not now. Come on. Step back here with me."

Tom turns back to Dante, the rumble in his throat grows louder and I think he's going to do it anyway, regardless what anyone says. Then he slowly lowers his hand, steps back two paces. The growling eases up. My whole body erupts in sweat.

Misfits' and Volvo's eyes have swallowed their heads. They step back quietly, climb into the back seat of the buggy, all macho bullshit flung right out the window after nearly seeing their leader's cranium popped like a grape.

Texas Drawl still stands in the front seat. He doesn't look scared like the other two. He looks very, very calm.

I feel that glass shard inside my belly again, and suddenly there's a pistol in Texas Drawl's meaty paw. He points the barrel directly at my face.

"All y'all get in yer fuckin' car and go." He cocks the hammer on the gun. "Now."

My eyes flick to PigBoy's waistband. His gun is gone.

There's a series of short, sharp cracks and Texas Drawl's leather jacket suddenly sprouts two small red holes, his forehead sprouts one. He keels over and flops out of the buggy into a heap, moaning and twitching.

That's when I remember Gus, and the unidentified thing PigBoy passed to him just before all this went down. Stumbling out from behind the rock outcropping, the still-smoking gun in his hand, Gus whistles low. "Goddamn," he says. "I still got it."

I look back to Texas Drawl flopping on the ground beside the buggy. Definite brain damage. Probably take a couple of days to heal.

But he doesn't get the chance.

Tom, allowing full rage to course through him, stalks over to Texas Drawl, brings a foot down onto his skull, flattening it.

Texas Drawl stops twitching. Tom smears the mush of his

head into the dirt and turns his attention to Misfits and Volvo in the back seat of the buggy. Volvo jumps up into the driver's seat, starts the buggy, pops it into Reverse, stomps on the gas. Gravel flies. Pulling a one-eighty, the buggy roars off down the road.

Tom, looking for something else to pummel to dust, walks back toward Dante, growling like a lion again.

Gus, looking for all the world like a decomposed Wyatt Earp, holds PigBoy's pistol at his hip, trained on Dante.

Dante doesn't move. He's still just inches away from PigBoy's face. "They'll tell him what happened, you idiot," he says, and smiles, exposing brown, chipped teeth. "They'll tell Barnes. He'll assume I'm dead. What do you think a father would do if he thought his boy was dead? What would *you* do?"

He waits a second to let it sink in, grins again. Wider this time. Loving every second of it. "They'll tell him and he'll kill her. Unless I stop them."

The sound of the buggy's engine recedes.

But this is PigBoy's call. Not mine.

PigBoy is silent for what seems like forever, then he drops his head, says, "Stop them."

Dante turns around quickly on his heel, puts two fingers under his tongue, blows three short, high-pitched whistles. A couple hundred feet up the road, the buggy's brakes lock. It skids to a stop. The only sound is its idling engine.

A few seconds later, gears grind and the buggy reverses slowly toward us.

Behind and above us, two pigs fall through the hole squealing, bounce off the ledge and into the flame pit. Two small *woof*s mark their transformation from flesh to bacon.

Dante turns around. "Now tell Gramps to holster his heat."

Gus grits his teeth. Three or four fall out, sprinkle on the dirt beneath him. But he puts the gun into a pocket of his threadbare overalls.

"Why are you doing this?" PigBoy asks Dante. "What do you want her for?" His eyes are wet, threatening to spill over.

"Well, what do you think Hell-dwellers would do," Dante says, "with a fresh ten-year-old girl from Upside?" Shark's grin. Cold and mean.

PigBoy's face bunches up, tears spill down his cheeks. "You fucking—"

"I can whistle again and my boys will be off like a shot. I'd watch my mouth if I were you."

PigBoy shakes his head, lifts a leather-clad arm to his face, wipes a sleeve across his eyes. Says nothing.

THE DISTANCE TRAVELLED

The dune buggy trundles closer, slows to a stop about ten feet from us. Misfits and Volvo eye Tom warily.

"So are we going to keep doing this silly little dance, or do you wanna know how to get her back?" Dante says.

"Why would we trust anything you told us?" I say, keeping the ball rolling while PigBoy regains his composure.

Dante smirks. His eyes slide off PigBoy's over to mine. "What choice do you have?"

I hold his gaze, trying to think of something clever, trying to stay in control, but there's nothing to say. He's right. What choice *do* we have?

I drop my eyes.

PigBoy sniffs. "Alright, what do you want? Money? How much?"

Dante laughs. "Money? I've got more of that than I know what to do with."

"Then what?"

Dante looks back at his boys in the dune buggy. They exchange a meaningful look, then Dante turns back slowly, nodding slightly, his lips pursed.

"I want you to kill Barnes."

PigBoy turns to look at me. I shrug.

"You *want* me to kill your father?" PigBoy says. "I mean, I'd planned to anyway, once I got my hands on him, but you actually *want* me to?"

Dante nods, grim-faced.

"Why?"

"'Cause he's in my fucking way, that's why. At every bloody turn, he's looking over my shoulder, checking up on me, wondering what I'm up to. Where I've been, what I've been doing. Who I've been hanging out with. Everything! He's like a little yippy dog winding his way in and out of my legs, constantly trippin' me up."

Dante spits these words out, wipes a sleeve across his mouth. "And I'm sick of it. Sick of his questions, sick of his accusations, sick of him interfering in every nook and cranny of my fucking business. I'm not a little boy anymore, but that fat bugger won't leave me alone.

"So," he says, "I want him dead."

PigBoy takes a few seconds to digest the information. Frowning, he says, "So why don't you just kill him? Why's it got to be me?"

"Ah, yeah..." Dante says, and laughs. "Well, I've thought about that, haven't I? And I can't do it. I can't kill my own father, no matter how much I fucking hate him. Someone else has to do it. And you've got reason, motivation. Most importantly, you've got detachment. See, I can't live the rest of my life with his dead eyes swimming about in my head, yeah?"

"So why not one of your friends here?" PigBoy says, motions to Misfits and Volvo in the buggy.

"What, these wankers?" Dante laughs again—hard enough to throw himself into a small coughing jag. When it subsides, he continues, "These pussies couldn't whack someone's pet fucking *gerbil,* never mind someone's father. Besides, have you *seen* my dad? He's enormous. He's a bloody walking, talking side of beef."

"It's got to be someone who really wants it bad. Who really wants to see his blood spilled. It's got to be someone like you," he finishes, lifting his index finger, poking PigBoy's chest on the last word.

PigBoy seems to weigh the options in his mind. If he's weighing the same options of this situation that I am, he's about to realize there *are* no options.

"You promise you'll kill the son of a bitch, I'll tell you how to get to him—and in the process, your sister. However, if you promise, and don't carry through, I'll hunt you down and make you bleed. For a very, very long time. So what's it gonna be, mate?"

PigBoy holds up a finger, walks over to me, leans in close, whispers, "What do you think?"

"I think you're gonna tell him what he wants to hear," I say. "That's what I think."

67

He nods, his eyes darting around on the ground, piecing things together, picking out all the snags. If PigBoy promises to kill Barnes, he gets information he may or may not be able to trust. He doesn't promise, he gets jack shit out of Dante. Even if we subdue and torture him, he'll most likely just spout lies to save himself and we'll be no better off than when we started. And if PigBoy promises to kill Barnes, then for whatever reason can't follow through, he's a dead man.

"Oy, what's it gonna be?" Dante barks. "Ain't got all day, chum. Pigs to throw, you know? And what with your man crushing one of my boys' skulls, I've got to go find me another. So get with it already."

PigBoy shuffles back over to Dante, head down. When he's in front of him, he lifts his head like it's weighted down with rocks. "I'll do it."

"'Course you will," is all Dante says. Then he pulls back and slugs PigBoy hard in the chops with a left. PigBoy falls back and to one knee, bleeding from his bottom lip.

Tom growls, takes a step toward Dante, who holds up his right hand, shakes his left of the pain. "Ease up, big fella, ease up."

Tom looks at me. I nod, look back at Dante. Tom stands his ground.

Dante points at PigBoy in the dirt. "That's for making my crew one short," he says, turns around, and walks back toward the dune buggy. Volvo shifts over to the passenger side. Dante jumps into the driver's seat.

"Whoa, whoa!" I yell, walking toward the dune buggy. On the way by, I pull the gun out of Gus's limp grip, point it at Dante. "Where the fuck you think you're going?"

Standing next to the buggy, arm stretched straight out, I cock the hammer. The barrel is about a foot away from Dante's grinning face. "Tell us."

Tom is right behind me. "Sister," he says. It's a command.

"Oh that," Dante quips. "Right. Well…" He pops the buggy into gear. "You ever hear of Oliver's Great Big Rainy-Day Fun-Time Book of Prophecy?"

"Oliver? Who's Oliver?"

"Sister," Tom says again.

"Yeah, yeah, sister, ya great oaf, hold on, I'm gettin' to it," Dante says to Tom. He turns his attention to PigBoy. "Oliver," he continues with an air of learned distinction, "was a little boy what could tell the future, believe it or not. Our man Oliver's father wrote books. In these books, he laid out a pile of stuff his son claimed would someday come to pass." Toothy grin. A sidelong glance at Volvo. "He predicted something for your friend."

"My friend? What friend?" PigBoy says.

Dante points at me. "Him."

"Me?" I say, astonished.

"Him?" PigBoy says.

"Sister!" Tom says, becoming increasingly irate with the lack of forward momentum evident in the conversation.

"What's he got to do with anything?" PigBoy says. "You better not be fucking with me."

"Go," Dante says. "Read up on our Oliver. You'll find out what I'm talking about." He revs the buggy's engine.

I step out of the way, lowering the gun, bellow to be heard over the high-revving engine: "You don't even know my name! How do you know it's me in this prophecy!?"

"Don't need to know your name, mate!" Dante shouts back over the roar. "I know your face!" He pops the clutch. Gravel spits out from under the tires. A cloud of dirt plumes up. PigBoy staggers out of the way, spluttering.

I turn to watch them go. As he speeds away, cranking the wheel hard left toward the scree of the rock-hewn stairs at the base of the flame pit, I catch a glimpse of the back of Dante's shirt.

It reads, VIRGIL HAS LEFT THE BUILDING.

exas Drawl's brains are drying fast. The stew that used to be his head cooks on the cracked surface of the red-dirt road. The heat near this flame pit is so intense, there's actual popping and crackling sounds coming from the post-cranial mush.

Gus sits in the bed of the Camino, ready to go back to his pumps. Tom waits on the hood of the car, ass planted firmly in the giant dent he's made. With no more peanuts to munch on, Gus drops off, his snoring the sound of rocks rattling around inside a leather bag.

I walk over to Texas Drawl, lean down and grab his gun lying next to one twisted arm, pop it into my jacket pocket. I walk back toward PigBoy, who's heading over to the Camino, hand him the gun Gus had used.

Looking up at the stairs leading to the hole to Upside, I see Dante and his boys hooting and hollering on their way to fetching more pigs.

Shit like this would never have flown back in the day. When I first got here those thirty years ago, Hell was a place to actually fear—in a *hardcore* way, and on a constant basis; now it seems like it's a place to just sort of dread a little…from time to time.

But hey, maybe I'm just feeling a bit of residual resentment for having lost some of my control back there in that confrontation. Maybe I'm feeling a bit useless when fucking *Upsiders* need to take control of situations a Hell-dweller like me should be more than competent to manage. Yeah, I know, I regained control, it all balanced out, and we both have our strengths and they complement each other wonderfully and blah-blah-fucking-blah—it doesn't mean shit to me. I didn't land down here due to my patient, understanding nature. I'm severely pissed.

"So why you bringing me along anyway, hot shot?" I ask PigBoy when I catch up to him. "Huh? You obviously don't need me. You're great at this. Just go beat the crap out of everyone and drag your sister back home with you, simple as pie."

I'm talking shit and I know it. But I can't stop myself.

"Nah, that ain't true at all," PigBoy says and keeps walking toward the car. He opens the passenger-side door, slides inside.

I walk around to the driver's side, getting angrier with every step. I'm not sure what it is that's upsetting me so much. I mean, so what, right? The kid doesn't need me. If I want to buy into my own line of bullshit, why not just drop him off wherever he needs to go and head home, forget about it?

But I can't. I think I *want* him to need me more than he does, and the fact that he doesn't stirs up long-forgotten emotions in me. Emotions that are partly responsible for landing me here in the first place.

Now, let's get something straight: I'm not one of those wackos who always *wanted* to go to Hell. And I'm not one of those guys who never really cared one way or the other. You know those types. Like they're just *so* cool that anything The Big Red Fella can dish out they can take lying down, yawning and smoking a great, fat stogie, not even breaking a sweat.

Whatever.

I never had that kind of confidence. I was always terrified of going to Hell. Not that the fear stopped me from doing any of the things I did, of course. And over the years, I've come to pinpoint the reason for my anger: Weakness in people—even when it's me who *makes* them weak. The fucked thing is that even though I get mad at their weakness, I *need* them to be weak so that I can feel strong. Needed. Useful.

What's even more messed up—and this is why I never thought I'd go to Hell—is that I never meant to hurt anyone.

Sure, I broke some backs, snapped some ribs, severely humiliated pretty much everyone dumb enough to get in my way, and even paralyzed someone from the waist down, putting them in a wheelchair for life. And, of course, there's my grand finale, the icing on my fucking shit-life's cake: little miss Orange and White.

Little miss Dead and Gone.

But I never *meant* any of it, so I thought I'd be okay. I don't even know why I thought that 'cause I had no reason to; I just always thought I was safe from this melodramatic bullshit because what happened in my life was not my fault, was never my fault.

Pardon me, Mr. Lame-Ass Excuse? You're needed over here. You're taking the wrap for this pathetic loser's fucked-up, useless, hurtful existence. Thank you, sir. Your contribution does not go unappreciated.

So, yeah, standing next to my Camino's dented black driver's door, all these feelings, all this pure, unequivocal *hate* welling up within me, I just want to smash PigBoy's skull to splinters, watch his blood splash my arms and the red, steaming dirt. I want him to *hurt,* just like I wanted that kid I put in the wheelchair to hurt. I think if no one else had been around when I'd pushed him down those stairs, I probably would have killed him. I remember wishing so badly that no one else was there, watching him twitch in the hallway, wailing like a baby about his back and legs. Every time he opened his mouth to scream new pain, I wanted to shove my foot down it, stomp him till he shut up. All that stopped me were the other people, all soothing voices and helping hands. It disgusted me.

But now…

Now it's just me, these same feelings, and this wiry little punk from Upside.

Then the strangest thing happens.

It vanishes. All of it—the visions of the kid in the wheelchair, of crushing PigBoy's cranium to dust, the black ball of hate winding through me, growing with each heartbeat.

Just disappears.

I stand there blinking my eyes. PigBoy opens his car door, steps out.

"You two getting in or what?" He has the smirk of youthful arrogance, completely oblivious to the fact that I've just come *this* close to ripping his head from his shoulders.

Part of me wants that red rage back. It's a familiar place, comfortable. I know what to do with myself when I'm in that state. But it's gone now, as though never there. I can't even *make* myself angry, looking at his smug, piggy face.

"Yeah, I'm coming," I mumble.

Tom slides off the Camino's hood, lumbers up into the car's bed, plops himself down hard beside Gus again—there's really no other way he can do it—giving my suspension another rude jolt.

I lift the handle, get in the car, shut the door softly.

On the way back to Gus and Tom's pumps, no one speaks. We don't even look at each other. There's no cheesy '80s music playing now. No singing along. No sound except the car's engines and its tires on the red road.

This is not an adventure, and we were foolish to think it would be. Sure, it's different than every other day down here. But it's too heavy. It's like a weight on our chests that we can't push off.

When we pull up to the pumps and pile out, Miss Appleton is there to greet us. A friendly face. Something to settle our nerves.

"What's the word, Apple?" I say, twizzling my sparse little goatee. "Find anything out from customers?"

"Not much. Just what we already knew—that random drive-by piggings are going on and no one knows where all the livestock's coming from."

A breakout of livestock down here is definitely something of an event, since The Big Red Fella banned farms because he wanted to make it more 'challenging' to come by food. I know it's his job to make things tough and all, but come on. A fella's gotta have freshly cooked meat every once in a while. Of course, there're illegal operations scattered around, which The Big Red Fella and Barnes try their damnedest to quash but, just like Upside, no police force in creation can stop a well-run syndicate of organized crime. They've been trying to shut down the operation that supplies Hell's Kitchen with their sporadic delicacies of 'beef' and 'chicken.' That said, the animal-based products, though familiar in name, aren't quite like they are Upside. Only the best-cooked meat has any chance of absorbing a single iota of flavour or tenderness.

I guess that's what happens when Hell's DNA scientists try recreating this stuff entirely from memory. Not that I should know that. Not that anyone's supposed to know that, but there you go. Secrets are true bitches to keep down here. "Great," I say. "So all we have to go on is some dork prophet named Oliver." I lean against one of the rusted pumps, pop the last smoke out of my pack, flip it up to my lips, light it.

Inhale…Smooth as shards of jagged glass. Everything down here is artificially produced. Nothing is grown anywhere—kinda tough to grow things out of dust and ash. The ironic part about that, though, is that everything tastes just *like* dust and ash. Then again, can't be much better in Heaven, if there is one—I doubt that there's much good topsoil up there, either.

"Oliver?" Apple says. "Who's Oliver?"

"Prophet," I say. "Dante told us to read up on him. It's our only lead in any of this, so I figure we've got no choice."

I turn to Gus. "Let's head to your library, chum. Got us some reading to do."

Gus looks shocked. "Oh, so we're all just gonna pile into my library and sit around readin' ancient texts, are we? While who runs the damn pumps?"

"Big Tom can look after 'em," I say, turn toward him. "Can't you, old friend?"

"Tom sees Miss Appleton. Time to love and stay," Tom says, walks over to where she stands, puts his arm gently around her, pulls her close, and smiles down at her.

It's always a little frightening watching Tom touch Apple. You're never sure if he's going to squeeze her just a little bit too hard, out of sheer excitement, and break her in half. But Apple never looks scared. She just grins back up at Tom, snuggles in close. They walk together to the gas station's shop, open the door and go inside to enjoy the time together between customers.

At moments like this, I remember that I've been alone—with regard to women—for all thirty years I've been down here. I'm far past trying to kid myself that I'm not lonely. Most of the time, though, I'm fine with it. I just occasionally get those sharp stabs. The kind that creep up on you, leave you sad for about an hour afterward. But it goes away, and I do my best not to let another one sneak up on me.

"Alright," PigBoy says, "Tom and Miss Appleton can stay up here, watch the pumps. Me, Stu, and the old fuck—"

"Hey! Watch yer goddamn mouth, boy," Gus says, and takes a slow, wobbly step toward PigBoy. "I ain't too old to—"

"Yeah, yeah, okay, keep your dentures in, pops; I'm just fuckin' with ya. Jesus."

Gus doesn't respond, just ambles off toward the shop without a word.

"Hey, why don't you lay off Gus, Aaron? We're lucky—"

"PigBoy. Remember?"

"Okay. Fine. Whatever. PigBoy. Why don't you cut Gus some slack? We're lucky he's willing to let us check through his dusty stacks for this Oliver cat, you know? I mean, shit, man, this is your sister's *life* we're talking about here. You should be kissing that 'old fuck's ass instead of reaming it every chance you get."

"You done with the lecture, dad?"

"Oh, fuck you—"

"No fuck *you,* you pompous cocksucker. Telling me what my business is when it sure as hell ain't *your* sister's life on the line. You can cast all the judgements you want. You can act like you know all about me. Get all pissy when I show some confidence, take control of things. You feel threatened by little Upsider boy. You think you're hiding it well, but you're beaming it out in all directions like a fucking lighthouse."

77

Taking a single deep breath, PigBoy steps up to me, gets even more in my face.

"So don't tell *me* to lay off, alright? I'll give Gus an easy time when you grow up and quit acting like the older brother who's lost his youth and 'edge.' I'm not interested in a prick-waving contest; I just wanna find my sister before she gets fucked in the ass by demons or impaled and roasted on a goddamn spit. Is that so much to ask!?"

I'm silent. I just stare at him, my mouth parted slightly in shock. He steps back, lowers his head, looks away from me. "Look, man...I'm sorry, okay? It's just that—"

"I know, I know. Tension's high, that's all."

PigBoy's silent for a few seconds, then he looks at me again. Hard. But not in anger. I think it's confusion. "Why are you even helping me, Stu? I mean, what's in it for you? Sure, I saved your ass a couple of times, but you've paid me back. I'd say we're about even."

That weight on my chest feels heavier when the words are out of his mouth. "I don't know, man. I guess I just got wrapped up in it and now it's forward momentum carrying me through." But it's complete bullshit. It's so lame, it practically limps out of my mouth.

I'm such a dick; why can't I just say that I want to help him? It's been more than implied, and yet when it comes to stating it clearly face-to-face, it makes me feel weak.

PigBoy doesn't call me on it, though. He just nods slightly, says, "Yeah...forward momentum." He walks past me toward the shop, where Gus has finally reached the door. PigBoy gets there before him, holds it open. Gus looks at him for a second, as if expecting it to be some kind of trick, then slowly edges past him. A slice of Tom's and Apple's laughter floats out the door before it closes.

Standing out here alone, the distant internal-organ-rearranging thuds of the Lake of Sorrow eruptions shimmering through me, I feel at once both the weight of what's to come, and the lightening of a load—though what load I'm leaving behind, I don't know.

I flick my cigarette away from the pumps—just in case Gus is watching—and head in to join the others.

've never seen Gus's library, so I'm really looking forward to checking it out. Every other time I've asked to see it, Gus has come up with some pathetic excuse why I can't: "Need to clean up in there," or "Got one of the books out on loan to a friend, and ya should see it when they're all there. Can't see it half-assed." Well, hopefully he's got something on this Oliver guy—half-assed or not. If he doesn't, we'll have to start poking around public libraries, and that's a thought I don't particularly relish.

Our public libraries are like public parks after dark in major Upside cities. It's true that the freaks come out at night, but they stay all *day* at the library. If Hell had zoos, our libraries would only need to change the signs out front and they'd be ready for business.

"So, Gus," I say, clapping and rubbing my hands together, "am I actually going to get to see your legendary library, or have you got another lame-ass excuse for me? Like maybe your non-existent dog ate all your books, or you're having a maid come in to clean the place?"

But Gus is still in no mood for my not-so-clever quips. "Follow me, ya mouthy bastards," is all he says.

PigBoy and I exchange 'whoa, what did we do?' looks that we both know are entirely unwarranted. Guess even gentle ribbing is out of the question right now. We keep our mouths shut and follow.

Gus walks down the hallway that leads to the back entrance. About halfway there, he stops at a small door I've never noticed before on account of it being painted the same shit brown as the rest of the hallway. He turns to his right, reaches in his overalls, pulls out a fist-sized key ring, flips through the keys slowly, angling them this way and that in the dim light from the main shop.

"Gus," I say after about two minutes of key rustling, "you always been as slow as you are these days or is it a relatively recent development?"

I know I shouldn't get under his skin like this, but damnit, everything he does just makes it so easy. Luckily, he's concentrating too hard on finding the right key to give me much of a tongue-lashing. "Nope, always been like this," he says. "Won't rush for God or monsters, sonny."

Then: "Son of a bitch!" Gus cries, and triumphantly holds aloft the right key. He crams it into the keyhole, cranks it around a bit, breaks it off. "Aw, hell." He pokes around inside the keyhole and eventually fishes the broken piece out, lets it drop to the floor, forgotten.

80

More flipping through the remaining keys, some mumbling about having a spare somewhere…and then: "Sweet mother of Jesus, I think ya might be it," Gus whispers to another key, gently inserts it, twists it in the lock, sticks his tongue out, squints his eyes closed as if praying, and—

There is a faint click, and the door opens a few inches. PigBoy and I creep forward to see what mysteries he's unveiled, but Gus stops us. "Hold on, hold on, I have to get the lantern. It's…" He sticks his bony arm into the darkness of the open door, "…somewhere around…" leans in, pulls out a dusty lantern, "…here."

Gus smiles wide, blows the dust off the lantern; PigBoy and I wave the dust away from our faces.

"Haven't been down in a while, fellas," Gus says, grins a little.

"Down?" I say. "Down where? You got stairs leading under this place?"

Gus ignores me, reaches back into the darkness behind the door, and pulls his arm back with a fistful of long matches.

"Lost the box years ago," Gus says. He lets most of the matches fall to the ground, holds on to just one. "Gimme yer Zippo, boy."

I dig in my pocket, hand it over. Gus takes it with the hand that's holding the single long match. "Here, hold onto this for a second," he says, passes me the lantern. He flicks the wheel of the Zippo and a red-orange flame leaps to life. Moving the match to his free hand, he touches the flame to its tip. The hallway flashes bright for a moment, then settles into a hazy orange glow.

I pass the lantern back to Gus, who sticks the match into it, lights the wick. Again, there's a quick flash of brilliance before Gus turns the wick down, and we're back to the soft orange glow.

Gus hands back my lighter. "Now, watch yer step, ya dumb shits. The stairs are falling apart."

"Lovely," says PigBoy.

Gus ignores him, opens the door farther, pokes his head inside, takes the first step tentatively.

PigBoy and I follow quietly. The first few steps are solid, like concrete, but then the fifth or sixth one cracks loudly under Gus's feet. We all stop dead. Gus moves his other foot to the next step down to get the weight off the one that just cracked.

"Just use the outer edges of the steps. Should be alright," Gus says, and carries on down the staircase.

PigBoy and I manage to creep around the cracked wooden step. Gus's orange lantern glow seems to get hazier the farther down we go. He knows the steps, so his footing is surer than PigBoy's or mine. He's getting away from us.

"Hey, Gus," I say, "Slow down a bit. We're losing your light." No answer. Gus just floats away a little more.

81

Something brushes past me going the opposite way, up the stairs. A chill crawls over my scalp, shimmies down my spine. "Oh shit, man, you feel that?"

"Feel what?" PigBoy says.

"Someone in here with us."

"Sure do."

"Jesus," I say, and shiver again.

"Doubt it," PigBoy says.

"Gus!" I say, this time louder. "Wait up, you old fool! We can't see where we're going!"

His voice floats back up to us. "Only one way you *can* go, idiot—down!"

"Well, Christ, how much farther is it?"

"Quit bitchin' and keep walkin'!"

Something else whips by me, this time whispers words in my ear. But they're too fast; I can't catch them.

"Holy shit, man, what's in here? Things keep whipping by me, touching me, saying things…"

"Same here," PigBoy says, his voice a bit shaky. "So why don't we cut the chitchat and pick up the pace, shall we?"

THE DISTANCE TRAVELLED

I take the steps faster, caring less and less with every one whether I fall through them or not. Some crack, one even splinters—the sound enclosed in this tight space is nearly deafening—but they hold until my feet find a relatively solid landing.

My chest tight, my mind spinning, PigBoy bumps into my back as he joins me on the landing. I barely see the glow of Gus's lantern, but from what I can make out, the staircase spirals a little to the right as it goes down. Shadows flit here and there around the old guy's dwindling lantern.

"Keep moving," PigBoy says. "Come on, why're you stopping?"

I force myself to carry on.

Between tentative steps, I hear Gus fumbling with his massive set of keys again. PigBoy, also hearing the rattle of the keys, pushes me gently aside, moves past me.

"Hey, hang on a second!" I shout after him, and the walls blast it back in my face. I wince, wait for the echoes to die down. "PigBoy!" I lean forward into the dark and whisper. "Aaron!"

Nothing. Just his steps thudding down the staircase. Gus's keys have stopped jingling, and the glow from below is nearly entirely gone.

82

I hear a strange popping sound, like the clasp of a button coming undone, feel something brush by me again—softly, though, as if lingering to savour the touch. The popping sound is followed by a slowly unfurling umbrella—metal spokes and vinyl webbing expanding, straightening, flattening out until...*snap!*

It's completely open.

And there's breathing right next to my ear, almost on my neck.

I freeze, reach a hand out straight in front of me, terrified of touching something, but compelled to know what shares this part of the staircase with me.

I touch nothing.

I turn around, grope madly, blindly behind me. Still nothing. Yet a man's voice is right next to my ear.

"Why?" he says, softly. A voice I recognize. "Why do I keep following it, Stu? Do you remember?"

My thoughts scramble around inside my head for a few seconds, trying to understand how this man—how *any* man except the two men I came *in* here with—could be beside me, talking to me, asking me questions.

A man that I cannot touch.

"Do you remember?" he says again. Not impatient, just repeating the question.

I wet my lips to speak. "Because…" And then my tongue gets caught and I have to wet my lips again. "Because…you haven't yet been everywhere it has to go."

Poe's telltale heart slams in my chest.

The voice says, "That's right. And neither have you."

The umbrella breaks down, metal and vinyl collapsing this time. The clasp pops again, closed. And then something brushes by me, going up the stairs, though there are no footsteps.

I turn and barrel down the remaining stairs, heedless of crashing through them, just wanting to be away from that spot, out of this staircase.

It's complete pitch and I keep bumping into the walls as I spiral farther down, until I round the next bend and see the glow of Gus's lantern. Able to see where I'm putting my feet, I place them more carefully now, stop ramming my shoulder into concrete.

The final twist in the staircase is a sharp one, so I bounce off the wall near the bottom and careen in through the doorway. Rich amber light suffuses my eyes, and I fall in a heap against a long, thin table in the middle of a very small room.

"Whoa, watch where yer goin', boy! Jesus H in a sidecar, what's wrong with ya!?" Gus says. "Ya knock any of these books off the shelves and I'll knock *you* off yer shelf, got it?"

83

My jaw muscles lock when I try to explain. "Door…" I say, being completely unhelpful. "The door…gotta…" I see black spots in my vision, try to blink them away. I flail a leg weakly in the general direction of the open door, the darkness outside creeping into the room like fog.

No one gets the hint.

I open my eyes. Brittle, earth-toned books fill the floor-to-ceiling shelves around me. Craning my head back, I see PigBoy with his nose in one of them, oblivious to my pleas. I edge myself away from the table, fling my leg out, this time close enough to connect with the edge of the door. It swings shut and all is the soft orange of the lantern. I close my eyes, lean back against a table leg.

"Ya gonna tell us what *that* was all about?" Gus says and steps into my field of vision.

"Small room," I say, my jaw muscles finally loosening up.

"Yeah, it's a small room. Don't try to sidestep me, fella. I been alive longer'n Shakespeare's been dead. Now come on, out with it. What's got ya runnin' in here like a damn fool, nearly knockin' over my book-readin' table? Made that fuckin' thing with my own two hands."

THE DISTANCE TRAVELLED

My legs, still mostly jelly, send signals to my brain that, should I test them, they will flat-out refuse to support my weight. So I shoot a hand out in front of me, motion for Gus to help me up.

"Aw, Christ," he says, and pulls me to my feet with both hands. I lean against the table for support once I'm standing.

"Gus," I say. "What in hell is out in that staircase?"

"What, them things that fly by ya and whisper shit ya can't make out? Those're ghosts, dumbass. Shadows of death, ya know? That all it takes to rattle ya?" Gus shakes his head and shuffles past me toward one of the two bookshelves on either side of us. He picks one from near the top, pulls it out ever so gently, cracks the front cover, puts a finger in and follows the lines as he reads them.

I turn around, defiant, wanting to be taken seriously. "Hey, one of them spoke to me, and I could very clearly understand what it was saying."

Gus, without even looking up or taking his finger off his line, says, "Impossible."

"No, *quite* possible." I take a step toward him. "And I think— no, I'm *sure*—it's the same guy who I saw behind the gas station after Salinger carved me up."

Gus grins a little, closes his book, looks up at me. "The Fairy Cloud Man? I think ya took a mean bump on the head at some point in all this excitement, boy, and now yer hallucinatin'. Why don'tcha crack a book and make yerself useful already?"

"Look, I know what I heard, and—"

"It ain't possible," Gus says, replaces the book he's looking at, fishes in the stacks for another. "They don't speak—never have. I been comin' down here fer about a hundred years and never once have I caught a single word any of 'em have said. So what makes you so special?" He turns and looks at me hard. "I sat in that stairwell once for almost three full days, quiet as a god-damn church mouse, listening hard to try to understand even one syllable, but nothin'. Not a thing."

"Well, most of them I couldn't understand, you're right, but I heard the man with the umbrella. It was like he was right in my head."

"That's 'cause he probably *was* in yer head, ya damn fool. Now get lookin' fer this Oliver fella, or go back upstairs—*by yourself*—and help Miss Appleton and Tom look after the station. Your choice, but do one or t'other. I'm sick of yer voice today, boy."

There's one chair in this tiny closet library, stuck under the far end of the skinny table. Gus pulls it out, plops himself in it, thumbs carefully through a dark, fat tome, and pointedly ignores me. I know if I say another word, he'll try to brain me with the book, so I shut my mouth for the time being, walk over to the opposite shelf where PigBoy is, and pull out a book at random.

"Oh," Gus says, "and like I told yer friend there, ya rip out a page of one of these books, ya bend a corner, ya abuse 'em in *any* way, we're back upstairs and yer never gettin' down here again. Kidnapped sister or no. Got it?"

"Yeah, I got it, Gus."

I open the book I pulled from the shelf, start thumbing through—gently—and realize very quickly, by taking a quick look around the room, that we could be here all week. "No idea at all where to start, then, Gus? You've never come across any mention of this Oliver kid's prophecies?"

"Name rings real faint bells, but I can't remember which book I saw it in. Shut up and read."

So I shut up. And I read...

I read about Hell's history, the thwarted uprisings against The Big Red Fella way back in the days when he actually put in an appearance every once in a while. Not like now. Now there are only rumours that he's even still alive. But things continue to run as always, so someone must be in control, and there's no proof that he's not, so people continue to believe. I think it was Michel de Montaigne who said, "Nothing is so firmly believed as that which we least know."

Doesn't matter anyway, though. If it wasn't The Big Red Fella, it would be someone else. Chaos never rests. Death doesn't sleep. Torture and torment can't go on vacation, and someone has to keep it all in line.

I flip a chunk of the pages and settle on a section that tells about a place in Hell the temperature is far cooler than anywhere else. It became a mecca to those seeking a way out. Maybe not a way out of Hell, per se, but at least a new section where something might be *different*. A lot of what makes Hell so unbearable is its unchanging nature. Nothing is ever new. Everything is the same. Even daily destruction of body and soul can become commonplace, and people will look for a change wherever they can find it.

This place, which people referred to as "The North," soon became overrun with people trying to find a way out.

Black magic, massive mechanical drills, human and demon sacrifices—they tried everything they could to break this part of the underworld open. Of course, there was nothing special at all about the place; it just didn't circulate the air as well because of the slight angle it was on coupled with the situation of its many buildings.

Then there was the genius who tried to convince as many people in his immediate vicinity as would listen that Hell needed a sociopolitical structure. He said we needed sector leaders, a working economy, politicians and *a legitimate government*, god-damnit—we needed to organize ourselves, no matter the cost. Money not just going from individual to individual, as was now the case, but money that would go for the greater good, he said.

The greater good. In Hell.

Yeah.

So that guy was lynched and his body mashed into unrecognizable mush—and then the mush itself smeared into the ground until there was hardly a trace that he'd ever existed.

People don't want reminders of Upside. At least not *those* kinds of reminders. There's no democracy down here. No communism. No armies. No alliances. No voting, health care—no real structure at all. It's every person for themselves. A certain amount of cash is distributed every once in a while to people's mailboxes, and that's that. You deal with what you get. You want more than you have? Go steal it. Go swindle people out of it. Prey on the sick, the retarded, the old, the weak, the dying. No one makes money honestly here. Hell wouldn't really live up to its name if they did, would it?

Flip, flip. Turn the page.

More dumbasses. This history book is littered with idiots trying to salvage some semblance of their old lives. They all die. Murdered, slaughtered, struck down by The Big Red Fella (if you dig back far enough, when those sorts of Biblical things were still in vogue). Or for the truly unlucky ones—shunned by everybody, blackballed, excommunicated. Napoleonized. Left to waste, rot away, with no one by their sides.

No matter what existence you call home, loneliness is—and always will be—the worst thing there is.

So there're only the sounds of very old book pages turning, like leaves scraping gently across cold earth. Then—

Something else. Quiet at first. Coming from outside the door.

Maybe footsteps on the old wooden stairs. Very high up, though, if that's what the noise is.

I turn to Gus. "You hear that?"

He doesn't look up from the book he's scanning. Flips a page.

"Shhh," I say. "Listen."

PigBoy looks at me, stops turning his pages. Gus doesn't raise his head from the book, but he stops flipping the pages.

Nothing. Then…there it is again.

"Hear it?" I say.

"Didn't hear shit," Gus says. Flip, flip.

I look at PigBoy. "You?"

"Yeah," he says dreamily, "I think I did hear something."

"Just the ghosts is all," says Gus.

"Too heavy for ghosts," I say.

"Yeah," PigBoy says, "'cause ghosts are lighter on their feet than that."

I give him a look. He gets my drift, keeps his mouth shut.

The noise is even, very paced. Methodical.

And getting louder.

Gus looks up slowly from his book, closes it, squints his eyes. Listens hard.

The noise continues, getting closer.

"Definitely footsteps," he finally says. "Must be Tom."

"Why would Tom come all the way down here?" I say. "He's bloody enormous. Would he even *fit* through that little doorway, and around those spiral twists in the staircase?"

"Dunno," says Gus. "Guess we'll find out, won't we?" He twists a little in his chair, turns it more toward the closed door, as if settling in to watch a movie. He crosses his arms. Waits.

I stand glued to the spot, to the left and behind him a bit. PigBoy is closest to the door, but as the sound gets louder, PigBoy puts the book he's checking out back on the shelf and shuffles a little closer to me.

"Gotta be Tom," PigBoy says. "Definitely ain't little Miss Appleton—unless she suddenly gained about 300 pounds."

Closer.

"You know who else is big," I say. And wait.

No answer. More footsteps.

"Salinger's big. And Salinger's *real* fucking mad at us," I finish.

"Don't suppose," PigBoy says, "this place has a back door, huh, Gus?"

"Nope."

"Fuck me."

Now we're all three of us just staring at the door, waiting for it to open, and for whoever's heavy, plodding footsteps those are to burst into the room, slice and dice us, rip us to shreds, mash our bodies into stringy gristle.

One thing that's systematically pummelled out of a person

down here is any form of sunny optimism. You're either a realist or a pessimist—and eventually the realist submits, too.

"And no weapons, either, huh?"

"No, sir," says Gus. "Just my withered old dukes, fellas. Sorry. Didn't figure I'd have to protect my little library with automatic rifles and the like."

The steps are coming around the final corner, slowing down. They stop.

Three kicks to the door, near the bottom. Then a muffled grunt.

We exchange furrowed eyebrows. *What the fuck?*

Three more kicks, this time harder, rattling the hinges in the door. Another grunt. Two more kicks.

"Whaddaya think?" I whisper. "One of those Upside pigs, maybe wandered in the back door upstairs, came down here looking for food?"

"Or," PigBoy offers, "maybe Salinger grunting and banging himself against the door like a zombie. His brains have been scrambled rather nicely, you know? I imagine a slug to the head at close range will do that to you. Speech might be a skill he hasn't quite mastered yet."

More kicking and grunting, more emphatic than before.

"Well," says PigBoy, "if it's a big fat pig, we can just sit tight and wait for it to get the idea that it's not getting in. It'll eventually wander off, right?"

88

"Right," I say, still keeping my voice low, "or it's Salinger and he'll keep healing while he bugs the shit out of us with that banging. Then he'll remember how to use a doorknob and we'll be fucked."

PigBoy scoffs. "All three of us, in hand-to-hand combat? No way."

I lock eyes with PigBoy. "If we hadn't had a gun earlier today when I was on that rack, there's no way we'd have ever escaped. Salinger is a walking tank. He'd have torn us limb from limb if we'd stuck around…probably even *with* half his head and throat in tatters.

"So yeah, all three of us. If that's him behind that door, and we wait around till he regains all his mental faculties and physical strength, we'll be very, very sorry."

We're quiet, just listening to the banging and ever-increasing grunting that has almost taken on some semblance of speech in its frustration.

"Why doesn't he bang near the top or middle of the door?" PigBoy says. "He got no arms, or what?"

"Who knows?" I say. "Maybe only his feet are in proper working order. Maybe the signals to his hands aren't being received properly. Not sure. Never had my skull scrapped by a bullet before, so I don't know how such a wound would heal."

Seeing movement in my peripheral vision, I glance over at Gus. He's nodding his head as though having come to a decision. "Let's open the door, take our chances," he says. "What else we gonna do?"

And the shit thing is: he's right. There's nothing else to do but get it over with.

"Go ahead, then, Gus," PigBoy says. "It's your bright idea. *You* open the fucking door."

"Fine," Gus says, "I will," and walks over to the door. PigBoy edges a little farther away from it. I look down at all our fists—they're bunched up, as if our blows would do anything to stop Salinger.

Gus reaches out to turn the doorknob, and it's like every horror movie you've ever seen, except slower. It seems like it takes hours for that bony claw to clasp around the gold-plated knob of the door. When it finally does, he twists it in his hand, and yanks back hard.

I instinctively flinch back, my head turned to one side, waiting for Salinger's half-healed skull and throat to appear, a destroyed jack-o'-lantern, leering in the dim orange light.

89

Instead, what bends down and squeezes itself into the room is big Tom China, carrying a full pot of steaming coffee in one giant mitt, four grey mugs in the other, and in his mouth a small, white, two-compartment rectangular container of sugars and creams.

He grunts at us, his face red, little beady eyes narrowed, accusatory. "Mmmph!" he says in several tones of distinct unhappiness, until Gus's paralysis breaks and he moves forward to remove the sugar-and-cream container from Tom's mouth. When he pulls it away, drool slops onto the floor with a wet slapping sound.

"Wrong!" Tom bellows from his hunched-over position. "Brought coffee! Closed doors won't let me in!"

"Yeah, Tom, it's okay. You're in now," I say, walk over and pat him on the belly. "Come on over here, big guy." I take him gently by the elbow, lead him closer to the table in the middle of the room. "Set that coffee down and—"

Then Tom leans on me, like he's losing his balance. I try righting him, but he staggers, leans forward, his hands open, the coffee pot and mugs shatter on the floor, and Tom keels over like a giant crane blown over in a windstorm. He lands squarely on the table, crushing it to splinters under his huge frame. On the way down, one of his arms catches a lower bookshelf, sending nearly a full shelf of volumes sprawling from their places, scattering on top and next to him.

There's a moment of shocked silence—PigBoy, Gus, and I just staring at eleven feet of downed HellRat.

"Holy Christ," says Gus a few seconds later. "How the hell'd that happen!?"

His voice snaps me out of it. I kneel down, try pulling Tom's body toward me to get him on his back. He weighs half a ton, though, so he's barely budging.

"PigBoy, help me," I say as calmly as I can. No use panicking him further by shouting orders.

PigBoy doesn't move.

I turn my head, look up at him. "PigBoy, look at me. Look at me." He does. "Help me turn Tom over onto his back," I say slowly to make sure he understands.

I turn to Gus: "Go upstairs, get Apple. Tell her Tom's collapsed. She might know what to do."

Neither of them moves a muscle.

Fuck this shit. Tom's not dying on my watch. Not today.

"MOVE!" I scream as loud as my throat will allow.

Gus jerks as if slapped, turns around and shuffles out of the room and up the winding stairs as fast as his old bones will go; PigBoy just narrows his eyes and kneels slowly beside me, still apparently partially dazed.

"On the count of three, pull hard," I tell him. "Yank like hell."

He nods, seeming to be more in control of himself now. "Okay. Hard."

"Yeah, as hard as you possibly can. Here we go: One…two…three!"

I pull till I feel veins pop out on my forehead. Beside me, PigBoy's face is red and sweating hard. "Come on!" I say through gritted teeth. "PULL!"

Our hands seek better purchase on Tom's greasy overalls. We pull back hard again, and this time his body moves a bit. He comes up on his side about two inches, maybe three, then our arms give out and he flops back onto his face.

"Fuck!" I say.

"Hey, maybe he's already…you know.…Shouldn't we check for a pulse or something?"

"No pulses on HellRats. No pulses on any of us down here."

"Oh, right.…"

"Shit, we gotta do something. Run up and get Apple's ass down here faster. Gus probably nodded off in the stairwell or something."

PigBoy gets up, bolts up the stairs.

"Come on, buddy," I say, and slap Tom's exposed furry cheek. "Don't you check out on me now. I need your help with this shit."

A few seconds later, I hear footsteps coming down the stairs. Fast. A moment later, PigBoy and Apple rush into the room. Apple covers her mouth for a second, closes her eyes, then bends down next to Tom.

"Where's Gus?" I ask PigBoy.

"He's coming. He was only about halfway up the stairs when I streaked by him. He'd started back down again when Apple and I passed him, so he should be here any minute. But dude, he was trying like a motherfucker. He was giving it all he had."

PigBoy and I turn to watch Apple talk to Tom. She's holding one of his big hands. She can barely get both of hers around two of his fingers.

"Tom…Tom, can you hear me? Come on, honey, snap out of it. Don't give in yet. I need you. We all need you."

"Do you have any idea what happened?" I ask her. "Has this happened before?"

She shakes her head side to side. "No," she says, squeezing his hand. "He's had some dizzy spells and some pains in his stomach and chest, but he's never fallen over from them.

91

"Tom, come on, baby. Come back to me," Apple says and shakes his body. "Please…"

Gus stumbles in through the door. "Aw, Jesus, he's still down?"

No one answers the obvious.

"Look, let's try turning him again," I say. "All four of us. Maybe something will shift inside him—maybe whatever it was that went wrong."

PigBoy and I quickly move over to the side where the lower bookshelf got knocked off, kick the tomes out of our way, hunker down, put our shoulders as far under his bulk as we can. Gus and Apple take the other side—they're to pull, we're to push.

I count to three again, and this time he gets halfway over, threatens to come back down on us, then with a last hearty shove, PigBoy and I send him over the rest of the way.

No sign of movement.

"Come on, baby," Apple says again. "Say something. Anything." She leans over him, kisses him on the lips softly, whispers "Please, Tom" over and over. "Please don't go."

THE DISTANCE TRAVELLED

Tears drop from her eyelids onto Tom's face, mix with his fur. She strokes his forehead. Her chest hitches and she weeps, leans her head against his.

Something inside me sinks. My flesh turns cold. The room spins a little. This can't be real. Tom doesn't deserve this. Tom needs to come back. Tom needs to sit up, return Apple's kiss. He needs to smile for me, tell me that time is fun. My own tears threaten, and Apple's still whispering to Tom, telling him she loves him, crying on his face, stroking his cheeks, his head. So come on, Tom, old buddy, you gotta see how much she loves you, you gotta wake up, you gotta open your fucking eyes, you gotta sit right up and—

One eye cracks open.

His chest kicks. He coughs, groans, moves his head.

Apple must not realize it because her head is still hung and her lips move with the same words she's been saying for the past few minutes.

"Goddamn!" says Gus. "He's back!" He whoops and claps his hands together.

PigBoy just grins, pulls the chair away from the wreckage of the shattered table and bookshelf, plops himself in it, lets out a long, slow sigh.

92

I kneel down and grasp Apple's shoulders gently. "Apple, he's alright. It's okay now. He came back."

Apple keeps shivering and crying until my words sink in. Then she lifts her head and looks at Tom's face. His eyes are open wide. But he's not looking at Apple. He's not looking at anyone. His gaze is locked on nothing at all.

"I was gone," he says. "Tom was dead."

We say nothing, just wait for him to say something else.

"Nothing there. Nothing there." His voice is small, not at all like the Tom we all know. "Nothing for Tom to see. All the lights out…"

"It's okay now, Tommy boy, you're back here safe with us. Let's get you up and into the chair," I say. PigBoy stands up, helps us haul Tom up and over to the chair. I brush chunks of fake wood from his back while Apple does the same for his front. She is still crying, but she realizes that Tom's okay now, and just has to let it work itself out of her.

I didn't know they were this close. I knew that Tom always had a really good time with her, but I didn't know it was this serious. I guess I didn't figure Apple for the type to completely return the feelings that Tom had for her.

While Tom blinks his small, dark eyes every once in a while, as if waking from a bad dream, PigBoy and Gus clean up the books that Tom knocked over on his way down.

"Damn good thing he didn't bust my shelf, that's all *I* gotta say," Gus grumbles. "Might just be imitation oak, but it still cost me more fer raw materials than I'd care to disclose. And good thing I put the lantern on the edge of a bookshelf, not on the table, ain't it? We'd have no friggin' light at all, and imagine what *that* would be like with those goddamn—"

"Gus," I say.

He straightens himself after picking up a dusty tome barely held together by brittle leather. "Yuh?"

"Give it a rest, would ya?"

He grumbles something I can't quite make out and goes back to his books.

Apple strokes Tom's forehead, holds one of his hands, which resembles a rat's paw only in the way that its fingers curl up— otherwise, it looks just like any large, male human's hand...except about three times as big.

"So," Apple says, her voice still shaky, "any luck with the search for Oliver?"

I shake my head, walk over to the library's open door, crunching glass and porcelain from the shattered coffeepot and mugs under foot. "Watch out for this broken glass and shit, you guys. I'll go up and grab a dustpan and broom. Be right back."

93

"Tom's real sorry, Gus," Tom says, just before I head up the stairs. "Get us new ones. I'm real sorry. Clumsy and dumb...stupid, stupid."

"You're not stupid, Tom," I say. "You just misjudged your step is all, okay? Everyone's alright, so it'll all be just fine. Back in a flash."

I close my eyes as much as I can up the stairs. I even try to plug my ears so I don't have to listen to whatever haunts this staircase. I have enough to deal with right now, without listening to dead people's problems, as well.

'Shadows of death,' Gus called them. So not really dead people's souls, I guess, but their shadows. Echoes of distressed lives, maybe? I don't know. Any which way it's sliced, I want nothing to do with it just now.

Up and into Gus's tiny kitchen, I spot a handheld dustpan and broom shoved between the counter and the stove. I hunt around for a garbage bag. Can't find any new ones, so opt for the one already started in the metal bucket under the sink.

Before heading back down into the gloom of the stairway, I stop near the door and look behind me, broom, pan, and bucket in hand. Apple and Tom must be the ones who do the cleaning 'cause it's nearly spotless in here. When Gus was on his own those years I knew him before he met Apple and Tom, you couldn't see an inch of countertop, and you'd've been lucky to've slogged through the knee-high rubbish without getting slimed by cans full of maggots or cockroaches.

Nothing grows in Hell, it's true, but cockroaches and maggots are eternal. It's as if they have no beginning, no end; they just *are.*

Back down the stairs, thinking how grateful Gus should be for Tom and Apple, helping him out the way they have. No way his business would be doing even half of what it is, if it weren't for them.

Faint voices as I spiral down. Ghostly tugs on my sleeve as the shadows try to latch on to me from some other dimension, try to pull me into their plane, or gain entry to this one. It doesn't matter, and I don't care what I see or hear—now that I can't cover up my eyes or ears—just as long as I don't hear *him.* Umbrella Man. Cloud Guy. Whatever his name is.

How does he know me? What does he want? What do I have to do to get rid of him? All I want is some peace and quiet to think through this situation with PigBoy and his sister, and this prophecy crap. But shit keeps cropping up; things keep getting in the way. I can't concentrate long enough to—

Someone in the library shouts. The sound reverberates off the walls, floats up to me. I'm about halfway down and can just see the glow from the lantern. There's another shout, then a whoop from big Tom.

I barrel the rest of the way, clanging the metal bucket off the walls as I go. I make so much racket, I have no way of knowing what came after those first few shouts. But I don't need to know any more than what I glean from looking around the room when I finally stumble through the doorway.

Someone's found Oliver.

efore I get a chance to ask who found it and where it is, Tom is up out of his chair, half-stooped, the upper part of his back brushing the ceiling.

"Tom China," Apple says, arms crossed, "you sit right back down here in this chair. Let Stu take care of that. You need your rest!"

But Tom isn't having any of that. He ignores her, crushes what's left of poor Gus's handmade table farther into the ground with his giant clodhoppers. "Tom's mess. Gotta clean. Not yours for worryin', Stu. Sit and let me."

Tom holds his hands out, nods his head.

"Alright," I say, because I know the feeling a man gets when he needs to clean up his own mess. "You clean it up, Tom. But then," I say, and poke him in the ribs, "you let Apple take you upstairs to rest. Deal?"

"Deal."

I hand over the dustpan, broom, and bucket.

While Tom sweeps up the remains of Gus's table, coffeepot, and coffee mugs into the pan, I walk over to PigBoy carefully, doing my best to avoid the larger chunks of debris. PigBoy stands beside Gus clutching a slim, two-volume set of books to his chest. He grins like he's got a pot of gold.

Apple saunters over to us—it's not like she's trying to be sexy, she just has that absolutely effortless swing to her hips that you can only call a saunter—her eyes still wet from crying, puts one delicate little hand on my forearm, one on PigBoy's, looks us each square in the eye for a full second, says, "Is this it?"

PigBoy answers quickly. "Yeah, I think it is. I think these are the books." He smiles wider, pats the two books still crammed against his chest.

Maybe I'm reading too much into the way she asks the question, but I'm not so quick to answer. Feeling how tight she grips my forearm, the look in her eyes...I think she's asking if this is the last time she's going to see her Tom.

When I find the right words—or at least what I think *might* be the right words—I look down at her, into her soft brown eyes. She needs the truth.

"Yes. I think this is it," I say, and watch her reaction closely. She looks away from me, lowers her head, takes her hands away from mine and PigBoy's forearms. Stepping back a few feet, she finds the seat of the chair with the backs of her knees, sits down slowly.

When she looks up at me, she has tears streaming down her cheeks, but her eyes are hard. Dark stones staring straight at me. She says, "Then I'm coming with you."

I nod.

96

The moment stretches. Time draws out. I hear every little piece of porcelain, glass, and fake wood Tom sweeps up. PigBoy beside me, the only living, breathing creature in here and he's not nearly as scared as the rest of us. He doesn't know what's going to be in those books he clutches so tightly to his chest; he doesn't know, but he thinks it's going to lead him directly to his sister. He thinks his bravery, courage, and willingness to keep going when everyone else has given up are going to serve him in this journey, like they would undoubtedly do if he were Upside.

But he's not, and whatever is in those two books is not going to lead us *directly* to his sister, prophecy or no. Nothing down here is direct; nothing is surface-level. There is always—*always*—a better, easier way to do something, but the way that you decide on, or the way that is thrust upon you in desperation, is the way you inevitably choose. We are playing in a hot little sandbox designed by an angry, jealous fool who is the very *antithesis* of direct. Everything is a game, a trick, subterfuge; everything serves His purpose in some way or another.

That's what we believe, so that's the way things are. Maybe things could be different, but the people down here aren't here because of their bravery, their courage. We're here because we're weak, cowards, bottom-feeders.

That's what we believe, so that, too, is the way things are—

the way things will stay forever, because we don't have the strength to change, to become something more than we are.

But despite all this, I don't say anything to dash PigBoy's hopes. I let him clutch the books to his chest.

Once the moment has drawn itself out, smeared itself all over this tiny room, and all those little pieces of fake wood, glass, and porcelain are swept into a dustpan, deposited into a metal bucket with a loud crash, we shuffle out one after the other, up the stairs, in silence except for the echoes of the dead all around us.

Since Gus's coffeepot is destroyed, we're positioned around the front desk in the office, drinking weak tea and sitting on crappy gas station chairs. You know the kind—the ones with black vinyl covers and barely any cushioning for your ass.

PigBoy's got both books in his lap, about to open the first one. I tell him to wait a minute, there's something I have to ask.

Regardless what lies ahead of me, it's going to require a lot more of my friends than I've ever had to ask of them before, so shit has to be clear from the outset.

"Tom," I say, "you sure you're gonna be up for this trip? Someone can stay behind and keep the pumps going, you know. You don't have to come. You and Apple can chill here, keep each other company till we get back."

Apple speaks first: "I'm going wherever Tom goes." She strokes his hand where it sits in her lap...okay, where it nearly *covers* her lap.

Tom says, "Feelin' fine, Stu. No pain. We'll come on along. Whatever gets done. Miss Appleton and Tom. Beside you as friends." He grins and gently squeezes Apple's hand, looks at her, then looks back at me. I see that his mind is made up, so I say nothing, just nod and smile.

That just leaves Gus.

"You've done enough for me, old friend," I say, and even though he's a grumpy bastard and doesn't like folks touching him, I reach out my arm, place my hand on his shoulder. He doesn't flinch away or give me a tongue-lashing.

"Mayhap I have, Stu," he says. "But I been thinkin' 'bout closin' up this old bitch of a gas station anyway. Drainin' what little life I got in me, it is. If I gotta go out, I ain't goin' out behind this shitty old desk, pumpin' gas fer folks what wouldn't give a second thought fer me if they never saw me again. I'm with you all, come good or bad."

It's not déjà vu, exactly, but just when Gus finishes telling me his decision, there's a feeling of being led down a path. Whether for better or worse, I get no sense, but something intangible clicks into place, and all of this feels as though it's *supposed* to happen.

"Right, then," I say. "PigBoy, open up those books, and let's see what this Oliver kid has to say for himself."

«« —»»

The first book is called "Oliver's Great Big Rainy-Day Fun-Time Book of Prophecy: Part One." It's a dark green book, just under 50 pages. The second book looks the same and is about the same length but is called "Oliver's Great Big Rainy-Day Fun-Time Book of Prophecy: Part Two."

Who knew prophesying could be so much fun?

100

PigBoy clears a spot on Gus's desk, we all gather round, and he opens the first volume. There is no copyright date in it, of course, since there's no time, per se, in Hell. We humans have our own perceptions of how much time has passed, and most torture sessions operate on a 24-hour model just to save trouble, but it's an assumption based on another existence, another realm entirely, and so cannot be counted on to mean very much down here. And The Big Red Fella has instituted no strict means of measuring time, because, I suppose, it furthers his goal of eternal suffering and such.

My own thirty years have been measured by a small pocket watch I bought at a travelling flea market when I first arrived. Since you arrive wearing the clothes you died in (not the clothes you're buried in, as rumour has it), some show up with watches on, others without. I never wore a watch Upside because, for whatever reason, no matter what kind of watch I put on, it stopped within a few days. Wasn't the batteries, wasn't any sort of mechanical problem, wasn't that I'd abused them in any way— they all just simply stopped working. Something to do with the electrical field my body gave off. I never fully understood it, and don't really care to now, since it doesn't affect me down here. The pocket watch works just fine—presumably because I give off no conflicting electrical field now. That said, I never particularly cared that I wasn't tracking time Upside, either, since most of my life was spent in confusion and a steadily building black ball of hatred, the source of which I still have very little clue about.

The state I was in, time didn't matter. Nothing mattered. All that mattered was making myself feel better about who I was by beating others down—either verbally or physically—to a level where I became superior.

Ah, memories.

The first few pages of Oliver's little book are filled with indecipherable scribblings. Not words, really, more just symbols laid one on top of the other, layer after layer. They look hurriedly rendered, as if upon waking from a dream or nightmare, in order to capture their essences before they faded from memory. About the fourth page in is the first distinguishable marking. In a child's unpracticed handwriting is the book's title. Under that, written in a different hand—that of someone quite a bit older—was: "The truth as the boy saw it." This is underlined twice.

A diagram fills most of the next page:

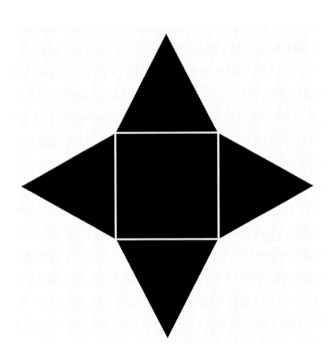

"Whaddaya suppose that is?" says Gus.

"Dunno," I say. But for some reason, I get a quick flashback of my grade five math classroom. I shake it off and say, "Keep turning those pages, PigBoy. There's got to be more writing."

PigBoy flips the next few pages quickly. More writing by the older hand, only shakier than before. Perhaps a product of time passed between writing, or maybe injury, but definitely the same person. Quite distinctive 'A's and 'T's. The writing is large, maybe fifty words per page, if that. Black ink. Choppy sentences. Illustrations line the margins, almost like picture frames, but they're similar to the first few pages of illustrations—difficult to make anything out in their multi-layered state.

This first page of writing says: "You who read this, it is the truth. The child saw it happen. His head does not lie. His head cannot lie. It sees everything, like a god's eye. This child of myth, of fancy, of ruin."

The second page of this writing reads: "So much has happened, but this will be the end of all those beginnings. The bottom will feed on the top, and the highest of all highs will be powerless to stop what cannot be stopped. The child's eyes are burning."

The third page simply reads: "Like haloes in the night."

On the fourth page is a scribbled drawing of someone that looks almost exactly like me, as well as the triangle that's to the left of the centre square of the diagram from the beginning of the book. Below it, more writing, this smaller and lighter than before: "Five pieces. First with kin. Below, below, where a giant 'S' glows." There is nothing but more drawings of strange symbols on the next several pages.

"What the bloody hell's that mean?" Gus says. "'Below, below'? We're as 'below' as anyone can go!"

I turn to PigBoy. "Is there anything else, any more writing?"

PigBoy flips through the rest of the book. "Yeah, there's some similar stuff near the end—more riddles, it looks like, only this time about the city."

"The city?" Gus says. "We ain't goin' there, are we? Jesus H. No good'll come of that."

"We go wherever this book *says* we go, Gus. What else can we do? It's our only lead."

Gus is quiet, just stares out the gas station window and picks his teeth, shakes his head.

Tom pats his old friend on the back, says, "Good'll come. Good'll come, you'll see." He smiles. Gus just turns away from him.

"You all don't know nothin' 'bout the city. It's worse'n it is here. A damned sight worse, to be sure. I used to live there, right in the heart of it. Right in the blackest part of that city, and I'll tell ya, it's filled with crazies. 'Least there's some kinda sanity out here, this far from the core. But in there...Goddamn, boy, in there, you go mad. I mean it, you go loony, start thinkin' weird shit, thoughts that ain't yers, thoughts that shouldn't be anyone's, but there they are in yer head, squirmin' around, makin' ya think things you'd never think. Makin' ya do things ya can't ever erase from yer memory. Turnin' ya into someone else, someone that—"

Gus stops, seems to realize where he is and what he's been saying...realizes that he doesn't want to be saying any of it.

"Well," he says. "Just let's see about this first bit. No use gettin' all worked up about somethin' we might be able to avoid, right?"

No one says anything.

Feeling the need to break the sudden tension, I crack a phony smile, join Tom in patting Gus on the back, and say, "Right! So, let's figure this first piece out, then, shall we? What do you think it means? Obviously, our young prophet saw things in short, particularly unhelpful bursts. Or maybe his translator is being purposely obtuse because that's how prophecies are. They have a reputation to uphold, after all. Can't just have a plain-as-day prophecy that's figured out in a matter of minutes, can you? What would the other prophets have to say about that, eh? Might get kicked out of the club."

My levity goes unnoticed, and everyone just sits with long faces.

"Come on, come on," I say. "We can't get down about this already; we've barely started!" More smiles, more cheer.

Nothing.

Tom just keeps patting Gus's back; Gus continues gazing out the window, likely at some shady, haunted past we all know nothing about; Apple holds Tom's other hand and stares at the floor, her brow furrowed in concentration, as if doing differential calculus in her head; and PigBoy stares at the crisp, brown pages of the book, drooling a little, his tongue stuck out the corner of his mouth—the gears are turning, but the machinery needs oiling.

The giant weight of expectation lands squarely on my chest again.

I can't do this. None of us can do this. I should just go home, brew some coffee, sit in front of the TV and fall asleep. Forget any of this ever happened. I'm so far out of my depth, I'm already drowning. And there's no help from any of my friends. Everyone just stares at me, or at nothing, as if waiting for something else to happen, like they're waiting for me to lead them when I'm just as lost as they are. Why do *I* have to be the one to take control? Why does it have to be me? I like to be in control when it's something I *can* control, but this…Jesus. I'm no leader. I'm no—

"Subway," Apple says just then, slapping my pathetic train of thought right out of my skull.

"What?" I ask, the word not connecting itself to any imagery in my head.

"Subway," she says again, even softer this time. "Below, below, where a giant 'S' glows." Then she lifts her head, her eyes focus on mine. "We've got to get to the subway."

15

his is probably the last time I'll ever see my Camino. Goddamn.

After scavenging around Gus's office and back room for flashlights—we manage to find three with decent battery power—we head toward the car where it's parked out front…with the exception of Gus.

Like me with my car, Gus knows this is probably the last time he'll see his pumps. Tom gives the place a quick goodbye, but he's not quite as affected, since he wasn't the one who started the place up. He was a hired hand that became a friend and, eventually, a partner in the business, but it's different when something is your baby, your own creation. Even when it's just a rundown gas station in a mostly forgotten corner of the underworld.

Though we've left him to it inside, and can't know for sure, I picture Gus saying a fond farewell to his little library in the basement, locking it up for good, hoping that if anyone ever comes here to take this place over, turn it into something else, they'll have the same love for the printed word, and for history, as he does. I picture him grabbing a few things from the drawers of his desk—maybe letters from people we don't know, trinkets from women given to him ages ago, photographs, scraps of paper, postcards, even though we have no postal service here.

People continue to make things that have no purpose because it reminds them of home, their old lives. Not that you can ever completely forget where you are, of course, but if you surround yourself with reproductions of things from home, and allow yourself to believe in them, you can certainly fool yourself once in a while.

I have no urge to take anything from my house with me on this journey; Tom and Apple have nothing, either, and PigBoy, obviously, has just the clothes on his back, and the need to find his sister. But Gus...I've no idea how long the old guy's been down here, and when I ask him, he just says stuff like, "Since before it was called Hell, boy," or "I was part of the construction team, fella." So I know it's been a long, long time and, as far as I know, this gas station has always been his home.

Big Tom China's in the bed of the Camino, nearly taking up the entire thing but trying to squeeze himself over to one side enough to let Gus in for when he's finally said his goodbyes. I'm in the driver's seat, PigBoy's in the passenger seat, and we've Apple between us, Oliver's words of wisdom trapped in two small volumes tucked into her black purse.

The Camino rumbles, Tom shifts around in the back, getting comfortable, PigBoy fiddles with his zipper, Apple occasionally licks her lips and glances to the gas station door, awaiting Gus. And I just sit and stare straight out the window, seeing nothing ahead of me. I am motionless. Calm. I wait as if in a vacuum, a bystander, an observer in my own life.

If all of this has been preordained, then what can be done to stop it? If it was foreseen by some strange child of Hell eons ago, then what is there to be afraid of? I'll simply follow the clues in the book, plod along righteously to my destiny, and wait to be written about in one of those history books that smother Gus's library shelves.

But since I don't know exactly what I'll be doing down in this subway, or much of anything thereafter, either, I'm still flying by the proverbial seat of my pants.

That's assuming, the prophecy isn't just a load of crap, which, of course, it could very well be.

Still waiting on Gus, but released from my ruminations for the moment, I turn to Apple, say, "Got a smoke?"

Without looking at me, she says, "Where are yours?"

"I forget. Must have left them somewhere, or maybe I ran out. Dunno. My memory has always sucked pretty hardcore, and having my brain flash-fried these past thirty years certainly hasn't helped."

She delves into her purse for a few seconds, pulls out a pack, pops up a cigarette, puts the pack away, hands me the butt.

"Thanks."

"Sure," she says.

I push in the car's cigarette lighter, tap my fingers on the steering wheel.

"You okay, Apple?" I ask. "You seem distant."

"Yeah, I'm alright," she says, puts her head down, looks into her lap, strokes her purse strap. "You're not the only one who's gonna be parted from a car, though. And I barely even got to drive mine. Always busted, hood up, rotting away."

Oh, right—the rusting Mustang. Tom's perpetual hobby.

"Caused you nothing but trouble, that old piece of shit; you should be glad to be rid of it. Get yourself a new car after this is all done."

"Won't be the same," she says. She turns to look at me as the lighter pops out. I grab it, lift the burning coil to the tip of the smoke, puff twice, re-slot it into place. "And don't you let Tom hear you calling it a piece of shit, either. He works his guts out on that car."

"Whoa, whoa, no way," I say, holding up my hands. "I wouldn't say that kind of thing to your Tom. I know he works his tail off fixing the old girl, and he loves doing it, too, because it's for you. But honestly, I've never known a car to break down as much."

Apple doesn't respond for a minute. I puff away silently, letting my mind drift off with the curling wisps of smoke coming from the end of the cigarette.

107

Then Apple breaks the quiet, saying, "Just 'cause it doesn't run well very often doesn't mean I don't enjoy driving it when it *does* run well, you know?"

And I do know what she means. It's worth the trouble just to get to drive it once in a while. "Yeah, I know what you're saying. Same can be said for some people. You deal with them, weather the storms of the relationship 'cause it's worth it when things are smooth. That sort of thing, right?"

"Yes, exactly," she says, looks me square in the eye.

Apple's eyes are like honey. Dull, very light brown, far lighter than her hair. There is great warmth in them, which makes me wonder what her story is, what she did to get here. I wonder those things only to know how she manages to keep the warmth. Most down here didn't have that kind of warmth to begin with, but to retain it through the daily torture, the feeling of failure you get once you realize you're never going back.

Maybe one day I'll ask her, but now just doesn't seem like the right time.

And thinking of time makes me think of how much of it Gus is taking.

"I'm waiting one more minute for Gus," I say, "then I'm

going in to drag his decayed, rotting ass out of there. We got shit to do."

When the minute's just about up, the red lights of the 'No Vacancy' sign wink out. The internal lights of the store go out, too. Then Gus finally comes shuffling out of the gas station. Once he's through the door, he turns around, locks it, pockets the giant key ring. I'm surprised when his hand goes inside the pocket of his overalls and the key ring doesn't just fall through the hole-ridden thread.

"Fucking magic," I mumble.

Then Gus begins the long trek over to the car. But we don't have time to sit around and wait this go-round, so I flick my smoke out the window—it ricochets off one of the nearby pumps, lands in the dirt—pop the Camino into gear, pull around to Gus, stop beside him. "Come on, old timer. Hop in the back." I look at his right hand; he's holding a small pouch.

Memories, like I'd thought.

"Go on, you can share those with big Tom on the way, okay?" I smile, and for once, Gus returns the smile.

"Thanks, Stu," he says.

108

I won't say he has a lump in his throat, and I won't say he looks weepy-eyed, but his voice isn't as strong as usual. Memories soften every man, one way or another.

"But say," he continues, "since the road swings by a corner of the Lake of Sorrows, can ya slow up a bit as we go by?"

"Sure," I say. "What for?"

"Gonna throw these here keys in there, that's why. If I'm givin' this old place up, it ain't gonna be to no freeloaders. They want in, they're gonna have to fuckin' work to get in. No open doors to a place I built from the ground up, sonny. No open doors, ya hear?"

"I hear ya, Gus. Now get in the back there, and let's get movin'."

Tom reaches over and picks Gus up under the armpits, lifts him into the bed of the Camino.

I stick my head out the window. "You lovers comfy back there?"

Tom laughs, while Gus puts together a string of obscenities so long it must have started at his toes.

Tires spit gravel as we swing away from the station. On the way out, Gus taps on the back window for me to stop. I put on the brakes near where the sign reading "Gus and Tom's Gas" is posted. Gus motions for me to get closer to the sign on his side of the car. I back up, get as close as I can. Gus reaches out and yanks on the sign. Tom understands what he's trying to do, and leans over to tug on Gus while Gus tugs on the sign.

I just sit in the cab and hope Gus holds together.

A few more grunts and groans later, the sign comes free. Gus lifts it over the side of the car, plops it between his legs, motions for me to keep going.

Once off the small track and onto the main road, Gus again taps on the window when we come near the closest corner of the Lake of Sorrows. With Tom's assistance, Gus stands up in the bed of the Camino, looks a moment into the lava-filled depths of the lake, then chucks the sign in. It burbles and melts into the red heat-haze.

This close to the lake, and with no anti-Hell-heat equipment on, we're all soaked in sweat within a matter of seconds. Except PigBoy, of course, with his little mind-over-matter theory.

"We'll melt right along with that sign, if you don't hurry up, Gus!" I shout out the window.

Gus doesn't answer, just fishes the gas station key ring out of his overalls pocket, places it in one hand, then the other, hefts its weight. He hangs his head for a moment, as if in thought, then he tosses the key ring in a high, wide arc. Before it even hits the surface of the lake, it's swallowed from sight in the wall of shimmering heat.

Gus sits back down next to Tom, taps the side of the car twice. We churn up more gravel, and wait silently for the quiet blue 'S' sign Apple says marks the entrance to the subway stop.

Before we get to it, we pass my house. PigBoy and I exchange a quick smile about the sheet metal currently serving as my kitchen window. It seems so long ago since that cheeky pig skidded across my kitchen floor and ate the rest of my Boo Berry.

There's a fleeting moment of surrealism as the house fades off into the distance, and we drive away from the Lake of Sorrows. I've never been out of sight or hearing distance of the lake. I feel like a kid venturing out into the woods surrounding his house for the first time.

When my place is completely gone from the rearview mirror, I'm seized by momentary panic. I imagine the hands of destiny pushing me farther away, promising me that I'll never come home again.

With the lake behind us, a dimness seems to settle over things. My spirits sink further, and a knot in my stomach pulls tight.

Ahead, a faint blue light glows.

The good thing about Hell's subway system is that—like all subway systems—it's underground, which means it's cooler than it is up here.

Slightly cooler, anyway.

That said, there are several hundred other things that are most decidedly *not* good about it, which accounts for the main reason I've never taken the subway. Thirty years and I've not gotten to know much of my home at all.

The blue subway sign looms closer, and Apple says, "What about our torture sessions? Won't Barnes, Salinger, and the others notice when we all don't show up for our dailies?"

"Yeah," I say, "I suspect they'll have people out looking for us. We'll just have to be careful."

"Gus still have my gun?" PigBoy says.

"I expect so, though it's gotta be running low on rounds, doesn't it?" I say.

"Yeah, must be. Probably only two left, if my count is right. Shouldn't be too tough to get more in the underground."

I look over at him. "How do you know about the availability of firearms and ammunition in 'the underground,' as you so nonchalantly term it?"

"Books, newspapers, TV, radio—just kept my eyes and ears open; it was in my best interest to do so, you know?" he says. "Just 'cause *you* haven't paid much attention to your surroundings doesn't mean *every*one has to ignore them, right?"

And there's his fucking smirk again.

"For the week I've been here, I've read the newspaper every day," he continues, "watched the tube whenever Dante and the guys stopped somewhere between chucking pigs—convenience store, bar, wherever—and listened to the radio every morning in the buggy. I'd sneak into Dante's library at night, too, skim through his books, or maybe Barnes' books, I don't know. Seemed like pretty high-class reading for the likes of Dante.

"Also, don't forget I spent every moment—that I *wasn't* reading and listening and watching—with those four pig-hurling badasses. Despite how goofy some of them seem, they know their way around things. How do you think they've been able to get away with pigging people's houses for a full week? They know their shit, and they're very well connected. They'd started showing me the ropes to become one of their little crew, and I was an attentive listener, which makes people, in general, all the more willing to dispense information."

I say nothing.

"A guy can learn a lot in a week, Stu. If he puts his mind to it," he finishes, turns his head and looks out the window again.

Feelings of inadequacy well up inside me again, but there's no time to indulge them. The blue 'S' looms large through the windshield.

I pull the Camino off the road, head toward a broken-down wire fence about fifty feet away from the subway entrance.

Since nothing natural grows here, us Hell-dwellers can't hide our cars under bushes or giant tree branches to give us more time to escape when we're on the lam from the law. So I park the Camino near the broken pieces of fencing, cut the engine, get out, and lift as much of the wire as I can onto the hood and cab of the car.

"Piss poor, that," says Gus.

"I know," I say. "But do you see much more to work with around here, Gus?"

"Nope."

"So what do you suggest?"

"Nothin'. Just sayin': piss poor."

"Helpful to a fault. You're a true asset; don't let anyone ever tell you different."

I pick up several handfuls of dusty red dirt from the ground, chuck it onto the hood. "Good enough. By the way, Gus, check that gun in your pocket. How many rounds left? We might need some firepower down there."

Apple shuffles across the seat toward the driver's side, eases herself out of the car with grace. "Bit melodramatic, that, isn't it, Stu?"

PigBoy rolls his eyes. "Just a bit," he says, steps out onto the dirt from the passenger's side.

"Well, whatever," I say. "Sorry I'm not the tough-guy action hero, but we already have one of those." I glare at PigBoy.

Gus fishes around in his overalls, finally produces the weapon. He examines it like it's a deformed baby, turning it this way and that. "I know how it fires," he says. "Just like all guns— pull the trigger—but I'll be damned if I know how to get into it to check the ammo. Some modern, new-fangled contraption, I guess." He tosses the gun to PigBoy, who immediately presses something that releases the cartridge. It falls into his waiting hand.

"Yep," he says. "One in the clip, one in the chamber." He slots the clip back inside the gun's handle, tosses it back to Gus. His hands flail for it, but he completely misses; it clatters into the bed of the Camino. Tom reaches down, picks it up in two mammoth fingers, hands it back to Gus. Tom glares at PigBoy.

"You know, you're not exactly making friends acting like this," I say.

PigBoy looks at me, lifts an eyebrow, shrugs. "Is it my fault the old bugger can't catch? Shit, I tossed it as lightly as I could."

113

Tom slides slowly down to the end of the Camino's bed, steps out, stands up. He looks taller than before, maybe another couple of inches. His fur doesn't look as healthy, either. It seems to have lost some of its shine. But he seems alright, able to carry on, anyway.

"Well," PigBoy says, "Now that the car's well hidden," — another shit-eating grin, a roll of his eyes— "let's see what's what, shall we?"

He turns his back on us, walks toward the glowing 'S.' "From what I've read, you shouldn't leave your belly exposed among these people. They'll slice you, steal everything you've got."

Anger. Once again. Harder to control.

"You'd think," I say, slamming my door, stalking after him, "that a guy would be more grateful to the people trying to help him find his *fucking* sister."

PigBoy stops in his tracks. Behind him, someone emerges from the stairs leading up from the subway. But with the red backlit sky and the bright, glowing blue 'S' overhead, the person's nothing more than a silhouette.

Turning to face me, he says, "I *am* grateful, Stu. As grateful as I have to be, considering you have no choice."

THE DISTANCE TRAVELLED

"No choice? I can jump back in my car," I say, motioning behind me, "take my friends here and go back home, leave you to figure this out on your own. How's that for a choice?"

"You won't do it. Your conscience won't let you. Maybe I'm a prick—hell, most *certainly* I'm a prick—but you won't, *can't*, hold that against my sister." He lets that last hang between us for a few seconds. "So quit the fucking cockfighting and let's go try to save her, okay? This insecurity of yours is getting seriously old…and it's getting in the goddamn way."

The person who emerged from the subway walks by us. In the dim blue-red light, I can just make out that it's a man, but he's wearing a hooded sweatshirt and walking head down with his hands in his sweater pockets. PigBoy hears his approach from behind, turns and holds an arm out.

"Friend," he says. The man stops, looks up slowly, unhappily. "You know where I can get some heat? My friends and I are embarking on a little journey that may see some dangerous times, and we—"

The man just scowls and keeps walking.

"Thank you ever so much for your kindness and patience!" PigBoy shouts after the man; he does not respond.

Several more people come up the steps, some with backpacks, with full anti-Hell-heat regalia, others with nothing, like the man in the hooded sweatshirt. I suppose they're all going to their torture sessions. I had the luxury of being within walking distance of my appointed areas, but I guess everyone can't be so lucky.

PigBoy scans the small crowd as they filter by, stops one guy, scuffed leather jacket, the most dishevelled of the bunch, asks the same question he asked the first guy. This man, however, looks around him furtively. "You got money?"

PigBoy nods. "A few bucks."

He eyes us suspiciously. "Well, give it over and I'll hook you up."

I open my mouth to protest, but PigBoy's already digging in his jacket pocket. "Here's five," he says, turns to me. "Give him what you got."

I frown, turn around, look at the others. They're positioned around the car. No help there—the most I get out of them is a slight shrug.

Yeah, let's just let the bloody Upsider run the show. Christ.

I yank my wallet out of my jeans pocket, open it to see a fifty and a ten. No way I'm forking over the fifty. I pretend there's only the one bill inside, snip it out, close my wallet fast, pop it back into my pocket. "Here," I say, relinquishing the ten spot. "Better be the telling the truth."

The guy in the shitty leather just sniggers.

Why the fuck does *no one* take me seriously?

"Right, then," the guy says, leans in close, breath like a backed-up toilet. "Down the steps, through the stiles. Guitar player. Coupla revolvers. Maybe a rifle, not sure. Tell him Jesse sent ya. Later."

"Whoa, whoa, m'man," PigBoy says. "How much for the jacket?"

"Huh?"

"Your leather, dude. How much?"

"Uh…"

"Why do you want his crappy leather coat?" I say.

"I don't want it, man—you do," he says, and luckily for him, he doesn't offer me his trademark Bruce Willis smirk. If he had, I'd've lost it, gone seriously ballistic.

"What do I need—?"

But he's already waving Apple over. "Yo, Apple, come 'ere a sec, would ya!?"

Apple saunters over. The guy in the shit leather drops his jaw appropriately.

"Okay, bro," PigBoy says. "What's your price?"

115

Having wiped the drool from his lip and wrenched his eyes away from Apple's figure eight, the guy says, "Um, shit, man, I don't know. Forty bucks."

"You got a fifty, Apple?"

Apple digs in her purse, comes out with a smaller red purse, about the size of a child's hand. Fucking adorable. Of course. "Here," she says, hands the bill over to PigBoy.

"Off with it, chum," PigBoy says, dangles the fifty in front of his face. The guy shimmies out of his coat, offers it to PigBoy. They time the exchange so that each of their hands is filled with what they want at the same time. "Now, give him your coat, Stu—put this one on."

PigBoy tosses me the jacket. Again, I open my mouth to object, but what's the point?

"Fucking hell," I say, remove my jacket, toss it to the guy.

"It's not much," PigBoy says to the guy, "but it'll protect you from a little bit of the heat anyway, man. Thanks."

The guy nods, holds the fifty up, smiles, walks away.

"Whoa, boyo, hold up," PigBoy says, holds his hand out. "You've got sixty-five bucks, chum. We're only paying you fifty-five. Dish the ten back."

The guy just laughs, keeps walking.

I turn to PigBoy. "What'd you do *that* for?"

"Dude, your coat sucked *ass*. You'd've been knifed in the gut before you could say 'lame-ass jacket.' It was a kid's coat, Stu. I've actually *seen* ten-year-olds wearing ones exactly like it."

My jacket, for the record, was light blue, with an elastic-band waist. 100% Polyester. I paid a pretty penny for it at a travelling flea market several years ago—same flea market I got my pocket watch at. It most certainly did not suck ass. But whatever. Mr. KnowItAll has this all planned out, apparently, and I'm just along for the ride.

"Fine, whatever," I tell PigBoy. "My fucking coat is a ten-year-old's. I don't care anymore. But we're looking at what's written in that second book or I ain't budging from this spot. We don't even know that the prophecy extends to my saving your sister. Maybe Dante is just fucking with us. Maybe the prophecy leads us into some heavily nasty shit and we're about to just walk right into it."

He squints at me for a second, realizes I'm talking reason, and says, "Alright, fine, but let's make it snappy. We should have already been down in that subway, gotten our guns, and been on our merry fucking way."

He stalks back to the others. I follow.

"Lemme see the second book, Apple," he says, abruptly.

"Please," I say, prompting him.

"Fuck your please," he turns on me. "Time's draining, Stu."

Apple produces the second book from her purse, hands it to PigBoy. He flips it open quickly, scans. We wait.

And wait some more.

When he reaches the end, he sighs.

"What?" I ask. "What is it?"

He hangs his head. "Says nothing about my sister, about *any* girl at all."

"Ah, shit, hang on, man. Look closer," I say, move toward him, take the book from his hands. "The location of the other two triangle pieces were described in riddles, right? So maybe these last three are just harder to figure out."

I flip through, slower than PigBoy. I read over the short riddles. They definitely seem harder—they mean nothing to me right now—but Pigboy's right, there doesn't seem to be even a hint that any of the answers involves a little girl. But that doesn't necessarily mean anything. Maybe Oliver didn't "see" her very well, and his riddles are a roundabout way of leading us to her. The fact is, we just *can't* know unless we go through with it.

The weight of it all again threatens to overwhelm me, but I won't let it. I can't give in. Not in front of PigBoy.

I close the book, calmly hand it back to Apple. "PigBoy's right. There's nothing overt in there about his sister. But let's think about this once we get to it, okay? I mean, maybe there's no mention in the second book because once we find the fourth piece, the riddle to the fifth is revealed there and then, you know? It's a possibility anyway, right?

"Besides, there's nothing else we can do, unless we just want to throw in the towel here and now—which I, for one, sure don't want to do. There might very well be a little girl at the end of all this who needs us. You guys can let her down...but I'm not going to."

There's a moment of silence, then Apple cracks a tight-lipped smile...and bursts out a shot of laughter, trying to stifle it. It's no good; her outburst gives way to a full-fledged guffaw, then the others join in. Even Tom.

"Dude," says PigBoy, between his own bursts, "you're such a cheesehead." But he's smiling, and it looks like a genuine smile. And within seconds, I feel the tension in me releasing. It whips up my windpipe in a gasp of forced air, my cheeks puff out, then explode.

Tom moves forward, his whiskers wiggling against his face as great booming laughter comes up from his chest. He pats me on the shoulder, says, "You're good on the heart, friend Stu. Tough coat now, too. And your head full of the cheese."

117

More laughter. People continue walking out of the subway entrance, staring at us with hollow, wondering eyes. Wondering what we could possibly be so happy about. But it's not happiness, just release, though you'd be hard-pressed to tell the difference the way we're carrying on, bent over, hands on our knees.

We're lost out here, and likely lost in what's to come, too, but we're still laughing, and I think that says something for us. But then, maybe I'm just being a cheesehead again. Soft, malleable. Gullible.

Right now, I don't care.

Right now, I'm among friends.

17

ur laughing jag over, flashlights packed, Oliver's confounding prophecies stowed away in Apple's purse, and me with my new, tougher-looking coat, we're finally ready to go.

The others start ahead of me; I hang back for a few seconds, lean over, kiss the roof of my Camino. "Farewell," I say, and hope that the next owner of this old girl loves her as much as I do.

There're more pathetic saps like me down here than The Big Red Fella would ever admit.

Catching up to the others, I ask, "So what did the first half of the first riddle say again?"

"Five pieces. First with kin," Apple says.

"Right," I say…and say nothing more, 'cause I've no clue what it means. "Any ideas?"

"Not yet," says PigBoy. "Let's see what we see, Stu. Don't go looking too hard. Sometimes things plain as day are missed when you look too hard, you know?" He turns to Tom. "Hoist Gus up on your back, m'man. No time to dawdle."

Gus only objects once—as vehemently as possible, of course—before seeing the reason in this suggestion. Tom bends down on one knee while I push Gus up Tom's back; Gus wraps his arms around Tom's tree-trunk-thick neck, loops what he can of his legs around Tom's mid-section.

We shuffle past the last of those coming up from what was

presumably a full subway train of people. Reaching the top of the steps, we start down, the glowing blue above and behind us the only light into the dark below.

When we reach the bottom of the staircase, the faint blue glow dissipates, and we're left in darkness until our eyes get used to the torches burning dimly in several spots on the walls around the inside of the station. The ticket booth is shrouded in almost complete dark. The ticket-taker wears a bright white mask. It glows with a fierce luminosity, as if lit from the inside, like a jack-o'-lantern.

"How bizarre is that?" I whisper to the others.

"Relatively bizarre," says PigBoy, as if the subway ticket-takers Upside wear them all the time. Sure, we just shared a pretty hefty laugh, and I'm currently counting him as a friend, but he still says shit that makes me want to ring his fucking neck.

When PigBoy speaks, the ticket-taker looks our way. He says nothing, just watches us walk. His main interest, understandably, seems to lie in the giant HellRat hunched over carrying a dilapidated old codger in a threadbare pair of grease-stained overalls.

I hear the strains of an acoustic guitar coming from farther down a hall that branches off from this main part of the station. "Hey," I say to PigBoy, "sounds like our man."

He nods. "Sure does."

We continue toward the ticket booth. "Let me guess what you're going to say next," I say to PigBoy. "'Let me do the talking,' right?"

"No. Let Apple do the talking," he says, turns to her. "You've been down here before. Said you sang at Hell's Kitchen. So you gotta know your way around here better than the rest of us.

"We'll be memorable enough," he says, now addressing us all, "with Big Foot here walking around with Grumpy Gus on his back, so any degree of anonymity we can achieve will be welcome when word gets out that we're missing."

Before we're to the ticket booth counter, I have enough time to make out one of the ad posters plastered on the wall to my left. A torch hangs above, illuminating it:

SEEN GOD?
WE WANT TO KNOW!
(All calls are private and confidential)

There's a telephone number beneath the lettering—1-800-SEEN-GOD—and a big, gold, sparkling halo beneath that. Before I have time to ask anyone about it, we're to the window of the ticket booth, so I just dig in my jeans pocket quickly, pull out the pen and small pad of paper I sometimes carry around to help me remember things.

For what reason I've no idea, I copy down the information on the poster.

"Five t-t-tickets?" the white mask stutters. The voice is deep as a well, and strong as brick. Mechanical.

Apple, at the front of the line says, "Yes, five, please."

"R-r-right," the mask says. A machine whirs behind the dark glass. Five tickets spring from a barely glimpsed automatic dispenser. A gloved hand whips out and retrieves them. Apple slides a ten dollar bill through the small opening; Sir John A. Macdonald's head catches a glimmer of dim light for a moment, then is snatched by another gloved hand. Before handing the tickets through the glass, the white mask says, "Carrying any w-w-weapons?"

"No," Apple says.

"Running from a-a-anyone?"

"No."

"Hell's p-p-public transport s-s-system will not be used as a means of e-e-escape. Is that unders-s-stood?"

"Yes." Apple's answers are quick on the heels of the question. Short, clipped.

Looking more closely at the face behind the glass, I see a small circuit board through the white of the right side of the mask.

121

"Will you be...be...be...be—"

"What's wrong?" I lean over and ask PigBoy.

"Looks like it's stuck," he says.

The mask continues stuttering. After about ten seconds of it, I feel the need to state the obvious trouble. "Well, it's still got our tickets."

"This always happens," Apple says, and sighs. "And it's always just before you're about to get your tickets."

Behind me, Tom steps up to the glass, pounds it with a giant fist. Nothing changes. "Oy!" he says. "Tickets!" And pounds some more.

The mask sputters momentarily. The light of the mask dims, flickers, looks as though it's about to go out, then: "—be needing any protection on your journey into the city?"

"Protection?" I say.

Apple points to the right of the booth. A grubby, bearded man clad in black leather chaps and a ripped Judas Priest T-shirt sits on an uncomfortable-looking metal stool. He picks his teeth with a fingernail, looks at us with genuine loathing.

"No, thank you," says Apple.

"Enjoy your visit to the inner realm," says the mask, its speech malfunction apparently corrected for the time being. The gloved hand relinquishes the tickets.

We push through the turnstile—Tom steps *over* the turnstile—and we're through. I cast a wary eye at the bearded guy on the stool. He just picks his teeth and hums under his breath, still eyeing us with unwarranted distaste.

There's another set of stairs before us, and as we start down them, I ask Apple what the deal is with the protection option.

Apple shrugs. "It's tough to fill boring job positions—especially as you get closer to the city. The guy on the stool back there was probably the old ticket booth operator. Lot more excitement in being a bodyguard than a ticket-taker, no? Job still needs to be done, though, so they rigged up machines to do it."

Only one torch lights the way down these steps, and I stumble a few times before we reach the first landing. The guitar is closer now—sounds like the player is into Spanish music.

"Know what was with the ad poster back there?" I say. "The one about seeing God?" I ask Apple.

"Yeah, if you see God, there's a number to call."

"Oh…" I say, and frown.

Coming to the bottom of the second set of steps, a gust of warm air blasts me in the face. I turn to my right to see the subway whipping off down the tunnel, close my eyes against the grit and bits of newspaper swirling around my head. When I open them, Apple is proffering a cigarette to me. I take it, put it between my lips. She lights it for me.

"Thanks," I say.

"You'll probably need it to calm your nerves. A lot can happen down here, even just on a single subway ride into the city. Keep your eyes open."

The fact that she doesn't warn PigBoy or the others isn't lost on me.

I know I have this insecurity issue. Believe me, I'm well aware of it. But having my face rubbed into the fact that no one thinks I can take care of myself is pretty humiliating. Realizing the truth doesn't make everything alright, and it certainly doesn't make it sting any less.

Especially coming from Apple.

The funny thing is, I loathe others' weaknesses, have no pity for them. Yet I get my back up when my own weaknesses are pointed out—even when they're pointed out and treated with kindness, like Apple's doing right now. It doesn't seem to make a difference.

So I feel sorry for myself, start beating myself up about the way I am, the way I react.

And this is definitely not what is needed right now. Strength is needed, not sulking and moodiness. Stupidly, I wonder why no one turns to me when strength is needed, but the answer's right here, right now. It's happening inside my head while I puff away on this cigarette given to me to calm my nerves, relax me, so I don't lose my cool if the shit gets thick.

I am such an immediate asshole, given so quickly to shrinking inside myself the second an ill word is spoken of me. I tell myself I don't need anyone's approval, but even *I* know I'm full of shit. Who am I kidding? I need people's approval so I can feel superior to them, then beat them into the ground when they fuck up.

Spanish music drifts on the heavy air, coming from our right. A skinny young man with his head bowed in concentration strums an acoustic guitar; the case sits open at his feet. There are a few coins in it, but not many, and no bills.

Looking behind and to the left of the guy, I see that some joker has painted a blazing red pentagram on the wall, written "666" in three of the triangles inside.

Cute.

Just down from this are a few huddled shapes with their backs against the wall, legs stretched out in front of them on the ground. Possibly dead bodies. Possibly just those who've given up, content to while away the hours watching people come and go, till their next torture session.

A lot of people go to the sessions of their own free will—maybe to create some sort of order in their worlds, a reminder of a 9 to 5 they used to have. But even if they don't go on their own, torture is inescapable; someone will come for them, drag their sorry asses to those torture blocks, then haul them back here, dump them in a bleeding heap right where they found them.

Unless they run.

Apple flicks ash, walks toward the guitarist; the rest of us hang back a bit, but still within hearing range should shit turn nasty.

"Tough day at the office?" Apple says, that hip swing of hers in full effect. The guy doesn't look up, keeps strumming. "Tough day?" Apple tries again. The guy flips ice-blue eyes at her, brings them back down to his playing.

Apple turns on her heel, gives us a shrug, turns back to the guitarist. "Jesse sent us," she says.

The guy stops playing. Looks up again, this time longer. Seems to appraise Apple. Gives us the same once-over.

He raises the guitar strap over his head, sets the instrument down gently behind him, against the wall. Bends to one knee. Looks to his left and right. Satisfied, he lifts off the top layer of the guitar case, reveals his weapons stash beneath.

Authorities wouldn't detain this guy for selling us guns, since guns and other weapons are a part of everyday life down here, the ticket-taker's warning likely more just rote than any serious inquiry. But I assume from his apprehension, there may be others around who *would* mind him selling us guns, as he might be horning in on their business.

Apple kneels down, checks out the selection. The guy's crisp eyes flick to her again. "Before the next train comes."

Apple nods, points to two items I can't make out from where I'm standing, says, "Plus some ammo."

The guy licks his lips, thinking. "Hundred bucks."

Apple takes out her little red purse, digs inside, removes two fifties, hands them over. The man examines the money in the dim torchlight, turning it this way and that, checking for authenticity. Apparently satisfied, he pockets the money, lifts Apple's choices out of the guitar case, grabs what look like two boxes of shotgun shells, and some loose revolver bullets, hands them over. He puts the top layer of the guitar case back inside, stands up, straps on his guitar, and continues playing, as if Apple no longer exists.

124

The rumble of the next train approaching filters through the tunnel. Headlights appear around the corner to our left.

When Apple returns, PigBoy shouts over the growing din: "One for me, one for Gus! He's a crack shot!"

Apple looks confused. "What!? Why!? I bloody well paid for them! And Gus already has one!"

"Yeah, but with only two bullets. Come on!" PigBoy shouts. "Tom's got his hands full, and we need Stu to, um, help navigate or something."

Very smooth. I guess I'll just defend myself with my brooding personality and erratic mood swings.

"And you—" PigBoy breaks off, just as the nose of the train pulls into the station.

"Me what?" says Apple, frowning. She's holding a shotgun in one hand, a revolver in the other.

PigBoy turns around, looks behind him at the blur of the train. "Well, can you *handle* one of those things?"

Apple raises her eyebrows.

The train slows behind us.

"Can I *handle* one of them?" she says, head titled, face flush with anger.

PigBoy just stands and looks uncomfortable, the way most men do when confronted with an unhappy woman. Unsure what they've said that's so out of line. And unsure what to do about it.

"Of course not," Apple says, "I'm just a girl." She mock-smiles and hands the shotgun, revolver, and the accompanying ammo to PigBoy, who hands the revolver to Gus, who snaps his jaw into place in excitement.

"Right, well…" he says. "Now that, uh…that's settled, we can, umm…"

I know why he's distracted. The look on Apple's face tells him that this is most decidedly *not* settled. Not by a long shot.

Eager to get on to other business, and not particularly concerned that he'd not finished his last sentence, PigBoy turns abruptly as the train doors open with a soft *ping*, walks inside—

—and then is suddenly walking backward, pushed by a mammoth hand attached to a giant arm attached to an immense HellRat, who ducks and pushes until he's clear of the ceiling of the train, then stands up straight. He's not quite as tall as Tom, but is only about a head shorter.

PigBoy's expression is priceless.

"I know you," the HellRat says after a few moments of looking PigBoy up and down suspiciously, plate-sized hand still open on his chest. He looks up at us all. "I know all of you."

125

Well, Christ, what do you say to that?

Exactly. You say nothing, and hope the big son of a bitch moves peacefully out of your way soon so you can catch the next subway *away* from him.

No such luck.

While we're all frozen, standing there on the platform, wondering how this guy could possibly know us, there's another *ping* and the train's doors shut swiftly. The train pulls away.

When the rumble and wind die down, the HellRat speaks again: "Where were you going? Into the city?"

PigBoy just nods, gulps, blinks.

"No-no-no, nuh-uh," says the HellRat. "You're coming with me."

This is not, all told, a particularly auspicious start to our journey.

PigBoy then remembers he's holding a shotgun. Problem is, there're no shells in it yet. I watch these two things register on his face: from inspiration to defeat in a heartbeat.

Gus, too, is carrying a weapon that could get us out of sticky situations, but is in the same boat as PigBoy. And the gun with only two rounds in it is useless, too, since it would take at least four or five rounds to pulp the Hellrat's massive head.

The Distance Travelled

The only one of us who could take this guy one-on-one opens his mouth and says, goggle-eyed, "One of me. One of me."

The HellRat looks at Tom, smiles. He's wearing thick, horn-rimmed glasses, a baggy grey turtleneck sweater, and what appear to be dark blue pajama bottoms. "Yes, I'm one of you." He takes his hand from PigBoy's chest. "Look, you don't want to go to the city. Not yet. You must first come with me. I will show you things that will help you on your quest."

"Quest?" I say.

"You are on a quest, are you not?" he replies.

"Well, uh, I don't know if I'd exactly call it a *quest*, but—"

"You seek something, yes? A girl."

"Yes, we do, but how did you know—?"

The HellRat beams, stamps his foot heavily on the platform. "Then you *are* who I think you are. You *must* come with me, let me show you the things I've been waiting to show you for nearly a hundred years."

"Nearly a…" I trail off, stunned.

Goddamnit, at this point, I just want to finish a complete sentence.

"Come! Come!" he says, walks in the direction of the guitar player, keeps going right past him, and farther down the platform. When he gets to the end, he jumps down onto the tracks, waves his arms. It's so dark where's he's jumped, only his furry arm can be seen flailing about. His voice floats back to us: "Hurry! Before the next train comes! I live just down here!"

And then he's gone from sight, the sound of his stomping footsteps echoing back to us.

In the distance, another train rumbles closer.

So I'm the navigator, am I? Well, so be it. If that's my role, then I'm going to live up to it. I'm going to make decisions for this group and they're damn well going to follow me.

I jump down onto the tracks, walk toward the sound of the receding footsteps and fading shouts.

Behind me, PigBoy says, "Where do you think you're going? We're going into the city! You're not going to just believe that lumbering monster, are you?"

Tom growls.

"I'm going by my gut, PigBoy," I say without turning around. "And my gut says to follow him. I don't know if he's crazy or what his deal is, but I'm going to find out. I think this is very important."

I smile at my decisiveness, feeling genuinely *powerful* for the first time in a long time.

126

"You can either stay here and wait for the train, or follow me—but if you choose the city, you'll be going there without your prophecy boy." I stop where the torchlight fades out, turn around. "The choice is yours."

I turn around, keep walking, on and into the darkness.

127

 hear muttering behind me—the others discussing what to do. I find myself not caring as I walk through this inky black, letting it swallow me up, suffuse my thoughts, relieve the pressure of a game I have no clue how to play.

I turn around while walking. The discussion seems to be getting pretty animated. The occasional shout reaches my ears.

I see that the HellRat has come prepared; there's a spark in the darkness and a small light bobs up ahead. The rumble of the oncoming subway train makes the walls tremble.

I smell nicotine, burning wax, and stale coffee. Where it's coming from, I can't tell, but I salivate at the thought of a good, strong, black cup of coffee. Yes, coffee would be lovely, but a flashlight would be nice, too. Unfortunately, like with most other things of any use, I wasn't trusted with one—Tom, Apple, and PigBoy have one each.

Bob, bob, bob, up ahead, and then—

—a shout of further encouragement, and the light makes a sharp right quickly and disappears.

Behind me, footsteps and voices.

Not like they have much of a choice.

I spin round, yell for the others to hurry up, the train will come up on them faster than they think.

A few more steps and I see the glow coming from what looks

like a hole in the wall. As I get closer, I see that it's a misshapen doorway. Very tall, very wide.

Another few seconds and I'm at the doorway, peering inside.

The HellRat sits on a big faux-wooden chair. He smiles wide, waves me in. "Come on! That city train's a quick one."

I look behind me to see where the others are; they're making good time, hurrying along, only tripping and stringing together long ropes of curses occasionally. Behind them, the train has stopped at the station, and is now just getting up a good head of steam to carry on.

I look back inside the little cavern that this strange HellRat calls home…and a vague sense of disquiet comes over me. This felt so right before, but for just a moment, I feel as though I've made a big mistake leading my friends in here. It lingers for a moment, this feeling, as I step inside the cavern walls, then it disappears, as quickly as it came.

I have a moment or two before the others spill in to look with me at the paper plastered over every square inch of the walls. Trying to focus on any one newspaper clipping, though, proves to be more than my tired eyes can handle.

I need to rest.

130

We sleep the same way it's done Upside, only for different reasons. We rest because our bodies ache after being awake and moving about for a while. We might even dream, I don't know. I can never remember my dreams, if I have them.

My eyes focus on a few clippings as I scan around the room. Most of them look like religious rants from some of the weirder groups that have banded together down here to try to invent a new mythology—something to combat the bottom rung of the clichéd one they currently find themselves suffering in. It's really sort of a let down when you first get here and realize that you got sucked into believing all this crap. You wonder all the time how things might have been different if you hadn't swallowed the bullshit, hadn't believed in such obvious black-and-white sides. Would you still be here? Maybe, maybe not…and I suppose that's part of the suffering.

By the time everyone piles in to this dreary little cubbyhole, the rumbling of the train is deafening, its lights blinding. I turn around, squint at the doorway. The *whoosh* as the train passes pops my eardrums. The wind from its wake flutters all the pages on the walls, blows off a few that aren't stuck on properly.

"My friends," says the HellRat, bending down to collect some of the displaced pages, "I am Portnoy. Portnoy Spavin. I knew you'd come; I just didn't know exactly when."

There's the shuttling of a shotgun shell behind me. PigBoy sniffs, brings the massive gun to bear on the HellRat. "Enough bullshit, freak boy. What's all this stuff on your walls, and what do you *really* want with us?"

"I'm sorry," I say, "did you say your name was Portnoy?"

The HellRat swivels his head in my direction, while still trying to keep an eye on the shotgun. "Uh, yes, yes. Portnoy Spavin."

"Portnoy," I say, roll the word around on my tongue. I love tasting words like this. "Portnoy," I say again, drawing it out.

The HellRat eyes me suspiciously. "Yes…Spavin." He frowns, turns his attention back to the shotgun. "Do you mind…?"

"Come on, PigBoy," says Apple, pulls out and lights a cigarette. "Give it a rest, would ya?"

"No, I *won't* give it a fucking rest! How do we know what this guy wants? Look at all the freaky shit on his walls. He could be some kind of whacked out serial killer or something. We *are*, after all, in Hell, you know. Not everyone's peaches and cream, like us."

"This is true," says Apple, blows smoke in PigBoy's face, making him squint and cough. "But I trust Stu's judgement."

Portnoy grins, puts his hands up in supplication, walks slowly over to a small desk in the corner of the room, pulls out a tube of some kind of poster paste. He finds some of the pages that wouldn't stick the first time he tried to put them back, picks them up, slaps some goo on their backs, and goes around the room pasting them back in place.

Just above his desk, and to the right of about five stacked, filthy mattresses that form Portnoy's bed, there is a window painted onto the concrete. The window looks out onto a blue sky, with a few puffy clouds here and there. Portnoy sees me looking at it, says, "I read about them in books. Skies, I mean, not windows. Vast expanses of blue, strewn with beautiful white clouds."

"I've almost forgotten what a sky looks like," I say. "But PigBoy—he's from Upside. A real, live human. He can tell you about skies." I turn to him. "Can't you, PigBoy?"

He stands with his legs spread apart, shotgun still trained on Portnoy. But I can see him softening. He looks from the painting of the window to Portnoy, then back to the window again. He sets his lips tightly. "Yeah, skies are fucking brilliant. So what. You mess us around, big boy, I'll blow you into little pieces. Got it?"

Portnoy nods, says, "I'm not the most passive of my species—I can push hard when I need to—but I'm by no means the most aggressive, either. So believe me, the last thing I want to do is hurt any of you. Okay?"

PigBoy narrows his eyes, waits a beat, then lowers the gun. "Okay...for now."

I look over at Tom, wondering what his reaction to all this is. He's just staring, standing stock-still, with Gus still on his back. Gus is picking his teeth with a bullet—sadly, the gaps in the top row of said teeth are big enough that a bullet is just the perfect size toothpick for him.

I get Gus's reaction before Tom's: "He's a fuckin' loon, you ask me. But never mind my opinion—it ain't my shindig." He goes back to picking his teeth.

Tom, not taking his eyes off Portnoy, finally moves. He lowers Gus to the ground gently, walks forward, brushing past PigBoy. Portnoy looks slightly alarmed at how close Tom is. The two stare at each other from about a hand's width apart. Then Gus reaches his arms out to Portnoy, clasps his shoulders tight, and says, "One of me. Really, really. One of me!"

Portnoy smiles, returns the gesture, clasping his hands to Tom's shoulders. "Yes, so you said before, and the truth still remains. Though I've never seen one quite your size. You're a head bigger than me, and forgive me for being blunt, but your coat doesn't look quite...healthy. Is there something—?"

132

"No pain," Tom says, shakes his head. He turns to me, drops his hands from Portnoy's shoulders. "No pain, right, Stu?"

"Yeah, big guy, no pain. No pain at all." It's the hardest smile I've ever had to wear. And by the look in Portnoy's eyes, he can tell it's not genuine. But he says nothing.

"Well, that's good, then, Tom. Good to hear." He claps his hands on Tom's shoulders heartily before lowering them to his sides.

Tom stands and grins, apparently content just to look at another of his kind, right here, in the flesh.

"There aren't many of us left, you know, Tom," Portnoy says, sits back down in his chair. "I've only seen two or three with my own eyes in the city, and there are only supposed to be about another ten, maybe twenty in all of Hell.

Tom nods, deep in concentration. Then he says, "Time is fun, so we oughtta have it while we can, right? I say that sometimes."

"You're right, Tom. Time *is* fun. That's a good way to think of things."

"Once the time is done, the fun might be done, too."

Portnoy nods sagely, as though Tom is dispensing age-old wisdom. "Truer words, my friend. Truer words."

The expression is lost on Tom, so he just smiles, steps back a couple of paces, puts an arm around Gus where he leans against the wall near the entrance.

"This is real touching and all," PigBoy says, "but like King Rat here says, we've got a girl to rescue, so let's get to it." He turns to Portnoy. "Spill already. How do you know so much about us?"

"Because of Oliver, of course," Portnoy says. "The prophecies, as I said before. I have a copy of the books, too. They're relatively rare, but a few copies are still floating around for true collectors."

"How do you know we have a copy of the books?" says PigBoy. "We haven't shown them to you."

"Well," says Portnoy. "How else would you have gotten here?" He smiles, chuckles a little.

PigBoy just frowns, realizing his suspicions are steadily mounting up to a whole lot of jack shit.

"You know the scoop on this Oliver kid, then, do you?" I ask, taking the opportunity to interject before PigBoy can think of something else stupid to ask.

"A little, yes. I know that no one's quite sure where he came from, since he never said a word his whole life. He just drew things and wrote the occasional word now and again. It was his father, Jonathan, who pieced his son's prophecies together, seeing in his boy what apparently no other could see. Everyone else just thought him dumb or mute. The father was a recluse, so not much is known of him, either. Most of any information now is likely 99% legend, 1% truth."

133

"What do you mean when you say that no one knew where he came from?" Apple says, exhaling, flicking her spent cigarette butt out the cavern door.

"Well, there's apparently no record of him coming through from Upside—same with his father. And they're definitely not naturals, since they were human. A lot of people think they were both sent here by some form of divine intervention."

I remember the phone number on the pad in my jeans pocket. "God?" I say. "*Here?*"

"Could be, it's hard to know. There are no reliable sources to go to, except the prophecies themselves."

Portnoy gets up, goes to his desk, pulls out one of the upper drawers, and gently removes a swathed rectangle, roughly the size of a book. He unravels the burlap-type material carefully, opens the book—not enough so the spine might crack, mind, just a little. "One thing, though, that's not written in any book dealing with this prophecy is that I've travelled the road that you're about to embark on," he says, touches the book—the second of the two—reverently.

We all just stare for a second. Then PigBoy, being the first one to find his voice, says, "Come again?"

Portnoy grins, apparently satisfied at our stunned reaction. "I've already been down the *very* path that you're all about to go down. But I'm just a minor player in Oliver's foretelling. Nothing was properly revealed to me. I wasn't able to get any of the pieces of the puzzle depicted in the first book because I'm not" — Portnoy turns to me— "you."

I gulp, and feel distinctly like I'm getting a little too big for my britches here.

"So I travelled on the road, but wasn't able to stop to see any of the sights, if you follow my meaning. I didn't even get to meet the people who hold the five pieces; I was just able to figure out the riddles—to the best of my ability, anyway—and get in the ballpark of where the pieces are. The rest, I suspect, was hidden from me by...well, by something watching over the puzzle."

Something occurs to me, and I allow a sliver of hope to creep into my voice: "Did you copy your answers to the riddles down on paper?"

Portnoy sighs heavily. He points to his desk. "One of the drawers in there contains a bottle of single-malt scotch for me to dive into whenever I think about that."

"Ah," I say, spirits deflating.

"I did not think to do so, and I have no idea why. Perhaps whatever oversees the proper path of the prophecy made me forget what I knew. Maybe I was so far off in my guesses at the riddles that for me to tell you my answers would lead you astray instead of help you. I simply don't know. But now that you're all actually here and it's finally coming true...those reasons don't seem to hold much water. It seems far more likely to me now that I am just a stupid creature who got carried away with something I should probably not even be messing about with. Even if it's true that I'm a part, however small, of the way the prophecy unfolds."

"But hey," says Apple, likely trying to brighten the mood, raise the spirits of the person who, right now, is our only decent lead, "this all means that you can show us what you know of the route, right? Why don't you come along, show us the way?"

PigBoy immediately raises the shotgun again. "No way. No. Way. Not gonna happen. How come you guys want to trust this wacko? Have you all overlooked the very obvious sanity problem he has? Hell, even *he's* doubting his need to be involved in this stuff! And look at these walls! How do you explain all this?" He waves the gun around, pointing out the newspaper-clipping wallpaper.

"Even though I'm sick of justifying myself to you," Portnoy says, clearly annoyed, "I will do so one more time.

"These newspaper clippings are just snippets of mentions of Oliver's prophecies. I collected them so I'd be ready for when you came. I've always hoped I was destined for something bigger than my own paltry life. And yes, I have doubted my own involvement in this because I sometimes feel that all the attention I've paid to it has done—and might yet still do—more harm than good. But regardless of any of that, I *knew* someday you'd come, knew it from the very core of what makes me who I am.

"Haven't you figured it out yet?"

"Figured what out?" I say, after a moment's stumbling thought.

"I'm the 'kin' Oliver mentions in his first riddle. 'First with kin,' remember?"

"Ohhhhh," says Apple. "Holy shit. Tom's kin."

"So then—" PigBoy says, putting the puzzle together in his head.

"You've got—" I add.

"The first triangle," finishes Portnoy. "Yes, I do."

135

«« —»»

"When an event bigger than any one man's life unfolds, it finds ways of making things happen, of creating 'coincidences.' Do you know what I mean?"

Portnoy walks over to his dirty bed, sits down on it, reaches his hand into a concealed slit in the second mattress down, pulls out a small object wrapped in the same burlap sort of material as the second book was. He smiles down at the tiny thing in his hand. "I've held onto this for so long, I can't remember a time when it wasn't with me."

The five of us remain silent while Portnoy strokes whatever's inside with the love of a proud parent.

Now comes the real test, though. If what's inside that little folded-over piece of burlap isn't one of the triangles pictured in the book, we'll know that PigBoy was right all along, and we'll have wasted so much time.

"Things just work out," Portnoy says, dreamily. "Sometimes you're made to wait a long, long time for them, but eventually,"

THE DISTANCE TRAVELLED

—he pulls the burlap back with his other hand— "all the forces working together to create a particular history pull taut...and show you the way."

Sitting in Portnoy's hand is a metal triangle, about the size of a human fist.

I've said it before, and I'll say it again: "Fucking hell."

I'm reminded of part of a spoken-word performance I saw back on Upside given by Henry Rollins. He was talking about a trip to Jerusalem he'd just been on, and how everyone always talks about the 'vibe' of the place. Saying things like, "Whoa, you gotta go to Jerusalem! The vibe is incredible!" He says he never understood about the vibe of any place until he went to Jerusalem himself, and was absolutely, unequivocally blown away.

This, right here in front of me. This beat-up metal triangle sitting in a HellRat named Portnoy Spavin's giant hand...

This is my Jerusalem.

136

fter a little more convincing and cajoling—even in spite of the overwhelming evidence that Portnoy is no more insane than the rest of us—PigBoy finally agrees to stop pointing his shotgun at the beleaguered HellRat every five minutes, and allow him to come with us to the city.

"Alright, alright," PigBoy says. "But for the record, I *still* have a bad feeling about this. Don't come crying to me when he rips your face off and breaks your spine over his knee."

Portnoy says nothing, just packs a duffel bag with some personal belongings, hands the triangle, still wrapped in its burlap covering, over to me—which makes PigBoy look even more foolish.

"For the love o' Jim, give it a goddamn rest, boy," is Gus's advice to PigBoy.

Ready to go, we stand at the cave's doorway, waiting for the next train to pass.

"Don't suppose you have any Irish Cream down here to pass the time, do you?" I say. Portnoy just eyes me.

I shrug. "Worth checking."

In the distance, the soft glow of a train's lights paints the bend in the tunnel wall. We watch it stop at the platform, unload and reload. Then it's coming toward us fast.

"Okay," says Portnoy, "everyone step back a bit. Hold on to your hats!"

The Distance Travelled

Lights fill the cave's doorway, and the blur of the train screams by. Wind shoots hard up my nose, fills my dead lungs.

"Hoo-wee!" shouts Gus from high atop Mount China. "Let's wait fer another'n!"

We file out into the tunnel in the train's warm wake, Portnoy in the lead. Tom, at the back of the group, quickens his pace, weaves his way through the rest of us, puts a hand on Portnoy's back. When Portnoy turns around to look at him, Tom says, "Fine gentlemen. Fine, fine gentlemen for our helpings," and smiles.

"Thanks, Tom," Portnoy says. "I appreciate your warm words."

Tom pats him heartily on the back, and continues to walk alongside.

"Now don't go thinking," says Portnoy, "that getting the next triangle will be as easy as getting mine from me was. I knew you were coming; it would be unreasonable to think that those who hold the other four pieces know of your coming, too. It's more likely, actually, that they'll not even be aware of their piece's significance, and they'll have come to treasure it. Which will make getting it from them peacefully a very tricky business."

We shuffle along the track, eventually reaching the platform. We climb up, walk to the middle, near the platform entrance. I look at the guitar player as we walk by him. He doesn't even raise his head.

138

The rumble of the next train echoes through the tunnel. Lights appear.

The train pulls up, the doors *ping*, and we file in. There's barely anyone aboard this train. A couple of scraggly-looking guys poking each other in the ribs and making fairy jokes about The Big Red Fella—that's about it.

There're no advertisements, either, just grimy walls and dirty metal bars. Everything is sold through word of mouth down here. Good to see the city shares that trait with the rural sections.

The train pulls away from the station, picks up speed. We all stand, having seen some of the seats and decided against placing our asses anywhere near them.

"What the hell's on *that* one?" says PigBoy.

"Got me," I reply.

"Actually," says Gus from Tom's hunched shoulders, "it sorta looks like a half-eaten loop of intestine that—"

"For chrissakes, Gus! There's a lady present!" I say.

Apple smiles at me, shakes her head—like she doesn't hear this kind of shit, and probably much worse, when she sings at Hell's Kitchen.

"Well," I add. "*Sort* of a lady, anyway."

I duck the punch aimed for my shoulder, and sock her one in the upper arm. "Ha!"

"Ow! Watch it, boy, or I'll sic Tom on ya!" She laughs, jostles Tom where he stands scrunched uncomfortably into the rounded ceiling of the train.

Tom giggles—as much as a giant HellRat *can* giggle—and squirms around until Gus knocks his head off the ceiling and shouts for Tom to stop.

"I know a guy whose place we can stay at in the city," says Portnoy, as our laughter subsides. "Pretty near the station."

I nod. "Cool." I'm lost in thought, not really looking at or for anything, just sort of spacing out a bit, letting my mind wander...and then my vision focuses and I see someone near the back of the car we're in.

"Hey, I didn't see that guy before," I say quietly, leaning over to PigBoy's ear. "Did you?"

"Who?"

"That guy," I say and nod my head in his general direction, avert my eyes, look toward the ceiling.

"Dude with the newspaper up in front of his face?"

"Yeah, him."

PigBoy shrugs. "Not sure. Might have seen him; I wasn't really looking, though, you know?"

"Yeah...."

There's a furtive peek from the newspaper, then it snaps back up tight—the glint of an eye under the brim of a dark brown fedora. The man's crossed legs switch positions: Right over left to left over right. He coughs.

Real subtle, buddy.

The subway rattles on, bumping over the tracks. We're on a slight incline for a minute or so, then the fluorescent lighting flickers momentarily, and we shoot out into the open.

Red.

Everywhere.

A wide view of the outskirts of the city to each side of us. Some scattered torture blocks, full to brimming with bodies in various states of torment.

Just like home.

I sigh. I was so hoping for something *different*. When a fella's off saving little girls from the clutches of evil, is it too much to ask for a little change of scenery along the way?

Ah well, things'll probably look different in the city proper.

The train swings around to the right with a shuddering jolt, revealing a large section of the city.

Whoa. Now *that's* what I'm talking about.

As though slapped down hard from on high into the middle of this red desert, there sits a roughly circular portion of the city. Squat buildings—none higher than probably five floors, tops—built by an architect evoking M. C. Escher on crack. All edges and sharp, bizarre angles.

"Check out the fog," I say, my eyes riveted to the train's windows.

"Oh, that," says Portnoy. "That's the work of The Big Red Fella. Since there's no ecosystem to naturally produce the stuff—and since he clings to cliché like a baby to a clothesline—he had machines installed to perpetually cover the city in a shroud of fake fog. Pathetic."

Portnoy looks out the window with distaste.

"Well, pathetic or not," I say, "it certainly *looks* cool. Damn, check that out."

The fog is a white shroud covering the streets. Some of it floats up near the tops of the stout buildings; other bits of it seep into the outskirts. It's like a living thing, crouching low over streetlights, winding its way through fire escapes, clinging to windows.

As the train banks left once more, the view of the city is taken from me. I feel excitement again instead of dread. I can't wait to get off the train now, start exploring. The thought has me wriggly like I used to be Christmas morning, bounding down the stairs at 6 a.m., shaking dreams off as I went.

I sometimes wonder if the boy I was then could have done anything differently, taken a different turn in life, and avoided eventually running over that little girl. It seems malicious to me that all the time spent in my skin, doing the things I did—the bad as well as the good—all culminated in my killing someone's daughter. Is that all my life was about? Is that what I was born to do?

Jesus Christ.

Who needs daily torture sessions when you can just sit in a dark room and think about the life you wasted, the time you threw away?

My case of the wriggles drains out of me quickly, and I'm back to dreading what's to come.

My mom used to call me an emotional teeter-totter. Dad used to call me Flip-Flop. All my ex-girlfriends called me 'moody,' or 'difficult,' or just plain 'asshole.' But any way you slice it, I'm fucked up.

Dying didn't change that.

"This is us," Portnoy says.

Wrapped securely in my cancerous thoughts, I feel the train

slow down; it pulls up to a grungy open-air platform, unloads its few passengers. The others go out before me. I hang back to see what Mr. Subtle does.

Newspaper still up in front of his face, he doesn't move. Guess his stop is deeper into the city.

Good thing.

Just as the doors are about to squeeze shut, I slip through them, catch up to the others as they head down a flight of stairs. Apple's still at the top, straggling at the back of the group. "Where were you?" she says.

"Just hung back to see if that weird guy with the newspaper glued to his face was gonna follow us."

"And?" she says, glancing around the platform quickly.

"Nope. Didn't move. Didn't even peek out from behind his paper."

"Great. So why do you look so out of sorts?"

"Do I?"

"You do."

I try to think of something less embarrassing than, 'Oh, just thinking about what a useless piece of shit I am, that's all.' Nothing springs to mind, so I just say, "Sour mood, I think. It'll pass. Nervous about this whole prophecy thing, you know?"

But Apple's a girl, and girls can see right through a man's bullshit at a hundred paces. No way to fool them—especially girls like Apple.

141

She puts an arm around my shoulders, smiles a little, and we walk down the steps.

Back with the rest of the group, we pass through the dingy, poorly lit, rancid-smelling foyer of 'Inner City Stop 1.'

More stairs lead up to a plain white doorway. In black ink and the plainest sans-serif font in existence, the sign on the door reads "Street."

"The Big Red Fella has quite the flare for catchy names," I say.

We move through the doorway, and emerge onto the street.

Bleak. That's my first impression.

Well, sure, you say, it's Hell, it's *supposed* to be bleak. But I don't mean it in a death-and-dismemberment-everywhere sort of way. It's not bleak like there's a cornucopia of atrocities being committed and we're powerless to do anything but watch. I mean bleak in a London, England sort of way: people dressed in rumpled trench coats shuffling along, directionless, beaten down by the interminably rotten weather, by the fog that, in this case, quite literally won't let up.

The Distance Travelled

The dark cobblestone streets are narrow, houses butted up against one another. The weird, sharp angles and staircases make me blink my eyes several times trying to focus properly, wrap my head around them. The material of the houses is grime-stained and green with lichen, as though it's been underwater for decades.

I glance around to the lower corners of buildings, looking for these fog machines, but see nothing.

Through the white blanket, milky globes float high above my head, on either side of the street. Remembering only the bright fluorescent electric lights from Upside, it takes me a moment to realize that these hazy orbs hovering over the street are gaslit street lamps.

The Big Red Fella definitely had a certain ambience in mind when he designed the place.

People pass into and out of heavy fog patches like flickering spectres. No one speaks to anyone else: head down, slow shuffle, like the weight of the entire city is on their backs.

Portnoy fumbles in his pants pocket for something, pulls out a slip of paper. "Come on," he says. "We need to hail a cab, get to my friend's place."

We turn left, walk down the street. On one of the old-style streetlights, I see a rumpled piece of paper pasted onto the side. Coming closer, I read:

TOURS OF HELL'S INNER CITY!
CHEAP—ONLY $25!!

A phone number follows.

"Those are shite," Portnoy says, pointing to the sign as we pass. "The shyster just takes your dough and shows you about four tourist traps—places a blind man could find—then calls it a day. The *real* tours cost about twenty times that much."

"So what do you see for $500?" I ask.

"The worst of the worst, Stu. Stuff you'd never, ever forget if you saw it," he says.

"That all?" I say. He turns around, unamused.

I lower my eyes to the ground, keep walking.

As we cross an intersection, I look up to the street sign. There's nothing printed on either green placard where the streets' names should be.

"Hey, what's up with that?" I say, point to it.

"The streets don't have names," Portnoy answers. "People have carved and spray-painted names into them before, but they never stay for long. City crews come along and replace them, so it's a no-win situation.

"It's all part of the wearing-down process. Displacement. Makes you feel like you're nowhere all the time, like no matter where you go or how far you travel, everything's the same. Sure, you have different businesses and such, and those sort of act as landmarks, but they don't do a lot to tie the place together in your mind, so you never get any true sense of home. Humans are used to street names. So it's even more frustrating that they leave in the posts and little green placards, because there's a partial connection to their instincts, to what they grew up with. But it's not fully realized, so that part of them that recognizes what the street signs are for feels an even stronger need to fill in the blanks than if they were never there to begin with."

Everyone to this point—except inquisitive little me, of course—had been silent, just taking everything in, trying to absorb the fundamental *weirdness* of the place. But Gus in particular had been more broody than just quiet. Surely by now he'd have hollered something loud and disruptive, or threatened PigBoy with violence of some kind, just for the fun of it. But there was nothing.

I look up at Gus, perched high on Tom's back. His back is bent, head down, his face stuffed against Tom's neck, like he doesn't want to see any of this—is, in fact, *hiding* from it.

Remembering his little episode at the gas station when we mentioned going to the city, I think of how to gently word the question. "So, uh…Gus. Buddy. What's the fucking deal with you and the city?"

Okay, so I'm not the best at 'gentle.'

Gus shakes his head side to side. "Piss off, boy; Don't wanna talk about it, ya hear? Just let me alone and keep walkin'."

"Oh, come on, man. I'd tell you if the roles were reversed."

"Yeah, well, the goddamn roles *ain't* reversed; you won't get shit outta me."

I decide to press some buttons. Something I'm fairly good at. I quickly run down the general possibilities in my head, then fire them off:

"Money troubles?"

"No, now leave me alone already."

"Death of someone close?"

"Stu, you little shit, I mean it…" He turns and glares acid at me.

At least now his head is off Tom's neck.

"Dreams unrealized, a life left wanting?" I smirk.

"Quit it, or I'll jump down offa here and rip off your god-damn—"

"How 'bout girl trouble?" I say.

Now either Gus becomes stuck for an idea of what body part to rip off me, or I've hit the jackpot. Nothing comes from his open mouth. He clamps his jaw closed after a few seconds, turns away from me, plants his face back into Tom's neck, and shuts his eyes.

Beside me, Apple puts a hand on my shoulder. I turn to her, still smiling, that little shitheel part of my personality fully to the forefront. And in her soft brown eyes, I see what I'm doing. But like a terrier, I cling to the idea of pushing Gus further, maybe till he cries, definitely till he explodes and tries to get a piece of me.

I manage to let it go, but it takes a Herculean effort. The urge to crush another's spirit to dust slowly drains from me.

"Taxi!" Portnoy bellows from several feet ahead of us. At first, I don't see what he's referring to, then three lights appear in the haze—two headlights and the vacancy light on the top of a car.

I remember a program about rats I once saw on TV. It said they can't see very well—only in blacks and whites—but their senses of smell and hearing are excellent. Portnoy must have heard the tires on the cobblestones well before the lights appeared.

144

"Damn, Porty," I say, "you rats got fine-tuned ears."

The dirty yellow taxi swings over to our side of the road, stops at the curb. Portnoy turns to me, says, "We're HellRats, Stu—demon-rat hybrids—not your run-of-the-mill Upside garbage-eating variety. We see in colour. I saw the cab before you simply because I'm nearly twice your height." He shakes his head.

"Oh...well, uh, let's get in the cab. Fare's running," I say, and make to jump in the front seat. Portnoy holds me back with one enormous, hairy arm, leans in the passenger-side window, addresses the cab driver: "We'll need another cab; can you radio for one, please? Thank you ever so much."

The cabby, a portly fellow with a mullet and a chin weaker than single-bag tea, says, "Aye-aye, cap'n," picks up the radio, mumbles into it, and sets it back in its cradle. "Be here soon," he says, like he has a mouthful of marbles.

"Cheers," says Portnoy.

I notice there's an even more intrusive accumulation of fog at this curbside than at any other place we've been on this street. I look down, hoping to track the source. At my feet is a sewer grate. But peering closer, I see that it's more than that.

While we wait for a second cab, I step back, ask Apple to see her flashlight real quick. She hands it over. I turn it on and train it on the sewer grate. Nestled against a side of the tunnel leading down is a short, thick tube from which billows of smoke pour—or what the inhabitants of Hell's inner city have come to know as 'fog.'

"Well, I'll be damned," I say. "There it is."

Behind and above me, Tom leans over my shoulder to get a better look. His face is bright with awe.

It occurs to me that even though Tom's a natural Hell-dweller, he may never have been to the city. "Never been here before, big Tom?"

"Nope," he says, eyes bugging out of his face.

"Guess we're all just a bunch of country bumpkins, then, huh?"

Tom laughs. "Bumpkin."

"'Cept old Gus there, of course," PigBoy says, perhaps with designs on picking up where I left off with the old fella. A quick, sharp glare from Apple, however, acts like a stick in his eye, and he shuts his trap.

Several cars, from many different eras in automotive history, trundle slowly by—there's really no other way to drive in this soup—until the second cab finally creeps up to the curb. This one's not a yellow cab, but is dark blue, and dented all to shit.

This time, with Portnoy's arm not blocking my way, I hop in the front seat of the yellow cab unopposed. "Shotgun!" I say.

No way I'm getting in that dented hunk of crap. There's a reason for all those dings, and I don't want to be an up-close spectator for the next addition.

Portnoy slides himself into the backseat of the yellow cab, lengthwise. PigBoy, being thin, is able to squeeze in on the other side. After bellyaching and whining about the lack of elbowroom, he finally manages to close the door. Behind us, through the rearview mirror I see Tom scrunch in lengthwise, similar to what Portnoy did, except that there's no room for even Apple to fit in by the time they get the doors shut. Apple and Gus sit crammed in beside the cabby, Apple nearly sitting in Gus's lap. The look on the old bugger's face tells me he's not entirely displeased with the current seating arrangements.

Behind me, Portnoy says, "Just drive, please, sir. It's been a while since I've been here, so I need to refresh my memory regarding the look of the streets, if you don't mind."

"Aye-aye," says the cabby, and puts the car in gear.

We roll away from the curb, and disappear into the haze.

20

ou'd think there'd be mayhem.

Or hey, *I* thought there'd be mayhem, anyway. But as we drive through the streets, there is only the aforementioned downtrodden skulking around, looking broody.

"So, like, what do folks around here do for excitement?" I say to no one in particular.

"Left at the next street," Portnoy says.

"Why are there no street-hangings, public decapitations, quarterings—with or without the drawing?" I wait for the laugh, receive nothing but silence and the car's engine humming away quietly. "Where do they go for their daily torture sessions, Porty? What gives?"

But Portnoy is deep in concentration, likely trying to visualize a map of the place in his head, trying to remember which street is which, what landmarks ring bells, if any.

And weak-chin cabby ain't sayin' shit.

I glance in the rearview. The blue cab carrying Apple, Gus, PigBoy, and Tom swerves all over the road, nearly runs someone over on the sidewalk, rights itself, then scrapes one of its sides against a street lamp. Sparks fly.

"Make another right, please, cab driver. If I'm not mistaken, it should be just a couple of blocks away now."

A wave of exhaustion comes over me; my entire body feels like a slab of concrete. "We need to rest soon. Goddamn, I'm tired."

The Distance Travelled

"Start slowing down…yes…yes, okay, that apartment complex…here we are," says Portnoy when the cab finally comes to a stop.

The blue cab behind us slows, slows…and crashes into us. We're only jolted ahead a little bit, but our cabby is beyond livid. He jumps out of the cab, stalks back to the driver's side of the blue taxi, raps on the window hard, and comes out with a string of curses about a foot long. It's in Italian, a language I don't understand, but you don't have to be a genius to connect the dots.

"Leave a twenty on his seat," Portnoy says. "We don't have time for this."

I dip into my wallet, extract my fifty, drop it on the cabby's seat. "That's all I've got."

"Fine. Now let's get moving. I see a light on in my friend's apartment. He's usually out, so this might be our lucky day."

Fifty-dollar cab ride. Fuck that. "Okay, but you owe me thirty bucks, Porty."

I stick my head out the window and look up to see the light in the apartment. Through the haze, I see it, and I see someone moving across the curtained window. Definitely home.

148

I open the door, step out of the car. Once out, I move to the back to open Portnoy's door, help extract him. I yank on his legs while he pushes himself with his arms across the seat. He's a heavy bugger, and I'm sweating in no time. His lower body out of the car, he's able to handle the rest himself.

I straighten and look to the developing scene behind us at the trashed blue cab. Weak-chin is punching the glass in the driver's side door. Inside, there's a mild-mannered looking man with a weedy little child-molester moustache holding up his hands in supplication. His mouth is moving, but I can't tell what he's saying. Probably something to the effect of, "Please, Mr. Insane Weak-chinned Mulleted Fat Man, it was an accident! I want no trouble!"

Whatever it is, it does no good, because Weak-chin—fist bloody from the hammering—finally breaks through the glass. It shatters, falls into the cabby's lap. He screams. Weak-chin yanks him out of the cab, still cursing up a storm in Italian, and throttles the man in the street.

What does one do when witness to such violence?

Well, what do people do Upside when something like this happens in their streets? Just look the other way, that's right.

As above, so below.

None of the several passers-by on the street even lift their heads to see what's going on, never mind lift a genuine *finger* to help the guy out. But then, we're in the toilet of the universe. What can you expect?

Tom, on the other hand, has a different mindset.

And the incredible fucking bulldozer weight and power to back it up.

Once PigBoy and Apple extract him from the back seat, he lumbers over to Weak-chin, who is currently laying the boots to the other cabby.

Tom pulls Weak-Chin by his mullet to a standing position, but the guy is so enraged, his feet keep kicking, as if running completely on automatic. As if he has no clue how perilously close he is to going on to the Great Big Nothing.

Tom puts his other hand over the man's entire head, like a sheath, says, "Stop. I squeeze."

Weak-chin's kicks continue for a few seconds, but since a giant hand now covers his face, they're errant, not connecting with anything but air.

"I squeeze," Tom says again, this time with decidedly more threat in his tone.

Weak-chin calms down a little, stops flailing his legs, stops his motor mouth from rattling foreign obscenities.

"No more," Tom says. "No more hurting. Okay?"

Weak-chin is quiet for a few seconds, just standing in the middle of this dark, foggy street, fists bloody, mashed to pulp, and a massive HellRat standing over him, his head wrapped tightly in his hand, ready to pop it like a grape if he gets the wrong answer.

A muffled, "Aye, aye, cap'n," seeps out from between Tom's meaty digits.

Tom releases him, walks back over to us slowly, looking the most tired and depleted I've ever seen him.

He says nothing, just stands and waits for us to move, so that he can follow.

Weak-chin drags his sorry, bullying ass over to his yellow cab, opens the door, sees the fifty I left on his seat, picks it up, brandishes it. He waves and smiles at us.

Gets in his cab, drives away.

This is not the place to learn life lessons.

The mild-mannered cabby pulls himself to his feet from the cobblestones, wipes blood from his lips and chin. "Thanks, big fella," he says.

Tom does not respond.

«‹—›»

We are all so tired.

I don't know how many hours we've been up, but it's got to be more than I've ever stayed up before. We don't say anything to one another; the only one with any energy left to speak is Portnoy.

"Guy's name is Felipe. He has room in that apartment to sleep us all, so hopefully he'll be okay with us just barging in on him like this."

We stagger toward the funky-looking apartment complex. There are three sets of stairs in front, all leading up to a massive stone gargoyle. The gargoyle is grinning, perched atop a mountain of cracked skulls. Behind the gargoyle are yet more stairs, with several different apartments branching off from each staircase.

I glance up again to check out the movement situation in the lighted window above. There is still a figure moving behind the curtain—not a HellRat's, but a person's silhouette, so this Felipe guy is probably an ex-Upsider. Either that, or he's an Official—a humanoid creature employed by what passes for the government, like Barnes or Salinger. You can usually tell these fuckers apart from ex-Upsiders, though, since they nearly always have some freaky side effect either to their appearance or their personalities. Since Hell's government-employed scientists are just as fucked up as the rest of the population, their creations tend to come out a bit more 'original' than they might like.

150

At the bottom of the middle set of large stone steps, I stop momentarily to check out the badass gargoyle.

"Fucking righteous," PigBoy whispers in awe beside me.

"Got that right, man," I say. "Nothing like this out in the sticks. That's one mean-ass looking—"

Just above the gargoyle's head, and through a break in the omnipresent fog soup, I spot the cloud.

The One Cloud.

"Holy shit," I say.

"Yeah, unbelievable," PigBoy says, still referring to the gargoyle. He and the others continue up the steps.

I stay at the bottom, thinking quick. I call up, "Hey, I'll meet you guys out here, okay? I'm *seriously* tired and don't think I have it in me to dog it up the rest of these stairs."

"Okay," Portnoy says from about halfway up the steps, "but don't wander off. We'll be back in about fifteen minutes—twenty, tops. Felipe's a pretty good friend, but I haven't seen him in a while, so it might take some convincing for him to let us recuperate here.

"Regardless what he says, though, after this, we'll go to a bar and grill a couple of blocks away, where we can go over the books again, and have a quick pint. Sound good?"

"Yeah, yeah, sounds fine. I'll just park my ass here, sacrifice passing virgins to the gargoyle or something while I wait."

Portnoy smiles easily, twitches his whiskers at me.

Funny little creatures, HellRats.

Well, okay—funny fucking gi*antic* creatures.

The others continue the slow climb upward. Gus, apparently in better spirits now, calls out from Tom's back: "Hoo! I need one o' these here granite jaws affixed to *my* yapper—maybe that way it'd stay put on my face!" He cackles with laughter, which, as is often the case, dissolves into an extended coughing jag. He hawks, shooting something vile out of his mouth; it hits the ground with a phlegmy splat.

I turn my attention to PigBoy as he strokes the skulls under the gargoyle. I watch him long and hard as he runs his fingers over their eye sockets, jawbones, teeth, foreheads.

We're doing all this for him. For his little sister. A particularly shitty part of me wishes I knew his sister personally, so I could know for certain that it was worth going through all this trouble to get her back. The kinder, gentler, more altruistic (and significantly *smaller*) part of me, however, knows that it's not important. A child has been kidnapped, stolen from her family, and I have a chance to do something about it.

However, I have only the lunatic ramblings of a semi-legendary child named Oliver to guide me.

I sigh. Best not to think too much about that. And hey, so far, young Oliver has steered me true, so who am I to bitch?

PigBoy finishes fondling the pile of skulls, catches up to the others, follows them up the third set of branched-off stairs higher up. They reach the door of the apartment with the lighted window.

Portnoy knocks.

A crack of light filters out onto the landing where my gnarled crew stand waiting, Apple and Tom swaying a little from exhaustion, achy muscles—probably throbbing heads and strained spines, too. Some words are exchanged, though I can't hear them, can only see lips moving, hands gesticulating. Then everyone files into the apartment, except for Portnoy, who hangs back and waves down to me, gives me the thumbs-up.

Once the door closes, I look up, wait for the fog to clear a bit, and see the lone cloud chugging away up there. I walk in its general direction, wishing I'd bummed a smoke off Apple before she went into the apartment.

I notice the ceiling in the city is far higher than it is out in the rural areas. I can still see its black sheen, reflected by various fires and lights around the city, but it's got to be at least two hundred feet higher than out by my house.

Out by my *old* house, I guess I should say. Remembering that I can probably never go home again makes my footfalls even heavier on the cobblestones than sheer exhaustion already has.

Through breaks in the fog cover, I keep an eye to the sky to track the progress of The Little Cloud That Could. Puff, puff. Chug, chug. Go, little cloud, go.

Jesus. I'm getting punchy.

Removing my pocket watch, I see that I've about another fifteen minutes, tops, before I have to be back on that staircase. Better get hustling if I want to see if Cloud Guy's still following his destiny around.

I wonder as I walk how widespread word of our deviation has become. Should we get disguises, lay low, do all the things they do in movies when the crooks are on the lam? I don't know, but there's a calm about all this that makes me believe more and more in those two books Apple's carrying around. So far, the evidence is too compelling not to believe that at least *some* of it is true. Things are slotting together so well that I'd be a fool to think it wasn't meant to be.

152

In some ways, this is relieving, as it affords me a sense of calm, but in other ways, it makes me very, very nervous—not least because this prophecy was foretold in *Hell.* I mean, if the ceiling cracked open and this prophecy was handed down to me from On High, well, I'd be all for it. Sign me up. But such is not the case, so maybe my saving this little girl somehow serves as a catalyst for something atrocious beyond belief.

I could go round and round on this and never be any closer to the truth of it, because I have to follow it through, regardless. Simply because what if it's *not* any sort of catalyst to the end of the universe? What if it just is what it is on the surface, and some strange child foresaw it all, his father having the good sense to write it down in the hopes that it might one day save someone's life? Sure, there aren't many Good Samaritan awards handed out down here, but some people, I'm sure, have to be borderline. There's good in my friends, so there must be good in other people, right? Maybe this boy and his father were two of the better to be condemned to this existence.

Maybe, maybe, maybe.

Fuck it. Keep walking.

I round a corner, look up, spot the cloud again. I'm nearly right underneath it. I look around the street. No Cloud Guy yet. Maybe one more block over.

Check the pocket watch: ten minutes to get back. I'll have to run.

I sprint through a dark alley, fire escapes looming above me. People hang over them, talk across the way to each other. One of them spots me, starts chucking things—a bottle crashes beside my right foot, several pop cans sprinkle down on me. I don't look up, just keep running. Laughter floats on the still air, and then I'm out onto the next block.

A convenience store's sign glows bright in the dark: Pop's Stop. Flashing neon in the window blasts my eyes with the words:

OPEN FOREVER

I scan left and right quickly, feeling the timepiece in my pocket grow heavier. There's no one on the street, except—

And there he is, just turning down another alleyway.

I shout after him, "Hey! Wait a minute!" I break into a dead run. Crossing the street, I'm nearly ploughed over by a black stretch limo, hip-hop music thumping from its stereo system, as it appears like a silent ghost from out of the fog. Its horn blares and hi-beams flash as its front right corner glances off the side of my thigh.

I gain the alleyway. Halfway down, and there's the umbrella. I get a shiver when I see it, bobbing along quietly through the night, its owner on some demented quest to see what, perhaps, can never be seen.

"Hey!" I yell again. "It's me! Remember me!?" Jogging after him, I catch up just as he's about to round the next building onto a new street. I come up alongside him. He doesn't even turn his head at my sudden arrival, just glances skyward, twirls his umbrella a little, and keeps walking.

"Hey, didn't you hear me calling you back there?" I say, every muscle and bone in my body screaming for rest.

"Of course I did," he says.

"So why didn't you stop?"

"Should I stop for every person that calls to me?"

"Well, when you know them, you should. Don't you think?"

He looks at me for the first time, then turns his gaze ahead again. "I don't know you."

"What? Of course you do! Remember behind the gas station, and then again in Gus's library staircase?"

Cloud Guy just shrugs. "Perhaps you know me, but I certainly do not know you. I may have at one time, but I am getting on in years and find myself doing strange things and forgetting people all the time. Growing old gracefully is impossible. Age sees to that."

He walks, twirls his umbrella. Then: "So?"

"So what?" I say.

"So what do you want? You say you know me, so what do you want? I've no money to give you, and certainly not much more attention."

"Well…" I say, and nothing else comes out.

What *did* I want with him?

"Then please leave me alone," he says, walks a little faster, pulls away from me.

Then I remember what he said in our previous encounters. "Have you been anywhere following that cloud that you haven't been before?"

He stops walking.

I stop walking.

Fog pumps out of a nearby sewer grate.

He turns around slowly. "No," he replies. "No, I haven't. I'm beginning to think I've been everywhere there is to go. Sad as that is."

He straightens the lines of his sharp black suit with his free hand, turns away from me, moves his umbrella aside, looks up, gauges where the cloud is, and walks on.

"I'll see you again, won't I," I call after him, more statement than question.

He only twirls his umbrella in answer.

Out comes the pocket watch. Shit. The others will be wondering where I've disappeared to.

I turn and run back to the apartment complex as fast as my worn down body will take me.

«« — »»

I slow down just before I reach the main steps of the complex, try to act like I've just been walking. Everyone's there, waiting.

"Where the fuck you been, Stu?" says PigBoy.

"Just had to take a leak, so I went around the back of the complex and drained the old lizard. Felt damn fine, too, I'll have you know. Been needin' *that* little bit of release for quite a while now."

There's no use telling anyone about Cloud Guy again. They didn't believe me before, why would they now? Just easier to lie and get on with business, take my freaky little side-trips on my own time.

"Right, well, Felipe's been very forthcoming," says Portnoy. "We can stay here to rest up after our business at The Old Codger's Bar & Grill is taken care of. But he's entertaining people soon, so we can't complain about the noise.

"I had forgotten," Portnoy continues with a smile on his thin lips, "but every year Felipe has a Deathday party, at which he celebrates the day he died, with food, drink, and close friends."

"I tell you what," says PigBoy. "I can't wait to get some sleep, 'cause I'm sick to shit of carrying this shotgun around. It feels like it weighs a ton. So let's quit yappin' about our lovely new friend Felipe, with his cheesy 'hipster' pad full of lava lamps and crappy psychedelic artwork all over the walls. It's enough to make me vomit. Let's just get to the pub, have a pint, learn what there is to learn, and get back to flashback haven for some shut-eye, okay?" PigBoy hefts the shotgun, mock smiles, turns to Portnoy: "Let's go, chum. Lead the way."

Portnoy, looking uncomfortable with PigBoy's words, moves in the direction in which I went after the cloud. The others follow, except me and Apple. She can read my face like there're bold-type words printed on it. My fists are clenched and my arms are shaking.

Apple puts a hand on my forearm, rubs gently. "Look, I know he's being a complete ungrateful dick right now, Stu, but try to see things from his point of view. Despite his macho front, he's still a fish out of water down here, and he's under a lot of pressure, what with his sister missing and all. Imagine what he must be thinking is happening to her right now—most of it probably not even a tenth of the true horror. You know?"

But I'm seething and it's hard for me to turn that reaction off. I want to smash and pummel to dust everything I come across. Apple comes closer, puts an arm around me, holds me close to her. She nudges us forward by starting off on her own, gently pulling me along. "Come on…" she says, smiling.

And it's hard to resist. You've never seen a smile quite like this. It somehow makes you believe that everything somehow *will* be alright, that the tough parts are actually worth plodding through to get to the destination.

In that moment, with that smile directed right at me, I feel myself falling for her just a tiny, *tiny* little bit. But it's more than I want, because I would never do anything to hurt Tom China.

Apple tugs me a little harder, and within a few seconds we fall back in with the others.

Tom senses me walking alongside him, looks down, grins at me. I grin back.

No pain for you, big Tom.

No pain.

he whole way to the pub, I feel like we're being watched, followed. People haze in and out of the ubiquitous fog, and it feels like the watcher could be any of them. I grow more tense the longer we're out in the open like this. I want nothing more than to seek cover and watch the streets from a dark, shadowed alleyway.

I think about the suspicious man hiding behind a newspaper on the subway. He got off at another stop, sure, but he could have just been trying to throw us. Maybe he got off at the very next stop, made his way back here.

What if it's the authorities? Would they have noticed us missing yet? Surely some of us have missed torture sessions by now. Not me—my next isn't scheduled until later tonight, by my watch—but certainly someone else.

How fast would they move on this? Would they immediately suspect us of embarking on some epic quest?

Surely not.

Then what? Who could it be?

Or maybe I'm a paranoid twit who should just keep walking, slide onto a stool behind the pub's bar and order several stiff drinks.

I discover as we walk that this freaky fog has one good side effect: It acts as a blanket for my thoughts, makes it easier to think, with barely anything else for my eyes to look at but the fog itself, the soft yellow of the glowing street lamps, and the occasional bit of pointy black architecture poking through.

The Distance Travelled

As we walk through the soup, stirring up a floating wake behind us, I remember the question that Portnoy didn't answer during our cab ride.

"Say, Porty—"

"I'd really prefer that you use my proper name, please."

"Oh, alright. Sorry," I say. "Say, Portnoy Spavin—" He rolls his eyes at me. "—I was just wondering about what I tried to ask you back in the cab. Remember? About where all the people were?"

"Oh, yes, sorry about that. Deep in concentration."

"Probably can't walk and chew gum at the same time, either," mutters PigBoy, hefts his shotgun, pretends to shoot non-existent birds out of the sky.

Portnoy ignores him.

"So, how come so few people out and about? Where they all hiding?" I ask.

"I can answer this one," Apple pipes up. "I've been to the city probably more than Portnoy here."

Portnoy sweeps his arm in Apple's direction. "As you will, m'lady," he says.

158

"These few that are out," Apple explains, "are probably on their way to jobs or to visit friends or something, because city folk have *in-house* torturers." She waits a beat for that to sink in. "Yup, the rich don't have to move a muscle to suffer their daily atonement. While the rest of us are trekking along dirt roads to go to public humiliation with our peers, these lucky pricks are paying for their sins in the privacy of their own homes."

"That sure must be a tough pill to swallow for you guys, huh?" PigBoy says. "Same punishment for everyone, but you poor bastards have to work to get to it!"

There's more than an edge of satisfaction and Upsider arrogance to PigBoy's comment that definitely rubs everyone the wrong way—not just me this time.

We bristle as one.

"I remember people Upside always talking about how it doesn't matter how much money you make," Apple says, "'cause when you die, you can't take it with you. Well, not only can you take it with you, but if you're Canadian, you don't even have to get it converted once you get here."

We round a corner, see the faded sign of The Old Codger Bar & Grill just up ahead on the right side of the street.

"And as for going out shopping and such," Apples continues, "why bother when you can order everything in? Which is exactly what everyone does. You've seen the occasional delivery truck going up and down these roads, right? There aren't that many around this area, since a lot of these people aren't affluent enough to afford it, but you get to some of the *really* rich neighbour-hoods? All that's on the road are these trucks."

Apple pulls the pack of smokes from her purse, tosses me one, pops one between her own lips, lights us both. "Shit," she says, "would *you* want to be out here trying to enjoy yourself? Nothing to see, barely anything to do—most of the shops that used to be open around here have long since closed down due to lack of business. Oh, and the spoiled brats have central air-condi-tioning, too."

Gus and I gasp and repeat the phrase *central air-conditioning* over and again in disgust.

"So that's where everyone is, Stu," Apple says. "*In*side. Doing everything they can to forget about *out*side."

"Can't say as though I blame them, Apple. If I could afford to exist from the comfort of my home, I wouldn't go out much, either. Especially not around here. I mean, sure it's hotter out where we live, but at least back home there're vistas and land-scapes and shit—stuff to look at and appreciate, like a piece of art. But here...?" I look around, spread my arms wide.

"Sad place," Tom says quietly. And although Tom doesn't say much, when he does, he's dead on.

"You're right, Big Tom. It is a sad place. Depressing. I wouldn't move here for all the tea in China," I say. Tom smiles when I say his last name. The expression is probably lost on him, but he's smiling, so I feel no need to spoil that with an explana-tion. I give my buddy a pat on his thick, furry forearm, and smile back.

"Well," Portnoy says, "here we are."

Above us, a barely legible sign juts out from a black-bricked building, hangs over the narrow sidewalk. The Old Codger's Bar & Grill. The face of a scowling old man is beneath the letters. Beneath the face, in smaller, even harder-to-read type, is the par-enthetical phrase "More Bar Than Grill."

"Let's try to glean further clues from the books over a pint," says Portnoy, pulling open the heavy wooden door. He lowers his voice. "But let's pick a more secluded area before we delve into the texts, shall we? Don't want to attract any unwanted attention, or make ourselves seem out of place."

Portnoy holds the door for everyone as we pile into the cramped little pub.

I hope to see a mixture of people in here—or at least people wearing a mixture of different *clothes*, for chrissakes—but there's only more grey, more long faces, more trenchcoats, more muted conversations, like it's a funeral home instead of a pub. Add to this electric environment the smell of stale beer and fish and chips, plus a generous helping of sheer boredom and desperation, and you've got a recipe for suicide.

If everyone here wasn't already dead, that is.

"Let's order, then sit down over there in that corner," Portnoy says, points to a dimly lit corner of the place where a dartboard hangs nearby. On the dartboard is a cardboard cutout of a red devil with horns. Its face is pockmarked with tiny holes.

A Tom Jones cover band is on the jukebox.

We approach the bar. Several grey lumps sit on stools mumbling to each other. I'm right beside one of them, but I can't make out a single word. His ashen lips barely move. The only one with any apparent life in here is the bartender.

Portnoy says, "Pint, please." He's chipper, a bubbling pot of enthusiasm.

The bartender—a bald man with a barrel for a belly and arm hair thick as thieves—looks Portnoy up and down, says, "Tall bugger, ain'tcha!? What are you?"

"I'm a HellRat, sir," Portnoy answers. "Indigenous."

"Don't care how smart ya are!" the bartender bellows.

We exchange confused looks.

"Well, what can I do ya for, Professor?" the bartender says.

"Um…pint, please, like I said before." He smiles, but it's troubled now and slips a little from his lips.

"Pint of what?" The bartender yells like the place is bustling and he has to shout to be heard. But the jukebox is so quiet, and the patrons so subdued, the loudest sound in the room is old Gus picking his teeth.

"Whaddaya got?" PigBoy says, steps up to the bar, lays his shotgun on the counter.

"Worderschlot? Sorry, young feller, fresh out of that, but might I offers ya a pint of—?"

"Worderschlot?" PigBoy says, looks around to us. We all shrug.

"Fresh out of it, I said!" the bartender replies. "And I still won't have none if'n ya ask for it a third time!" He furrows his brow. "And by God you should saw that fuckin' shotgun off! Damn thing's useless like that, 'less you got a good, long trench coat to hide it under, which you ain't seem to got! Give it here!"

The bartender grabs the shotgun off the counter. PigBoy shouts "Hey!" and snatches at it, but the bartender's too quick. He disappears behind a curtain.

A few seconds later, I hear sawing, a piece of wood hitting the ground, then the bartender reappears. He's carrying PigBoy's shotgun, only it's shorter now. The bartender hands it back to him.

"There! Now you tuck that little bugger in your leather—make a slit in the lining near the coat's waistband to act like a holster—and no one'll be the wiser!" The bartender's face is red from yelling.

"Umm…thanks," is all PigBoy can muster.

The bartender just looks at him, like he's said nothing at all.

"What!?" he bellows suddenly, though no one has spoken.

"Oh, fuck this," I say. "Let's just go sit down."

We move away from the bar, toward the corner with Satan's likeness on the dartboard. The booths are a tight fit for Portnoy and Tom, but they manage, with zero room to spare. As a group, we take up two of them, side by side.

Pipe smoke drifts on the air. I make a special effort to breathe so that the scent fills my nostrils—always loved that smell. That and the smell of good, fresh coffee cannot be beaten.

No one in the bar even looks at us. Even though we're easily the most lively and colourful crew in here, they probably see us through the filter of their own dull, drab, sad little existences.

Fuck the city. The country's where all the action is.

Apple digs into her purse, carefully pulls out the first of the two prophecy books. She lays it on the table, opens it, flips some pages, finds the page after the first riddle. "Yeah, yeah, first with kin, below, below, already solved that one…what's next here," she says under her breath as she scans. "Pictures, scribblings, drawings, yeah, yeah, yeah, and—"

"Whoa, whoa, hold on," I say. "Flip back a page."

Apple goes back one page.

"Next one back," I say.

She flips another one. And there's Portnoy looking at me from the page. In amongst the other scribbles and bizarre symbols is a child's drawing of a big HellRat wearing glasses, a turtle neck, and the same blue pajama bottoms Portnoy has on right now.

A chill dribbles down my spine like ice water.

Because above his head is a cracked halo, bits crumbling from it.

"Huh," says Portnoy.

The whole table is silent until Portnoy speaks again. "I've studied these books for more years than I can count, and I've never seen that drawing."

My chill deepens, spreads through my entire body. "You've *never* seen this before? I mean, it's pretty obvious, man. Especially if you've *studied* the books, not just skimmed through them like we have."

"Yeah," says PigBoy. "Funky shit. So I wonder if that deaf prick's ever gonna come over here to take our order. Not that he'd get any of it right, but…"

Careful how I word the question, I ask, "What do you think it means, Portnoy?"

"Well," he says, gazing down at the drawing, thinking. "I guess the deal with the halo could be Oliver's interpretation of me. Since he wasn't indigenous like me, nor even from Upside, if what the legend says is true, then perhaps this is how he saw me. My race is, after all, called 'HellRat,' so one way to represent this would be to have a symbol of good falling apart near me."

His words make at least *some* sense, and I'm inclined to believe him, as he doesn't seem particularly nervous about the situation—just more sort of shocked, like the rest of us. We went out on a pretty big limb trusting him, so the idea that this trust is misplaced…

"Yeah," I say, chewing my lip. "Could be."

The others seem satisfied with his explanation—even PigBoy—and I've been getting increasingly more paranoid lately, what with the guy on the subway and my thinking we were being followed on our way to the pub. I try to run other explanations through my mind as to what the crumbling halo might mean, but I come up with nothing sound.

I'm distracted as pseudo-Tom Jones's voice fades from the jukebox and is replaced with the lifeless murmur of the grey, pipe-smoking, Worderschlot-drinking patrons around us.

Whatever the fuck Worderschlot is.

The bartender shouts at someone on the other side of the bar to turn on the TV. There's a small television set hanging like a bat in the far corner of the room. A stocky man wearing a dark grey trench coat stands on a chair, reaches up to the TV, switches it on with a fat hand the colour of rotting salmon. Thin wisps of black hair leap out from his skull in all directions. He sits down again, brings his glass to his lips, and downs almost half a pint in one swig.

I glance at the television set, see an ad for some brand of cigarettes. People in the ad aren't doing anything exciting at all. They're sitting in their homes puffing away, or they're out walking in the fog, looking destitute, like the only thing keeping them from jumping in front of passing trucks is this crappy little cigarette between their cold, dead fingers. Not that jumping in front of a truck would solve anything, anyway, since they'd just heal and be forced to go back to their shitty little non-lives again anyway.

The next ad shows a man smiling. He says he saw God today, that he called the number on the bottom of the screen and some very nice people on the other end made him feel so good about reporting it.

And he looks so happy, you almost believe him.

Too bad it's all such a crock of shit. I don't know what they do with the information they get from these crazies, or why they even bother to advertise the number. I mean, even if there *was* a God, what would he be doing hanging out with these morons?

The bartender finally comes around to our table. I tell him I want nothing; the others struggle and shout, trying to order a simple pint of bitter. I tune them out, go back to watching TV.

A white-haired newscaster in a crisp, dark blue suit appears on the tiny screen. The camera pans out from him, and a little picture-in-picture appears beside and to his left. And in that little square is Dante.

That little pig-throwing son of a bitch.

163

He and a few other leather-jacketed hooligans are shown in their dune buggy, driving by a house in the city, throwing a pig through its kitchen window. Glass shatters. They laugh and carry on for the camera, fully aware that they're being recorded.

By this time, the others are all watching the screen, too, having finally been able to communicate their orders to the bartender by writing the names of their beer choices on a napkin.

The report says these 'piggings' are becoming more widespread, that they're occurring in both urban and rural areas, where before they'd been limited solely to the country. It is suspected, they say, that the livestock (illegal itself) is being obtained illegally, as well, and that authorities are looking into the nature and sources of the crime. A number is given for people to call with information.

Then the camera zooms in again on Dante standing up in the passenger seat of the buggy. The driver guns it straight at the cameraman. Over his head, Dante swings a fat pink pig attached to a rope. The cameraman is quite clearly trying to back out of the way, while still maintaining the shot. The camera zooms in on Dante's laughing face. He releases the pig; the camera zooms back out. The squealing, kicking animal fills the screen, slams into the camera dead on, and the picture to the left of the newscaster turns to snow.

He clears his throat, shuffles his pages, moves on to the next story.

"Je*sus!*" Gus says.

"Bizarre or what," I say, shaking my head.

"Definitely fucking bizarre," says PigBoy.

"It's like," Portnoy adds, "the fabric of this reality is slowly unravelling or something. Maybe it's a side effect of this prophecy finally coming true. A way to balance the forces at work, you know?"

"Yeah," says PigBoy, his tone generously slathered in sarcasm, "or maybe it's just because of that giant goddamn *hole* into Upside."

"Ah yes, the hole," Portnoy says quietly. He wiggles his whiskers uncomfortably.

"Wait," I say, as the bartender returns with the table's drinks—some of which he gets right, others which aren't even close, despite it having been written out for him. "How do you know about the hole? It's not part of the prophecy, is it? Or is it somewhere in one of the books and we've just not read about it yet?"

Portnoy shifts around in his seat. "Yes, yes, it's...in there alright." He eyes us warily, as if we should already know this.

I try to shake the feeling that he's hiding something, and so decide to change the subject—or rather steer it back on course. "Well, anyway, let's take a look at the second riddle, see what we can make of it if we all put our heads together."

Apple takes a sip from her glass, grimaces, pushes it aside, and concentrates on the book again. She flips past the picture of Portnoy, to the page where the next riddle sits couched among what looks like hundreds of little drawings of half-formed nightmares and obscure symbols and letters.

She reads it aloud to us: "Second with pain. Metal glints. You'll see it again."

"What did you make of this when you first read it, Portnoy? Where did it originally take you?" I ask.

He looks cagey about answering for a moment, but then lifts his pint to his lips, takes a massive gulp, and seems to relax a little. "I had no idea what it meant then, and I've no definite idea now, really. I just walked around the streets in this neighbourhood for a while and then carried on to the third riddle. I figured the 'metal glints' portion of the riddle was just a reference to how the city would look in Oliver's mind. He would have seen the street lamps and the sharp architecture of the buildings, the dim glow of the light reflecting off of them...or something.

"Look, I know it's lame, but like I said before, I'm not the one who these things are to be revealed to, so any insight I have is very general, and subject to more than a grain of salt."

Portnoy grins a little, sheepishly.

You know that feeling you get when someone has built something up in your mind to almost mythic proportions, and then you discover that it's not nearly as exciting as you'd hoped, and the wind is completely let out of your sails? Well, that's the way I'm feeling right now, and the way I think the others are feeling, too, judging by their silence, and occasional glances to the floor.

They don't want to meet my eyes because they know they'll find distinct disappointment there; and they don't want to meet Portnoy's eyes, either, because he's the source of our disappointment, despite his good intentions.

It's not that we feel we've been bamboozled or even led astray—not on a conscious level, anyway—but more like we've had our hopes built up based on his enthusiasm and the way he talked about how he'd already walked our path and everything. When in reality, he'd only guessed at things, then followed those guesses around blithely in hopes of having something revealed to him. When nothing was, he just read the next riddle, and carried on, then went home and waited for the real thing.

I sigh. Heavily.

Far too tired to get into a giant argument right now, I say, "So what *do* you know of the remaining triangle locations, Portnoy?"

He senses my disappointment, and sulks like a little boy. If he had a thick enough bottom lip, he'd be pouting. He looks down at the table, fiddles with his hands, shrugs. "Well, from the riddles that follow, I think that after the city, the third triangle might be suburban…or maybe just somewhere less populated than this part of the city."

The rest of us exchange looks of exhaustion.

"I don't really know," Portnoy continues, looking to each of us for some sort of support. "The fourth, though, I'm relatively certain must be in Hell's Kitchen. And the fifth might be there, too, since the books don't really say anything much after the fourth riddle."

"Wonderful," says PigBoy. "If you're not mistaken."

Portnoy hangs his head.

"I'm really sorry, everyone. I just wanted to come along for this. I'm not much good at anything else, and this was something that I *knew* about, you know?" He lifts his head, and there's more actual conviction in his voice than ever before. "This was something I saw *into*, something I knew I was part of. There was a

165

window of opportunity—the only one I've ever seen open to *me* and me *alone*—and I was damned if I was going to let that pass me by. Sure, I embellished my story a little and made you believe I knew more than I did, but I *had* to make you believe that I was meant to be part of this."

We're silent; there's only the news quietly reporting the latest pigging developments on the TV behind us.

And I'm a big fat sucker, because I find myself feeling sorry for the poor guy. We're all of us at this table a little different from most everyone else down here. We're out here, far away from home, trying to save a little girl from something terrible, something she's not meant to endure. There are no children in Hell, and I have a theory regarding that: They aren't held responsible for anything they say or do until they're old enough to understand the difference between right and wrong. And as nice as it may be to think that right and wrong is all in the individual's perception, it's just not true. Or if it *is* true, the powers that be running Heaven and Hell do not subscribe to that notion. There's a line drawn in the sand, and when you die, if your life has been spent mainly on one side of the line, you are judged accordingly. There are no retractions and no appeals.

166

I smile a little at Portnoy, which eases everyone else's tensions. Soon, there are more smiles than frowns and long faces at the table. I say, "It's okay, Portnoy. I understand where you're coming from. I think we all do."

There are a few nods, and Gus says, "Christ almighty, let's get on with this already. I'm so tired, I'm about to fall apart where I sit."

There's nervous laughter, and the air around the table lightens up a little.

"So," I say, "any theories at all about this second riddle? Let's bat some ideas around and then we'll head back to Felipe's for some shut-eye, tackle this thing again when we wake up."

There are intense looks of concentration, but no one says a word. Gus's and Tom's eyelids droop, Apple's fully close, and PigBoy's are waffling back and forth. Only Portnoy has enough energy to actually look like he's actively thinking of a solution.

Sleep is no longer an option, but a necessity.

"Alright, you sad sacks, let's head back now and get some sleep. Maybe this riddle will come clear in the morning."

There are sighs of relief all around. Those with drinks down the remaining portions, we leave enough on the table to cover the bill, plus a relatively generous tip for the deaf, demented bartender.

On our way out, a tray of empty glasses in his hands, the bartender calls to us loudly, "Watch your backs tonight, gents! Miscreants out and about! Saw it on the news there! Punks throwin' pigs!"

"Thanks ever so much," Portnoy calls back, and tips an imaginary hat in the bartender's direction. "Have a good evening."

"What was that, old son!?" the bartender roars back.

Portnoy just smiles and waves. The bartender smiles back, nods enthusiastically, waddles back behind his bar with the tray, and into the curtained area beyond.

I open the door, step outside, turn around to make a feeble attempt at starting a final brainstorming session about the second riddle. One arm still holding the big wooden door open, waiting for the others to file out, I see a flash of black to one side and feel something cold slide quickly into the lower part of my stomach. I shut my eyes tight in pain and shock. The cold slices a hot strip up my middle, stops at my rib cage, pulls out. Hands flit about my jacket, searching, searching.

Gone.

And then I'm on my knees on the sidewalk holding a loop of intestine in one hand, my mouth hanging open. I see the others gathered around me, sharing my expression. Looking ahead, down the street, I see a black shape running, get swallowed by the fog.

I fall backward into unconsciousness.

«« — »»

"Mother*fucker*," I say, always the first word to come to mind after I've been rendered unconscious. I try to sit up, but the gaping wound in my stomach shoots pain through my system and I'm forced to lay back down on the sidewalk.

"How long I been out?" I ask. The others squat on their haunches or stand nearby.

"Just a few minutes," PigBoy says.

I nod. Then something occurs to me. "I was stabbed, wasn't I."

Everyone nods.

"Your jacket change idea really helped out, PigBoy," I say, try to laugh, but give that up real quick once the first firecracker of pain explodes behind my eyes.

PigBoy just smiles. "Hey, sorry, man. But think what he would've done to you if you'd been wearing that pansy-ass baby-blue jacket."

"Don't make me laugh, you fuck," I say, grinning.

"Dude, that shit sure looks like it hurts."

"Yeah, it does, but I'll be alright. Just need to sleep it off. Portnoy: You have room up on your shoulders to give me a lift?"

"Most certainly," he says, and smiles, likely just happy to be along for the ride after fessing up in the pub like he did.

Tom leans down and, as carefully as possible, picks me up, puts me on Portnoy's back. He grunts with effort, though, at something that would never have made him grunt with anything but satisfaction before.

Once Portnoy has me secured, I turn, look over at Tom, now able to see eye-to-eye with him way up here. "You still alright, buddy? Hangin' in there?"

"Hangin' in, Stu. Yep. Monkey, monkey, and hangin' in there." He smiles, hoists Gus up onto his back with another grunt. Portnoy crosses the road, and the rest follow. Tom's step is no longer as sure, and he looks about ready to drop in his tracks.

My gut bleeds all over Portnoy's nice grey turtleneck. "Sorry about the blood, Portnoy," I say. "Promise to buy you a new one when all this is over, okay?"

He laughs a little and keeps walking.

"Anyone see the fucker that did this?" I ask, completely drained and ready to pass out again at a moment's notice.

There are negatives all around.

As I'm drifting off, I replay the incident in my head, trying to slow my mind's eye down around the part where I saw the black shape in my peripheral. Two images swim up out of the confusion: a quick, silvery glimpse of the knife that cut me, as well as the hand that holds it.

Somewhere between Old Codger's Bar & Grill and Felipe's place, I'm swallowed again by the darkness.

When I next open my eyes, I'm propped up on a bright red couch, something that sounds vaguely like Jimi Hendrix is blasting out of a nearby stereo speaker, and dead hippies dance all around me.

I close my eyes and pray for the blackness to claim me once again.

o such luck.

When I reopen my eyes, all the funky hipsters are still there, grooving and bopping, making fools of themselves.

Sure, I listen to some right cheesy '80s stuff, but somehow I just can't get into the '60s and '70s crap. It stirs nothing inside me. Not sure exactly what's inside me to stir if the '80s fluff does it for me, but whatever it is, it definitely ain't the same shit that's inside these twits.

My head feels like it's stuffed with cotton, and my mouth tastes like I've been sucking on an aluminum can all night. I look down at my gut to see that no one bothered to stuff my stray loop of intestine back into its rightful place.

"How thoughtful," I mutter, cram the loop back inside, look around for somewhere to wipe my bloody hands, settle for wiping them on Felipe's couch.

I take a quick look around. Lava lamps populate every table in the place. The pachouli's so thick and the clothes so bright and nauseating, my brain screams to leap out of my head.

Looking to my right, I see the crowd part and Apple come strutting through—the antithesis of everything hippy—and it's like a salve to my beleaguered soul. She has two drinks in her hands. She sits down beside me, offers one of the glasses. "Drink this," she says. "It'll help ease the pain."

"Yeah, in more ways than one," I say, glance around the room, give her a sidelong glance and smirking grin. "Thanks."

"Don't mention it."

The music has devolved from tolerable Hendrix covers to out-and-out Grateful Dead rip-offs.

Sometimes I wish there was an open line of trade between Hell and Upside—at least that way we could actually get our hands on the real musicians' output, instead of having to listen to shitty cover bands groomed by the underworld's record executives trying to replicate, from memory alone, the work of famous Upsiders.

Unfortunately, not many big musicians wind up down here— they make too many people happy. You do that, you lose your shot at the luxurious life down under. You wanna be a musician in Hell? Better start killing people, or selling crack to little kids, 'cause if you're any good at all, and manage to put smiles on a few thousand listeners' faces, you can forget about rubbing elbows with the 'red elite.' We're picky about who gets into our club, so start fucking shit up.

Apple and I just sit and stare ahead for awhile, sipping our drinks. Mine's a whiskey on the rocks; hers looks to be a gin and tonic.

"Where are the others?" I say.

"Sleeping," she says.

"How come you're not?"

"Not tired. Well, I mean, I'm tired—bloody *bone* tired—but I can't sleep. Too wired, you know?"

I nod. "So how come I got dumped out here?"

"No more beds."

I dig her short answers. Can't stand a woman who fucks about, blathering, talking your goddamn ear off.

"Where's the host of this wonderful little flashback?"

"Still crumpled at the bottom of the main stairs out front, I imagine."

I turn my head, raise my eyebrows.

"He tried to hit on me, made to grab my ass," she says, looking into the bottom of her glass. "So I slapped his hand away, kicked him in the balls as hard as I could, and pushed him down two flights of stairs. He wasn't moving much when I walked back inside." She takes a delicate sip from her glass.

"He'll heal," I say.

We smile at each other, and there's a certain *frisson* exchanged that I definitely do *not* dig. Not with Tom's girl.

"So how's Tom holding up?" I ask.

Apple's features darken, she looks away from me. "I don't know how much longer he's gonna last, Stu. He tells you 'no pain, no pain,' but I see how much it hurts when it's just the two of us. And it's breaking my heart."

I put my arm around her, rub her shoulder.

It occurs to me that we've never exchanged Upsider stories. I figure now's as good a time as ever to bring it up. Get her mind off Tom, at any rate.

"Apple, what did you do Upside? What's your story?"

She smiles softly, lips curling back just enough to reveal her top teeth. "My story? I'll tell you mine if you tell me yours."

"Not much to tell," I say. "I was a prick most of my life, fucking people when they were down. I went from shit job to shit job, never earning more than minimum wage. Finally squirrelled away enough money to buy a crappy car. Wound up driving said shitbox over a young girl playing near the road, effectively crushing her skull to splinters. Her mother screamed and ran to the side of the road, lifted her little girl into her arms, and lost herself in immediate grief. Her father must have seen what happened from the living room window of their house, because he grabbed and loaded his shotgun, marched out to the road, aimed it into my face where I stood in shock near the mother and dead child, and pulled the trigger, blowing my head off.

171

"When I woke up, I was here in the big 'H,' lying on the floor of what would become my home for the first thirty years of my punishment.

"Now, when I close my eyes for longer than a blink, I see the colours of the little girl's blood-spattered shirt and shorts—orange, white, and red—smeared like oil paints across my mind's eye."

Apple nods. She's looking at me really, *really* hard.

"What? What are you looking at?" I say.

She studies my face for a few more long seconds before answering, "It's strange, that's all. I didn't figure you for having killed anybody."

"Yeah, well, neither would I before I felt the crunch of bone beneath my tires."

Silence, and I'm glad of it. I don't even care if she tells me her story now. I'm sick of my own voice. I'm sick of the events that make up my life, my pathetic existence. I'm sick of whining about it, too, so it's best when there's just silence.

"I'll need another drink to tell you mine," she says. "You want another?"

"Nah, I shouldn't," I say. "This gaping gut wound will never heal if I keep thinning my blood."

She nods, rises, walks off with her glass for a refill.

As she disappears into the kitchen, Blue Balls Felipe walks in through the front door, looking particularly out of sorts. His clothes are rumpled, his hair's a mess, and there're cuts and bruises all over his arms. Concerned people approach him to ask what happened; he brushes them off angrily, stalks into the master bedroom.

Go, Apple, go.

When she returns from the kitchen with her new drink, she sits down a little closer to me this time. "So, me, huh?"

"Yup, you. Spill."

"Alright, but you get the *Reader's Digest* condensed version 'cause I'm finally getting sleepy. This'll be my last drink, too, then I'm hitting the hay. Deal?"

"Deal, chick. Let's have it."

"Okay. I grew up in a poor family; moms and pops never had enough money to make ends meet and I—"

"Oh, fuck off," I say. She had well-off-but-well-adjusted written all over everything she did.

172

She laughs. "Okay, you got me. I'm from money—lots of it. Had shitloads of the stuff pouring out of my purse. But it meant nothing to me. I had an empty hole inside that just couldn't be filled by the almighty dollar. I longed for friends who truly cared for me and not just my bank account, so when I—"

"Quit already! I gave you the real goods; now come on, fess up, would ya?"

"Aw, shit, you're no fun...." She knocks back her entire drink, licks her lips, belches. "Alright, you ready? Here we go:

"Middle-income family. Lots of angst. Unrequited love as a teenager—older boy. Read lots of books to escape depression. Took up martial arts, dove in with both feet, earned black belt."

While my jaw drops, she stops to light a cigarette popped from her pack.

"Was intensely unhappy for many years. Fell in love again—younger man this time. Again, unrequited. Less so than as a teenager, but still not returned with anywhere *near* the degree I gave it. More depression. Some shitty secretarial jobs. Other part-time crap. Mother died of cancer. Father worked all the time, paid no attention to anything I did. Boo-hoo, poor me. Misery lumped upon misery. End of rope, end of tether. So I gave up. Cashed in my chips. Slit my wrists. Died in a red bathtub as the fluorescent light over the sink flickered. Woke up here in stylish clothes. Met and fell in love with Tom. Love anything *but* unrequited. Never been happier.

"And now he's dying," she says, gazes at the floor. The surrounding lava lamps splash colour across her face. She crosses her arms, takes a drag off her cigarette.

"Voila," she says, looks at me with glistening eyelids.

I say nothing. There is nothing to say.

I just stare straight ahead, think about Tom, think about the second riddle, think about wanting to kill everybody in the room for being so fucking happy and carefree.

That's when I see the man's hand.

He's just walking past, doing a little shuffle in time to the music. A glint of light catches his watch, pulls my eye to his hand again.

Son of a fucking bitch. No way.

Images scroll in my mind as I stand up: the flash of a knife, the hand that wields it, the scar on the hand between the thumb and forefinger a long gash that starts at the wrist.

And then nothing but the pain.

I walk slowly toward the guy, approach him from behind.

I vaguely hear Apple calling after me, asking where I'm going, what the matter is.

And I'm thinking about Tom, about Apple, about my own life, about this seemingly hopeless prophecy. Is it all worth it? Is it worth getting knifed in the gut by this hippie punk? Is it worth dragging poor Tom around during what are likely his final days?

173

That black ball of hate I felt a thousand years ago toward PigBoy but was able to control now winds itself through my system, digs deep into my heart, and I see red. I see this hippie fucker's head as a puddle of grey-red snot. Even as my stomach screams at me to sit down and forget about it, let it go, my brain is on fire; it roars at me to squeeze every bit of hate I've ever had in my life into one pristine moment of destruction.

"Fuckface," I say, loud enough to be heard over the shit pounding out of the speakers in all four corners of the room. He doesn't turn around, just continues passing people he knows, nodding and winking, shooting imaginary guns at them like he's *such* a cool cat.

I catch up to him, lift my arm to his shoulder and spin him around, wince at the pain in my healing stomach. Pain that I will no longer feel in a few moments, because there will only be the pain in my arms, legs, and fists from pummelling this piece of shit to a stain on the revolting orange-brown carpet beneath my feet.

When he's facing me, I wait for recognition. There is none.

The Distance Travelled

"Bet I'm the *last* fucking person you expected to see, huh, shithead?"

He frowns, attempts to do the math, but I can see that he doesn't have a clue who I am. I direct his eyes lower, to my abdomen. He sees the wound...and finally the lights go on upstairs. His eyes grow wide at his unbelievably shitty luck.

Red is the only colour my eyes will pick up. Everything else is out of focus, blurred.

I waste no more time.

I pull back quickly, cram a hard-packed fist into his face, feel teeth dig into my knuckles. He flies back against a nearby wall, puts a hand to his mouth, comes away with blood, looks up at me.

He is clearly terrified.

And for good reason.

I move in quickly with two more punches to the face. He ducks neither one. Blood splashes across the wall to his left as my second shot splits his cheek.

He puts his hands up in front of his face.

The room has gone quiet. No one is dancing. No one is partying. Everyone just watches while I beat this guy down.

I rabbit punch him hard in the ribs. He doubles over. I grab his head between my hands, lift my knee. Connect.

Blood erupts from his nose, sprays the carpet at my feet.

174

My own wound reopens and I'm forced to go to a one-handed attack in order to keep my insides from flopping out onto the ground.

Pushing him by the face against the wall, I kick at his kneecap, hear a satisfying crunch. He screams, falls over. Squirms.

Just like old times.

His weakness disgusts me, and my rage pumps up a notch.

His nose bubbles blood and snot from where he lies on his side in the corner of the room, near one of the four speakers. He is curled into the fetal position, mumbling something. I catch a few 'please's and that's it, that's all I can take.

I move toward the top portion of his body, lift my booted foot, bring it down twice onto his head.

Softening it up for what comes next.

Disregarding my stomach, I remove my hand from the bleeding wound, grab and lift the speaker over my head. A loop of intestine flops out, but I feel nothing.

The man's eyes are closed. He is gibbering, shaking his head side to side.

I grunt and bring the speaker down.

His skull cracks but does not shatter. His gibbering and mumbling stops.

I lift, bring the speaker down again. This time, I feel bone give way.

Someone turns off the music; there is complete silence, except for my mechanical pounding of bone and brain to pulp.

I lift and bring the speaker down a third time, harder than the last two—so hard this time that I feel the floor meet the bottom of the heavy speaker. Cranial matter splashes to each side, like water does when you jump high and come down in the middle of a puddle.

Other colours bleed back into my sight. Blues, yellows, greens. In my periphery, I see Apple approach. Her mouth is a wide 'O.' She reaches out, tentatively touches my arm in a subtle gesture of restriction. But I'm done anyway.

On the floor, there's a man with a speaker for a head. It looks like a surrealist painting.

Our lovely host, Felipe the ass-grabbing smoothie—having cleaned himself up enough to rejoin the party—saunters into his living room, all shark teeth and fake charisma. He stops dead; his smile retreats from his lips.

"Sorry 'bout the mess, Felipe," I say, stuff my flopping intestines back inside my body. Exhaustion of both mind and body overwhelms me; I waver on my feet. "Friend of yours?"

Felipe shakes his head, still goggle-eyed, trying to comprehend how everything could have gone so terribly wrong.

I nod, barely registering his reaction. "I need to get some sleep now," I say.

Apple steps closer to me, holds me up under the armpits. "Jesus-fucking-Christ, Stu, what have you done?" Apple whispers as I let my body go nearly limp.

I just chuckle, feeling giddy, and decide to take one last look at my handiwork. Apple moves us away from the body, but I stop her: "Whoa, whoa, hang on a second."

There's something hanging out of the guy's jacket pocket. I go down on one knee, crawl over to it. Apple starts to object. "Stu, for chrissakes, what are you—"

But then she sees it, too, and quickly shuts her mouth.

The first piece of the triangle. It's half in, half out of his left pocket—the one closest to the floor.

My mind flits back with its last vestige of energy to replay the knifing one more time in my head. I remember the knife, the scar, and…hands searching my pockets, fingers finding purchase even as I lost consciousness.

The Distance Travelled

I giggle some more, and it turns to throaty laughter; my shoulders shake up and down. A tear pops out of the corner of one of my eyes. I wipe it away, and remember one more thing: the knife.

I search his right-side jacket pocket, but there's nothing. Nothing, either, in his back jeans pockets. I try his inside jacket pocket, and there it is. I feel the handle, pull it out, lift it up to the light.

"Fucking hell," I whisper.

Embedded in the handle is a metal triangle that looks exactly like the other one I hold in my hand.

I remember the words of the second riddle: "Second with pain. Metal glints. You'll see it again."

"Goddamn you, Oliver. You little prick," I say, and laugh.

The crowd around me just stares, clueless. Some of them shuffle past me, out the door.

As Apple lifts me to my feet, carries me into her and Tom's bedroom, sets out some blankets on the floor for me, I realize that there's absolutely no way of escaping this. Oliver has my number. I'm locked into this whether I like it or not. And so far, I don't like it one bit.

Two down, three to go.

178

Sleep falls on me like a hammer.

hen I wake up, I stretch my hands out in front of me. The blood caked on my knuckles cracks and splits; bits crumble to the floor.

No sign of Tom and Apple.

I get up, stumble around the room looking for the washroom. I find it, wash my hands and face.

Despite what one might think, Hell's water supply is relatively clean—and yes, there's cold as *well* as hot.

Walking out into the living room, I see everyone sitting on the couch or surrounding chairs. They're all sipping from mugs. "Coffee," I croak.

Felipe nods, gets up slowly, walks to the kitchen slightly bent forward, very obviously favouring his nutsack.

I glance in the corner of the room where I'd pulped that guy's skull. Only a small, faded stain marks the spot. I don't care where he's gone; I don't want to know.

"Two pieces now, huh, Stu?" PigBoy says, takes a sip of his tea. I just nod. "How long I been out?"

"About 21 hours, give or take," Apple replies. She has a smoke in one hand, cup o' joe in the other. No makeup, hair all matted and pasted to her skull, and wearing only a man's bathrobe, yet still she's sexy enough to get an early-morning stir out of me.

"Good Christ," I say. "Twenty-one fucking hours."

"Yeah, we've been up and back to sleep again, but we let you rest," says PigBoy. "After what went down last night, we figured you'd need some time to let your dreams sort of…you know, clean out your system."

"I don't dream," I say, maybe a little too curtly.

PigBoy stays silent, brings his cup to his lips, looks out the window.

I'm in the shittiest mood I can ever recall being in. I wish that guy's carcass was still in the corner, so I could pick up where I left off last night.

Felipe wanders back in from the kitchen with a steaming cup of coffee. He hands it to me, I take it gratefully, thank him, let the vapours swirl up my nose, fill my lungs.

Tom's sitting in a big wicker chair near the window. His fur has lost so much of its shine, it's beginning to look like straw. His black eyes have lost some of their intensity, too. They don't seem as dark as before—more dark brown than black now. The skin of his face has fallen, and the way he's sitting, he looks like a well-worn coat that someone has draped over the back of a chair.

We've got to get moving.

I decide to adopt a fake cheery attitude. After last night, I sense a slight shift in focus, and it seems like the mood of the group depends on me.

"So!" I say loudly and clap my hands, startling Gus so much he spills about half of his coffee in his lap.

"Goddamn son of a—!"

"We have two of these fucking pieces," I say, cutting him off, "and there're three more out there somewhere that need tracking down. Swallow a last mouthful of your drinks, everyone, then let's dig into that next riddle."

My sudden change in attitude makes everyone a little wary, but they oblige, swallowing the rest of their drinks, then moving over to the coffee table in front of the couch.

All but Tom, of course. He makes to get up, but I motion for him to stay where he is.

Apple brings the second book out of her purse, plops it down onto the table, opens it, flips through the initial lunatic scrawling and jumbled drawings. When she hits the page with the third riddle, she stops, reads it aloud:

"He is everywhere, forbidden. Their hope is stronger than death. It is in what they worship."

There are frantic drawings of triangles around the words, and something that looks like a church steeple.

"So what was your guess on this one the first time around, Porty?" I say.

He looks doubtful, a little of the previous night's shame after the confession at the bar and grill coming to the forefront again. "Well, I asked around a little bit on the street, and it was actually Felipe here who pointed me in what I *thought* was the right direction. That's how we met in the first place."

Felipe nods and smiles.

It occurs to me that I've never heard Felipe speak. "What's the matter, Felipe? Cat got your tongue?"

Portnoy says, "Felipe *has* no tongue, Stu. It was torn out during a routine torture session and never grew back. Felipe thinks it's a sign from God."

"A sign from *whom*?" I say. Apple looks at me sideways; a little bit of guilt flushes her face. I wonder how it feels to have caved in a God-fearing mute's testicles.

"From God," Portnoy says again.

"There ain't no God," Gus says, sucks his teeth. "Just like there ain't no Santa Claus, Tooth Fairy, Easter Bunny, or none other o' that kinda crap. Fairy tales, all of it."

"So how do you explain Satan, then?" Portnoy says.

"The existence of one don't necessarily prove the existence of the other. Could be that the Bible is just The Big Red Fella's propaganda. Something to sucker people into believing in *his* existence by way of another—decidedly *nicer*—god's. You think he's retarded or something? Ya believe in one, ya believe in both. But if there's only the one to begin with, then he's got ya—hook, line, and goddamn sinker. I mean, he suckered all of *us* down here, didn't he?"

No one has an answer for Gus's theory, but Felipe looks genuinely disturbed by it. Perhaps he's never thought of the possibility.

"Anyway," I say. "Theological discussions aside for the time being, where did Felipe lead you, Porty?"

"To the church of God."

"Come again?"

"Church of God, Stu."

"Where?"

"Here."

"In Hell?"

"Yes. There is one, but it's obviously not officially recognized. It's quite secret, and Felipe went out on a big limb taking me to it. They'll kill him and anyone else who even knows about it, if they find out it exists."

It takes me a little while to absorb this information as truth. I mean, I'm trying to imagine the strength of soul to not only believe in, but *worship* God after being exiled to the absolute *ass-hole* of the universe for the rest of your conscious time in this existence.

"So you went there," I say, "and what—found nothing?"

"Basically, yes," Portnoy says. "Going by the 'it is in what they worship,' part of the riddle, I looked all over the cross at the front of the small enclave in which they worship, and found nothing."

"Okay, well, I guess there's nothing for us to do but go back there and see what we see. If there's only the one church—" Felipe nods an affirmative to me "—and there are drawings of a church steeple in the book…"

"I guess we pack and go," PigBoy finishes.

With a definite purpose again—a direction to follow—the mood is more upbeat. There are even a couple of smiles around the room now. But I decide to shame Felipe's right off his face. I point at him. "Now you listen here, chum. You wanna stand any chance of getting out of this place on good behaviour, like you're evidently hoping, I strongly suggest you quit groping hot young thangs like our Miss Appleton. You know what I'm sayin'?"

Felipe blushes, cups his balls, grins. Nods a little. He throws his head back, motions like there's a bottle in his hand, pretends to chug.

"No excuses," I say, and smile.

He laughs.

We stand up. I thank Felipe for his hospitality, apologize again for the messy decapitation in the corner of his living room the previous night, and we shake hands.

"You remember the way to the church, Porty?" I ask.

"Most certainly, though I'll double-check with Felipe quickly before we leave," he says. "It's not far at all."

"Right, then, let's get at 'er."

Gus and PigBoy check to see that their guns and flashlights are safe and sound; Apple packs the books away, checks on her own flashlight.

"We're leaving the guns, fellas. Present to Felipe here for his goodwill," I say.

My comment is met with confused looks. After a moment, PigBoy says, "Fuck that!"

"No, *don't* fuck that. We won't need them anyway. You see how easily these two triangles fell into my lap? Have we needed the guns at all yet? No, not for anything, and I'm convinced we won't need them later, either. We're being ridiculous. We've watched too many gangster movies. This shit is preordained. I believe that now. Nothing can get in the way of its forward momentum. A ball has begun rolling and it's a huge-ass mother-*fuck* of a ball that no gun, no person, no anything can stop."

I'm not even sure where these words are coming from. They don't feel right coming out of my mouth, yet I say them with conviction. I say them as though I'm *not* a cynical bastard who's never believed that anything can ever completely turn out right, that there will always, *always,* by special design of the universe, be something in the way to seriously fuck things up, no matter how perfect it all appears to be.

"Well, that's a sincerely heartwarming speech, Stu," PigBoy says, "and I'm glad you're so uncharacteristically confident, but I, too, have certain beliefs about this situation. And *my* belief is that the deaf bartender who sawed my shotgun off for me had particular reason to do so. Now, I don't know what it is, and I don't really fucking care, either, 'cause when a complete stranger just decides to grab a guy's shotgun without asking and modify it for easier handling, I figure there's got to be a good goddamn reason why."

Fair enough.

"Fine, then," I say. "But the revolver stays. I'm sure Felipe will make good use of it. At his next Deathday celebration, should some unhinged motherfucker like me start cracking skulls and making a mess of his nice plush carpet, he can whip out his heat and splatter some grey matter."

183

Felipe grins, chuckles.

Gus leaves his revolver and ammo on the coffee table.

"Good deal," I say. Then I remember the other gun, too. "Might as well leave 'em both, Gus."

Gus drops the other gun on the table beside the revolver.

"You're sure about this, Stu," Apple says, concerned.

"Definitely."

Apple looks worried, but nods. "Alright, then," she says. "I'll get changed and we'll get a move on. Felipe, you're small—can I borrow some jeans and comfortable boots? I'm getting sick of trying to keep up in heels and a tight dress."

Felipe obliges, then we say our goodbyes—Apple grabs Felipe's ass on the way out and we all have a good laugh.

As we pass the enormous gargoyle protecting the premises with its stone glare, I look up at its face. The lines in it seem darker, sharper, more etched.

When we reach the street, Portnoy says, "We have to take the subway again. The church, such as it is, is a few stops deeper inside the city."

THE DISTANCE TRAVELLED

Through the ever-present fog, the glowing 'S' of the subway station just looks like a blue glob from this distance. Our footfalls on the cobblestone echo back from the dark buildings lining the streets, swirl around the narrow alleyways. I become vaguely hypnotized by the offbeat rhythms emerging from the stones.

When we're close enough that the blue glow is reflected off the stones, I hear a brief scuffle ahead, where PigBoy and Portnoy walk side-by-side. I look up.

My stomach sinks into my boots.

I watch Portnoy—as if from a great distance, and in ultra-slow motion—reach in and pull the sawed off shotgun from inside PigBoy's jacket, shuttle a shell into the chamber, take aim at Gus up on Tom's back, only a handful of feet away, and pull the trigger.

The barrel explodes; the flash of light in the blanket of fog is brilliant, blinding.

Most of Gus's head is sheared from his shoulders. His body topples from Tom's back, hits the ground with a wet thud. Tom stops walking, looks down at Gus. He doesn't even look in Portnoy's direction, just sinks to his knees at Gus's side.

Portnoy opens up again, this time in Apple's direction. She ducks in time, though, and the shot misses her. Portnoy bellows, "I know about it all! I know what happens when you get the fifth piece!"

184

Somehow, some way, he's gone insane. Fire burns in his eyes, and he believes in what he's doing.

"I can't let it happen. I *won't* let it happen!" The shotgun empty, Portnoy throws it to the ground with a clatter. He marches toward Apple, ten feet of focussed aggression and purpose.

Portnoy closing the distance rapidly with his monster's stride, I am unable to do anything but watch, opening and closing my mouth. PigBoy, at least aware enough to know that he has to try *some*thing, launches himself onto Portnoy's back, wrapping his arms around the giant's throat.

Portnoy doesn't miss a step.

Still on her haunches from when she ducked the second blast, Apple reaches into her right boot, pulls out a slim knife, and whips it at Portnoy's head. The knife sticks into one of his eyes. He roars, clutches at the handle where it juts from his face. Apple sidesteps the blind behemoth. He stumbles around, PigBoy beating on his skull from behind.

Inspired by Apple's damage, PigBoy claws at Portnoy's other eye, jams his fingers in as far as they'll go. More roaring, and more words that make no sense: "I can't let it happen! You'll destroy everything!"

Blood dribbles from both eye sockets, and he finally stumbles against a building, trips over his own feet, falls flat on his face.

Apple rushes over to help PigBoy hold him down.

I'm still frozen in place, rooted to the spot.

Tom, still on his knees, reaches down, touches Gus gently, says, "Gus and Tom's Gas Station...Gus and Tom's Gas Station..."

He repeats this over and again, rocking back and forth, his hand on his friend, tears streaming down the fur of his face.

Looking at what's left of Gus's head, I see immediately that there's not enough remaining for it to heal again.

Gus's hands and feet twitch a little, then quit.

Tom slumps and cries harder.

I just stand there, Portnoy's words bouncing around inside my skull, trying to connect to something that makes any kind of sense whatsoever.

A few people poke their heads out of windows above the street, but when I look up, they vanish, shut the windows tight, draw the blinds.

The only thing I can think to do is walk over to Tom, put a hand on his shoulder. He looks up, sees it's me, and continues crying.

187

Portnoy has all but given up struggling now, and just lies facedown on the sidewalk, mumbling into the cobblestones. Apple sits on one shoulder; PigBoy sits on the other, and they've got both his arms secured with their own.

We're all so confused that no one says anything for nearly a full minute.

Then Tom gains his feet slowly, wipes an arm across his eyes, turns in Portnoy's direction, and steps toward him slowly. As he passes me, I see the look in his eyes, and I know what that look means.

"Tom," I say, following after him. "Hold on, now...let's, uh...I mean, we don't know where the church is. We should try to get that out of him before...Tom, slow down!"

But his steps are heavy, decisive. Apple and PigBoy look up at his approach, see the same thing I saw in his eyes, and get the hell out of his way.

Portnoy rolls over onto his back. His face is a mask of blood. He's still mumbling about having to stop us, that he's been meant for this since birth.

Tom reaches Portnoy's prone figure, reaches down, pulls the knife out of his eye. Portnoy screams, clutches his face. Tom gets down on his knees, grabs a fistful of fur on Portnoy's head, and saws through the meat of Portnoy's neck.

"Goddamnit, Tom!" I yell. "We need him to tell us where the *church* is first!"

Tom ignores me, just shakes his head from side to side while he cuts.

Blood erupts from Portnoy's neck, splashes the cobblestones. Reaching the spine, Tom twists the head this way and that. There is a snapping sound, and Tom continues sawing.

Apple and PigBoy just watch, silent.

When the head comes free, Tom drops the knife, picks the bloody ball of flesh and bone up, walks over to where Gus's carcass fell to the street. Again, getting down to his knees, he puts the head aside, lifts Gus's scrawny little arms onto his chest, then picks Portnoy's head back up, and places it between Gus's hands.

Tom stands back up, turns around to us, fresh tears on his face. He nods grimly. "Felipe," he says.

I nod, look at PigBoy and Apple.

On our way back to Felipe's, PigBoy stops to pick up the shotgun. He loads it, puts it back in his coat. This time, he zips up.

Apple grabs her knife, wipes it off on her jeans, slips it back into her boot.

Going up the stairs at Felipe's place, the gargoyle keeps watch, looking miserable now. Defeated.

I touch it as we walk by.

24

elipe, shocked at the news of Portnoy's and Gus's deaths, writes directions to the church down slowly, as if in a dream. He writes again and again how he can't believe Portnoy would do such a thing. We tell him what Portnoy said while he attacked us, and the words make no sense to him, either.

"I knew about his obsession with this prophecy thing," Felipe writes on a yellowed pad of paper, "but he didn't say anything to me about the prophecy's realization being able to 'destroy everything'—whatever that means. Nothing like that at all. He just went on about how his time was coming soon, that he could feel it. He just seemed excited more than anything."

We thank Felipe for the directions to the church—promise to burn them as soon as we've found the place—and say goodbye.

He insists we take our guns back.

I nod slowly and pocket them.

«« — »»

On our way to the subway station, we pass Gus's body, Portnoy's head in his hands on his chest. PigBoy, Apple, and I look at the body the whole time we're walking by, thinking our own thoughts, probably remembering Gus in our own ways.

But Tom doesn't even turn his head, just keeps walking.

Across the street, where Portnoy fell, the puddle of blood is enormous, filling the sidewalk from side to side. Tom does not look over there, either.

We're comfortable leaving the bodies where they are, out in the open, because it's not a custom down here to bury or cremate people. There are a few who still follow the Upside ways when a loved one dies, but most folks don't relish the idea of digging a hole in the hard red dirt—not just because it's tough going, but because apparently a very strange feeling comes over you. You feel like you're trapping them in this shithole, instead of letting whatever's left of them—if there's anything at all—go free.

As for cremation: A lot of people's time is spent being burnt during torture sessions, so it just seems like more of the same to let the flames finish the job. Best just to let the body *breathe*, as it were, let whatever would naturally happen to it happen in its own good time.

Lost in these thoughts, I suddenly remember the picture of Portnoy in the first book of prophecies—the crumbled halo. A warning sign? The further we get into this prophecy business, the more likely that seems. Everything seems to mean something. Nothing can be ignored.

The blue 'S' floats out of the fog, hangs overhead like it's on strings, until we can make out the dark brick building it's attached to.

We descend, pay the automated ticket-taker, and board the train quietly.

«« — »»

Staring out the train's windows, my thoughts wander once again:

The fucking guns.

What possessed me to say we should leave them behind? Maybe if I hadn't, Gus would still be alive. When I heard the scuffling, I didn't lift my head fast enough to see how much time Gus had before Portnoy fired. He might have had enough time to react, had he still had the guns.

Then again, if PigBoy had listened to me and left the shotgun with Felipe, too, Portnoy would have had to attack us with his bare hands—which, granted, would have been a handful all on its own, but four on one, we would have stood more than a chance.

In the two seats to my left, Apple and PigBoy exchange a few subdued jokes about when we first bought the guns, how PigBoy questioned Apple's ability to handle one. Now, reaching inside his jacket, he hands the sawed-off over to Apple. "Judging by your quick work with that boot-knife of yours, if you'd had this instead of me, Portnoy might not even have been able to wrestle the damned thing from you, and Gus might be on this train with us."

Apple smiles. "Thanks, PigBoy, but you hold onto it." She passes it back to him.

PigBoy takes the shotgun back. They sit in silence as the train makes its first stop.

Tom doesn't look at anyone. His gaze is locked on the floor.

I think about old married couples and how sometimes when one dies, the other is not far behind, because it's just so unbearable to lose someone who's been an intimate part of your life for so many years. Big Tom looks grey, faded. Drained. He has the look of someone who has disconnected, who doesn't care what happens anymore, but is just going through the motions until someone or something stops him.

Tom is with us, but he's not. I think he died, too, the moment Gus's body hit the street.

My mind wanders back to the question about why I was so insistent that we leave the guns behind. I know that if nothing had happened, I probably wouldn't even be giving it a second thought. Everything was slotting perfectly into place. I felt partially confident and partially controlled. It seemed like no matter what happened, the prophecy would be realized.

191

Thinking these thoughts, I feel young Oliver pulling my strings even now. I've never thought that all things happen for a reason, that's it's all scripted, but I can't seem to shake that feeling in this case. Even now, with Gus dead and Tom as good as.

Maybe I'm clinging to this as an explanation simply because the alternative is too fucking unfair to believe.

The train stops again. Grey people file in and out without a sound.

One more stop till we get off.

To my right, in the single seat next to me, sits a grubby, pear-shaped man with a portable TV on his lap. It's black and white and has rabbit ears on top. The man stares at the screen, drooling.

I watch with him as a sprightly young male newscaster talks about the recent piggings plaguing our great empire. In addition to the footage we saw earlier at The Old Codger's Bar and Grill, there's a special report investigating the pigs' apparent semi-intelligence.

"We've no idea," the newscaster says, the image of a pig, a brain, and a question mark floating to his left, "how these animals are achieving it, but there are reports from the victims of these attacks that the pigs—once they've settled down a bit after the trauma of being thrown through a window—display unmistakably human traits. They've been said to sit in front of a person's television set with the remote, turn the power on, and channel surf, showing distinct tastes, grunting in disgust at one show, or snorting with appreciation at another. They pick up the telephone, dial seven-digit numbers, then grunt and squeal into the receiver. One report even states that a pig that came crashing into an elderly woman's home slid hard against the opposite wall, stood up on its hind legs, brushed the glass from its back, spotted the game of blackjack currently under way at the living room table, pulled up a chair, and sat down—'looking very clearly,' said the owner of the house, 'as though he wanted to be dealt in.'"

The news wraps up, and another program begins:

"The Decidedly Violent Adventures of DOLPHIN BOY," the screen says. It's a cartoon, and the animation is terrible—barely more than stick figures.

A middle-class family sits at the dinner table, smiling, happy. The adults talk about their days at work. The children, two boys, speak of schoolyard antics; the father laughs, shakes his head in amusement, while the mother looks concerned but clearly amused, also. "You little handfuls," she says. "What ever will we do with you?"

192

Everyone has a good laugh.

Suddenly, a knife-wielding dolphin springs from the pantry directly behind the table. The dolphin wears a dark, pinstriped power-suit. There's a large tattoo of a knife-wielding dolphin on the right side of his head.

He squeaks shrilly, making the noises dolphins do, while he hops around the table, plunging the long, serrated blade into the family's necks. Arterial blood shoots from their throats, splashing the cupboards, windows, plates of food, and Dolphin Boy himself in exaggerated arcs.

Dolphin Boy is followed out of the pantry by another, smaller, dolphin with a large rubber mallet for a head. This one is wearing pajamas with small, bloody meat cleavers on them. He has a fancy water mister in his left flipper, with which he alternates spraying himself and Dolphin Boy, keeping their bodies good and moist while Dolphin Boy sets about his work.

Once the entire family has slumped from their chairs in a gore-streaked mess—Dolphin Boy still squeaking and stabbing away madly at the corpses—the scene cuts abruptly to a close-up of the father's dead, carved-up face. Bold white letters flash onto the screen: THIS COULD HAPPEN TO YOU.

The drooling fat boy beside me nods his head like he actually understands what just happened.

The train slows again. When it stops, the door *pings* and we file out amidst the rest of the walking dead.

As the train pulls away, I feel in my jeans for my pocket watch, pull it out. I stand on the platform looking at the watch's face.

The numbers mean nothing to me anymore. They're jumbled up. I can't read them. I realize that time is just a concept I've held onto as a reminder of the way things were Upside. And now, with no torture sessions to go to, it has become completely useless. I toss the watch onto the tracks, watch its face crack and shatter into a million pieces.

Up onto the street. Out into the fog. The air seems heavier this deep into the city.

I pull out the map Felipe gave us, decipher his manic scribbling, and turn to lead the way.

In search of God.

193

or whatever reason, the buildings in this part of the city have fewer staircases, fewer fire escapes. The architecture has more round edges to it, fewer pointy bits. And there are a lot more people on the streets, which leads me to believe that it's less ritzy, the majority of inhabitants being unable to afford in-house torturers and home deliveries. More businesses, too; they line both sides of the streets in some places. Also, less fog due to all the human and motorized traffic breaking it up.

Still grey people, though, for the most part. Occasionally a standout will walk by wearing red or dark green, the occasional shocking burst of canary yellow. Also, a few other races.

One HellRat, wearing a Lollapazuzu shirt, walks by with his dog—a pitbull. The dog stops, shits on the sidewalk. A teenager walking behind the dog, earphones on, just grooving away, steps in the shit, slips, cracks his skull open on the curb. Blood dribbles out of the boy's ears. The HellRat sees this, laughs himself silly, carries on walking.

Some demons carrying shopping bags whistle the theme from 'The A-Team,' doing Mr. T impersonations at one another.

And every single person smokes—not a pair of hands in sight without a butt in one of them. Red embers bob in an endless stream up and down the street.

"Another block, then we hang a right till we hit the end of the street," I say. "According to Felipe's directions, there's a building there with a metal door painted black. Says it's around back. We open that door, follow the stairs down, and there'll be someone standing guard. We give the person the password, and we should be let in. Felipe said to drop his name if the guard gives us any trouble."

Pushing through the people on the sidewalk, I meet a pair of eyes that stick to mine longer than they should—especially down here where New York City hasn't got a thing on us for eye avoidance: Look straight ahead. Never show interest in what anyone else is doing. You are disconnected. You are not involved. You do not know these people and have no clue what they're capable of, so keep your nose out of it. Look at your watch, the buildings, the stores—anything but another pair of eyes.

I turn around as he passes me, watch his head bob away into the crowd.

Another man bumps my shoulder when I'm turned around. I barely get a glimpse of him before he turns down an alleyway. Just as he turns, he looks like he says something into his jacket's lapel.

Turning right down the main street shown in Felipe's directions, I see a man wearing a fedora duck quickly behind a garbage dumpster.

"Keep an eye out, you guys," I whisper, slowing my pace. "Seeing some weird shit around here. Might have nothing to do with us, might have everything."

Since all she's got is her boot-knife, I reach in my jacket and pass my backup gun to Apple, the one with only two rounds left in it.

She takes it, looks at it. "Gee, thanks," she says.

"Hey, better than just a knife, right?"

She pops the gun in her purse.

The crowd thins out after the first two blocks heading in this direction. Fewer businesses, more residences. No lights on in any windows, though, and more fog to obscure vision. Barely any street lamps, too.

"Give this dumpster a wide berth," I say quietly as we approach it. We swerve out onto the road. I've got my hand on the revolver inside my jacket. PigBoy's hand creeps inside his coat, too.

We pass the dumpster; there's no one behind it. I glance up the alley. Nothing moves.

I ease up on my revolver.

Warning signals blare in my head. This all feels wrong. But what else can we do besides prepare for when the proverbial shit hits the fan?

So we continue walking.

When we finally reach the end of the street, there's a yellow 'Dead End' sign.

"To the left," I say, glance behind me quickly. No one's there.

We move up onto the sidewalk, then around to the left side of the building, and around back. Shoes scuffle somewhere behind us; I turn around, see nothing. A shadow falls across the wall from somewhere above. I look up, catch the flap of a trench coat as it disappears behind the wall of an adjoining building.

"Jesus H, they're everywhere," I whisper.

The back wall of the building is about twice as long as the sides. It's dark red brick, and there's no door, there's no door, there's no fucking—

And then there's the door, nearly kitty-corner, right at the end of the back wall.

Painted black metal, just like Felipe said.

I pull on the small silver handle sticking out from it. The door opens, revealing the top of the stairs.

"Come on, hurry," I say, and we slip inside.

«« — »»

The door swings shut behind us; we're thrown into pitch darkness. Apple and Tom dig out their flashlights, turn them on, illuminating a short flight of stairs. PigBoy brings out his shotgun. I just keep my hand inside my coat.

We descend, and I'm reminded of Gus's library stairs. A shiver wends its way through me.

The stairs are concrete, so no matter how softly we step, our footfalls reverberate loudly, announcing our approach—especially Tom, since a half-ton HellRat can hardly be expected to be the master of stealth.

We reach the bottom; I knock on another black metal door.

A small portion of the door about the size of a mail slot slides open, reveals a set of Oriental eyes. Neither the eyes, nor the voice of the person who owns them says anything. A blank stare; a silent tongue.

"Uh...Pepupea," I say.

The others exchange confused looks.

PigBoy says, "What the fuck is that?"

"Shh!" I say. I look again at the eyes in the door, say the word a little slower, concentrating on the enunciation Felipe taught me. "Pepupea."

The eyes narrow, look me up and down. The mail slot slides shut, locks unbolt on the other side of the door. It swings open.

THE DISTANCE TRAVELLED

A tiny Japanese woman is revealed. She's wearing an all-black skin-tight outfit. She still says nothing, just motions with her arm for us to come in.

Once inside, she closes the door, locks up again.

She walks along a long hallway lit by small torches. We follow.

PigBoy's still got his shotgun out. I motion impatiently for him to put it away.

"What did you say, anyway?" PigBoy asks, leaning close to me once the gun is tucked back into his jacket.

"I said the password," I reply.

"I know—which *was*…?"

"Bumhead."

"Bumhead?"

"In Estonian, yes."

PigBoy looks at me like we *must* be in the wrong place.

"Don't ask me why," I say. "It worked; that's all I care about. Now shut up and keep your eyes and ears open, alright?"

At the end of the hall is another door, also black. The Japanese woman pulls it open, too. We follow her inside.

Before this door closes, I dread hearing the first one we entered come alive with knocking, shouts for it to be opened, that it's the authorities, and that there's nowhere to run.

The door does close, but there're no sounds from the other side. I allow myself the tiniest hope. I don't know what they're waiting for, but there's got to be a reason why whoever's tracking us hasn't followed us inside. Password or no, they could just bust in here and shoot the place up. And since there are no trials in Hell—no one has the right to remain silent, the right to an attorney, the right to make a phone call—all you have the right to do is take what you get and deal with it.

This new room we enter is full of wooden pillars, most with crosses of varying shapes and sizes on them. There are so many candles, there's barely even anywhere to walk. The set-up is that of an old church Upside: pews, centre aisle, pulpit, and a large cross hanging behind the pulpit—the focal point.

There are people in all-black attire, similar to the Japanese woman's, filling most of the front two rows of pews. Their heads are down in prayer—the prayer itself I cannot make out, it's being whispered so quietly.

"Excuse me, but—" I start, but the Japanese woman puts a finger to her lips.

"One moment, please," she whispers, disappears into another room, closes the door.

We stand in the centre aisle, unsure what to do with ourselves.

A few moments later, the woman re-emerges with another woman. This one is of dark skin, and pale, striking blue eyes. She is clothed just like everyone else.

The Japanese woman walks past us, smiles, tilts her head, and goes back to her post at the front door.

"The password," the second woman says quietly when she reaches us. "Where did you get it?" She is serious, emotionless.

"Felipe," I say.

She nods slowly. "My name is Muriel. What do you want here?"

"We have come to worship along with—"

"Don't lie to me," she says.

Fair enough. Cut the bullshit.

"Okay. Well, um, I'm not exactly sure how to put this, or if you'll even believe me at all, but—"

"We want the fucking triangle," says PigBoy. He opens his jacket, shows her his sawed-off, like he's the muscle in some Scorcese film.

Muriel looks at him with distaste. "We have no *fucking* triangle, boy."

PigBoy raises his eyebrows. "Damn, lady, you sure don't talk like the Christians I know Upside—" At the mention of Upside, the woman clearly gets a jolt. "—but I like your style. Don't know many God-fearing people that'd cuss like that and make the word sound so natural."

"The word 'fucking' is not against God," she says coolly. "Now what is this about Upside? How did you get here?"

"Wouldn't you like to know," PigBoy says.

"Oh, quit acting like you're five, PigBoy, and just answer the woman's question," Apple says. PigBoy looks at her, makes a face.

"Alright, alright. Yeah, I'm from Upside. But look, we don't got all day here. So quit fucking around with the attitude, and just tell us if you know anything about the triangle."

Muriel ignores PigBoy, turns to me for an explanation.

"He's a dick," I say, "but he's right. We're looking for the third piece of a puzzle of five. The first four pieces are triangles; the fifth's a square. We've got the first two, now we need the third. If you know anything about it, please—any information you can part with would be greatly appreciated."

She weighs my words, apparently decides that there's a chance I might not be lying, and says, "Show me the first two pieces."

The Distance Travelled

I pull them from my jacket pocket—the one still wrapped up, the other loose. I pull back the wrapping on the second one so she can see them both, but keep my hands close to me, ready to snatch them away if she makes any sudden moves.

I lost one of them once; no way I'm losing them both.

Her eyes open wide at the sight of them. She crosses herself.

I'm reminded of something Portnoy said when we first met him, in the little cave in the subway tunnel that was his home. "You know about these?"

"Oliver's prophecies," she says, eyes glued to the triangles. "Yes, I know a lot about them. I just can't believe that..."

I put the triangles back in my jacket pocket. "Well, a...uh...*friend* of ours told us that it was incredibly unlikely that any of the holders of these puzzle pieces would be aware of their piece's significance."

Muriel thinks for a moment. "Was this *friend* of yours the first piece holder?"

I look to Apple, Tom, and PigBoy, get no signal that this is ground we shouldn't be treading, so I say, "Yes, it was."

200

"Well, what this person neglected to tell you—or perhaps he or she genuinely did not know—is that three of the five *will* know of its significance. The first, third, and fifth holders will, in fact, be acutely aware. The second and fourth will not."

I think of fuckface whose cranium I demolished at Felipe's place.

"Okay, great," says PigBoy, "so hand it over already, and we'll be on our merry way."

"Unfortunately, it's not quite that easy, *boy*," she says.

PigBoy visibly bristles. "Say, sister, you'd better quit with that 'boy' shit or—"

Muriel turns to me, once again effectively cutting PigBoy off. "I have read up extensively on the subject, pieced certain clues together, and am fairly convinced that the third piece is in this room—but I've no idea where. And believe me, I've looked. But I suppose it's not to be revealed to me. Only to you."

I run my fingers through my hair, glance around the room. "Well, shit, I don't even know where to start looking. I mean, hell, it could be—"

Someone coughs. I follow the sound.

I freeze.

My throat catches on the word 'anywhere,' refuses to let it out.

Hands. I see the hands of the man on the subway—the one who was holding the newspaper in front of his face. They're up on the railing of the second row of pews. The man's head is bowed, and he's wearing the same fedora.

"Oh, Jesus…" I say.

"What is it?" Muriel says, alarmed. "Do you see the piece?"

"No, not the piece. Stay here a second, okay? I'll be right back. Just have to, uh…" I trail off, my mind preoccupied with what I'm going to say to this guy, because there's no way this is a coincidental meeting. Not with the swarm of shadows outside, apparently just waiting for some signal to come into this place and tear it to pieces.

I walk toward the man, holding up a hand behind me, indicating to the others not to follow me. I reach into my jacket, pull out the revolver, let my hand drop to my side, hold the barrel of the gun flush against the back of my leg, hidden from view.

I sit down on the end of the third pew, slide over as quietly as possible to where the man sits in the second row. The dim lighting makes it hard to make out his profile features, especially with his head down, his fedora casting deep shadows on his face.

Just behind and to the left of him, I bring the gun up from my leg, place it behind his right ear, lean in close and whisper, "Why are you following us?"

The woman closest to him, on his right, lifts her eyes for a moment, turns at the sound of my voice, sees the gun. Her mouth opens a little in alarm, but I gesture for her to just turn around and keep praying.

201

The man whispers back, "To bring you lot back, of course."

I know the voice, but it can't be. Not here.

"Turn around," I say. "Slowly. Leave your hands on the back of the pew."

The man turns his head, and before I can even fully see the face, I know who it is.

Salinger.

Fucking Salinger.

A thousand questions bolt through my brain at once, and I settle on the first one I'm able to pin down. "How'd you find us?"

"I've been following you ever since you left, ya bloody wanker. When I lost you on the subway train, I called in some intelligence help, and we tracked you down at your buddy Felipe's place. Once you left his groovy pad, we had a little *chat* with him, if ya know what I mean, yeah?"

Salinger grins that awful fucking grin of his.

"He was only too willing to let us know where you'd gone, and what the password was to get in here, too."

Before I can clasp down on another of my thousand questions, Salinger continues: "Shame, though, what he done after we left…"

I jab the barrel of the gun in his neck. "Which *was*?"

"Topped himself, I think. Couldn't live with the fact that he'd ratted out his little secret society here. Bloody weakling. He must have a pretty merciful regular torturer, that's all I know, 'cause he didn't get nearly the scale of my usual treatment before he cracked." Salinger's weedy little laugh seeps out of his scrawny throat.

Yet another death in the name of this goddamned prophecy. I feel the rage building in me again. Rage I absolutely *have* to control if there's any chance whatsoever of us walking out of here alive.

"No worries, though, mate. Suicides always come back," Salinger says.

"What?"

"You didn't know? You can't do yourself down here. Against the rules. Too easy, that, isn't it? Nah, you do that, you come back, get reinstated. The Big Red Fella sees to that. Don't always come back looking exactly how you checked out, mind, since TBRF's 'doctors' have to reconstruct you from whatever mess you've left yourself in."

Wonderful. So, Felipe'll come back all fucked-up looking *and* wracked with guilt at having ratted out the only remaining church of his religion.

"Those your men out there, surrounding the place?" I say.

"You're fucking brilliant, you are," he says, winks at me.

"So what are you waiting for?"

"Nothing. We could've sacked this place ages ago—*well* before you got here. But I don't give a sod about people wasting their time praying to a God that doesn't exist. If he ever *did* exist, he's long since forgotten about anyone down here. So no harm done, yeah? Just like having a good, solid wank, this." He shrugs, looks around, curls his lip in disgust.

Taking a quick glance behind me, I see Muriel standing close to the others, obviously in some sort of planning huddle. I shake my head side to side—*nonononono*—hoping one of them looks up to see me, gets the hint that I need to handle this on my own. No one does.

Great.

I can see this turning to shit very quickly within the next few minutes. Especially considering PigBoy's tendency toward violence when experiencing even the slightest doubt.

Salinger says, "You can worship whatever dead or forgotten gods you like. Won't do you a jot of good anyway. But you can't just skip out on your torture sessions. You're all down here for a reason, yeah? Because you're colossal fuckups. And this is where you pay for being a colossal fuckup. There's no shirking payment, no skipping town to go on some grand adventure. Whatever it is."

So he doesn't know about the prophecy? Or maybe he's just lying to throw me off.

"Might as well put that gun away, too, mate. I don't walk out of here with you rabble in tow in about—" He leans forward slightly, checks his watch without moving his hands off the pew. "—oh, say, five minutes, my crew's gonna come in here and murder every single one of you silly fuckers."

Another shark grin, exposing his rotted teeth.

My brain spirals inside itself. I glance behind me again. The huddle is over, and now the others are just looking over here nervously.

If I shoot Salinger in the head—which would put me in a good mood for at least the next two weeks—in less than five minutes, my friends and I will be dead, these worshippers will be dead, and PigBoy's little sister will have no hope of ever getting back home.

If we walk out of here with Salinger peacefully, we'll be carted back to the open country, where life will resume as it was before—and again, PigBoy's sister will have no hope of ever getting back home.

Oliver, where are you?

I sigh, pinch the inside corners of my eyes with my fingers. "Fucking hell."

"You said it, mate," Salinger says. "Tough choice. But I have faith you'll make the right one. You're a smart boy." He takes his hands down from the back of the pew, confident now that I'm not going to shoot him.

I look around at these people, these stupid idiots praying to God, to the one who let them rot here. My little Hollywood moment with Salinger barely fazes them, even in the house of their lord. Catching little snippets of their mumbled prayers, I hear them asking for forgiveness, pleading for another chance, begging to be shown the light, to let the strength of the holy spirit infuse them, allow them to fight the evil of this place.

While their weakness stirs me up inside, boils my blood, it also makes me sad.

Because I wish I could believe.

Part of me sees a mewling bunch of blind sheep, content with using fairytales as a crutch and a scapegoat—a way to make it through the day without having to take too much responsibility for the way their lives turn out. Another part of me, though, sees immense strength in people who can still believe in those fairy-tales, even when at the lowest rung of the ladder. They cling to it—not just as a habit, but as an integral part of their lives. As something that *defines* them.

And I cannot have their deaths on my hands.

"We'll go with you," I say, hanging my head, putting my gun back in my jacket. "We'll go back with you."

Salinger grins wide, exposing blackened, pus-filled gums. "Wise choice, Stuart. Now hand over your weapon. My face is still a little numb from the last time you lot had a go at me."

I open my jacket, hand over my piece.

All for nothing, I think. *Gus's death, and all the rest of it, for absolutely nothing.*

"Oy!" Salinger says, standing up, startling the churchgoers. He waves a hand at PigBoy. "Take that shotgun out of your jacket real slow-like and slide it down the aisle, up to this pew. Got it?" He cocks the revolver, aims it at PigBoy. "Now, sweetcheeks. Ain't got all fucking day, you know."

PigBoy eyes him warily but relinquishes the sawed-off, slides it down the aisle as requested.

Salinger walks to the end of the pew, picks it up. He moves his trench aside, stuffs the revolver into his waistband, levels the shotgun at his hip with both hands. "Does the big guy have any-thing stowed away that my boys might not appreciate having stuffed up their arseholes?"

We shake our heads.

"What about the cunt?"

Apple burns a hole through his face with her glare, but says nothing. Just shakes her head.

"Right, let's move out, then. Come on, Stuart, you first. Out into the aisle."

My mind scrambles, trying to think of any feasible way out of this. At the same time, I'm wishing I had more time to ask Muriel some questions. Like what Portnoy's ranting before he attacked us might have meant, what else she knows about the prophecy, whether the fifth riddle is revealed somehow after the fourth, since it's not mentioned in the books. But it's slipping away with each step I take closer to the aisle.

I get to the end of the pew, come out into the aisle. Salinger pokes the barrel of the gun into my back, prods me forward.

Muriel just stares, backs up, as Salinger makes his way up the aisle.

"Go back to your storybook, sister. Forget you saw any of this, or I'll come back with my boys—and next time things won't go down so quietly."

Reaching where Tom, Apple, and PigBoy stand waiting, Salinger carries out a one-handed frisk job on Tom—as much of him as he can reach, anyway—and says, "You'll forgive me if I don't just take you at your words." Satisfied that Tom is clean, he moves on to Apple.

"Believe me, sweetie," he says, leering at her, patting between her legs, the sides of her breasts, "I wish I could trust you enough to do this with both hands."

Finished with the search, he motions for us to move out through the door. We march down the long, dimly lit hallway till we reach the first door we came through. The Japanese woman is still at her post.

"Outta the fucking way," Salinger barks. The woman stands aside, but Salinger pumps a shell into her stomach anyway. The report is deafening in the contained space. The woman crumples to the ground, holding her midsection. Blood pools around her on the floor. She moans and whimpers, squeezes her eyes tight.

Salinger leans over, sneers, says, "Where's your saviour now, eh?" and kicks her in the teeth.

He leaves the door open so the meager illumination from the hallway can light our way up the small flight of stairs that leads to the outside door.

205

The Japanese woman continues to sob; it echoes all around us.

A big part of me will be glad to go home, just forget about all this. Maybe reopen the gas station with Tom and Apple. Fix my window up properly. Get a better air-conditioner. Buy some more Boo Berry. Just wipe the slate clean and start again.

At least it will be over, then, and I can be alone with my misery.

Boo-hoo, I know. I feel like cramming my *own* boot down my goddamn throat. When did I become such a puling little bag of shit?

Tom, at the front of the line, opens the door; shallow light from outside seeps in. Tom looks back at us, a question in his eyes.

"Keep going," comes the command from the back.

Tom looks forward, steels himself, steps outside. I half expect to hear Salinger's men open up, riddle Tom with bullets. But there is only silence after his big feet smack the ground outside.

THE DISTANCE TRAVELLED

The rest of us emerge. I see black shapes on the roof and fire escapes of the building that this one backs out onto. There's a fence separating the two buildings. Several men stand along the fence, rifles and shotguns trained on us.

Salinger prods us on, back the way we originally came—Tom in front, followed by PigBoy, then Apple, then me. "Stay close to the wall, and stay in single file. Try anything stupid and you'll be full of so much fucking lead you won't know your arsehole from—"

Ahead of me, Apple flattens herself to the wall quickly, slides backward along it slick as oil, twists the shotgun out of Salinger's hand before he has a chance to react. She pushes the barrel upward, aiming it high; the gun goes off right in my ear.

All around us, shotgun shells slide into place, rifle bullets slot into their chambers, handguns are cocked. But Apple's using Salinger as a shield, one arm around his neck. He struggles with her, threatens to overpower her, then Apple says, "I didn't want to have to do this, but—" and her right boot comes up, the knife there slips out, twists around in her free hand so she's holding it business end down. She sinks it hard between Salinger's shoulder blades.

Salinger shouts once, quickly, clipped. Then bites his lip, draws blood. His face scrunches up in pain. He drops the shotgun to the ground.

"Okay," Apple says, "maybe I *did* want to do that—but just a little, honest."

"You shitty fucking whore," Salinger says, blood dribbling from his lip. "You can't get away. What the fuck is wrong with you!? YOU'RE SURROUNDED, you blind twat! Can't you—"

Apple punches the knife down farther between Salinger's shoulder blades, twists it, pulls it out completely, then plunges it back into a different spot, to the right of the first hole. He bellows louder and longer this time. She wrenches back with the arm that's around his neck. Something cracks.

"Tell your boys to climb down, drop their weapons, and line up along this fence," Apple says.

Salinger just spits blood and chuckles.

"Do it *now*," Apple says, twists the knife in his back. He groans, stamps his foot at the pain.

"Alright, al*right*, goddamnit!"

"Line up along the fence, like the lady says!" Salinger shouts to his men.

After a moment's hesitation—long enough that I think they're just going to open fire anyway, Salinger be damned—

weapons clatter to the ground, feet tromp down fire escapes, men attached to wires jump from rooftops. They land softly on the ground, walk toward the fence.

They line up, just like the lady said.

"Hands up where I can see them," Apple says.

A dozen pair of black gloves rise slowly into the air.

"Good," Apple says. "Now down on your knees, Sally."

Salinger sneers. "Why, you fucking little—"

"Shut up and get on your KNEES!" Apple roars so loud in his face even *I* flinch.

Salinger sinks slowly to his knees, shaking his head. "You're gonna pay for this, bitch. You're gonna pay hardcore."

"Uh-huh. Whatever, Sally," Apple says, down on her haunches behind him, still with an arm wrapped vice-tight around his throat. She looks over her shoulder at the others and me, motions with her free hand for me to grab the shotgun where it lies next to the wall.

When she turns back, one of the men standing along the fence has a foot in the chain-link. She barks at him to step back or she'll cut off Salinger's head. The man hesitates for a second, then steps back in line with the others.

Apple leans close to Salinger's ear, says, "I'd kill you, you weaselly little shit, but there'd just be someone else to take your place, anyway, so what's the point? And the new guy might be better at his job; you, I know I can take." Then she stands up quickly, brings back her foot, and kicks the knife in Salinger's back. It sinks the entire way in, handle and all. Salinger pitches forward onto his face.

The line along the fence tenses, looks ready to pounce, but I've got the shotgun trained on Salinger's head.

"Tom, you strong enough to carry him?" Apple says.

Tom nods.

"Beautiful. Hey, you there, Mr. Impatient Pants." Apple points at the guy who'd put a foot up onto the fence. "Lend us your pair of bootlaces, would ya?"

The guy bends down, undoes his laces, throws them over the fence, puts his hands back up in the air.

"You're a sweetheart," Apple says, bends down and ties Salinger's hands behind his back with both laces. She yanks hard on the knot, motions Tom over.

Tom bends down, picks Salinger up, cradles him in his arms like a baby.

"Right," Apple says, "You follow us around this building, my big buddy here will bite Sally's face off, and then my shotgun-wielding friend will cram the barrel in his mouth and blow what's left of his skull across the street. Are we clear on that?"

The line does not move. The line does not make a sound.

"Good enough for me," Apple says.

We walk around the side of the building. I keep an eye on Salinger's men. They stay right where they are.

Salinger moans in Tom's arms, probably in too much pain for coherent speech.

Remembering the revolver, I say, "Someone wanna grab that revolver from Sally's waistband? His hands are tied, I know, but I think we've all seen too many movies where a fella worms his way out of even the best-tied knot, and plugs every one of his captors."

PigBoy walks over to Tom, roots around behind Salinger's trench coat, digging at different sections of his waistline.

He finally comes up with the revolver, and is about to pop it into his jacket when he remembers his specially cut lining made for the sawed-off. "Dude," he says, "swap me heat. I got the holster for it, man. If the shoe fits, you know?"

I roll my eyes, toss him the shotgun. He throws me the revolver.

Up ahead on the main street ahead of us, people bustle around. That's where we need to be—mixed in with a large crowd.

We continue up the dead-end street, PigBoy and I whipping our heads around every few steps to make sure the street behind us is still clear.

We make it to the main street, take one last look behind us— nothing moves—and turn the corner.

Melt into the grey.

26

hat was it Portnoy said again?"

Apple's walking fast through the people on the street, pushing them aside. "What was it…something about Hell's Kitchen?"

"Yeah, I think so," I say, trying desperately to keep up.

Beside me, Tom plods heavily, pain in his face, not nearly as well hidden as it once was. No one even gives us a double take, despite the moaning body Tom's carrying in his arms.

"Slow down, Apple," PigBoy says. "Tom can't keep up. He's carrying a whole extra *guy*, you know?"

"No time to slow down. You think those guys will wait long before they call for backup? Hell, they probably did that the second we were around the side of the building."

We're walking in the opposite direction of the subway and, looking ahead, I see a bus stop loom out of the thin fog, so I assume that's what Apple's chugging toward.

Tom stumbles a few times, calls out. "Miss Appleton…" He winces, barrels someone over, falls against a store window, rights himself, keeps walking. "Gotta be slow for me. Tom's not as fast today…"

A bus's headlights cut through the fog. Apple yells, "Come on! We can't miss the bus!"

PigBoy, Tom, and I pick up our paces a bit. PigBoy and I lose Apple in the crowd, but Tom—being over twice everyone else's height—says he can still spot her. His eyes are nearly completely closed from the pain now.

Salinger's dangling legs kick people as Tom ploughs through the crowd. Someone mumbles, "Hey, watch it"; another guy says, "Have an eye." They sound like robots, just repeating phrases they learned in another lifetime.

The bus pulls over to the bus stop. A few grey people and a green-haired demon shuffle on, the demon's two-foot mohawk scraping the ceiling of the bus.

Finally spotting her again, I see Apple bound the last few steps to the open door of the bus. She climbs aboard, disappears, then re-emerges a few seconds later, waving her right arm frantically, hanging onto the guard rail inside the bus with her left. "Hurry! He's gonna leave without us!"

We dash the rest of the way to the bus, pile on.

Apple pays for us, double-checks with the driver that this bus goes to Hell's Kitchen. He hands us three transfers, says, "End of the line, use these," and pulls away from the curb.

Apple turns around, looks at Tom; her eyes shoot open. "Wait!" she yells. The bus driver slams on the brakes, startled.

"Tom, honey, leave Salinger behind—we don't need him anymore," she says in a soothing voice, puts her hand gently on Tom's shoulder.

Tom just stares at her for a few seconds, then a light goes on behind his eyes, and he smiles quickly, laughs a little, turns around, and marches down the three steps at the front of the bus.

The door opens. Tom tosses Salinger out into the street.

Salinger lands on his back with a sharp crack. A small Chinese man runs him over on his bicycle, rings his little bell, spits curses at him.

I smile as the bus door closes again.

The driver pulls back out into traffic, while we move to the back of the bus, sit two on one side, two on the other.

"Well," I say, as we drive safely past the dead-end street where the church was. "That was beyond brilliant, you getting us out of that, Apple. PigBoy just keeps getting to eat his words over and again, doesn't he?"

PigBoy flips me the bird; Apple laughs; Tom tries on a tired smile, nods his head.

"Only thing is," I say, "there's no fucking way we can go back there. Not unless we stock up on some serious firearms—and even then, it would hardly be anything but a suicide mission. And as confident as I've grown in your formidable ass-kicking capabilities, Apple, you have to admit, we'd be dead in a matter of minutes."

Apple looks at me steadily, a smile growing slowly on her face as I talk. Her grin infectious, I find myself smiling, too.

"What? What is it? Why're you smiling?"

"Well," Apple says, leaning back in her seat, "it just so happens that we don't have to go back."

My eyebrows knit together; I look at PigBoy and Tom. Smiles sprout on their faces, too.

"Alright, what gives?" I say. "Unless I missed something, we didn't get the third piece of the puzzle, and since we need all five, this is a *bad* thing. No?"

Apple leans forward, digs in her purse. She pulls out a beautifully adorned cross-shaped trinket box about the size of her outstretched hand. It's studded with jewels of all kinds.

"Goddamn..." I say.

"Fuckin' A," PigBoy says.

Apple hands the cross to me carefully. "Open it," she says, that big smile still shining from her face.

I pull the top off the box, and inside is a beaten, weathered triangle.

The third piece.

"But...how?" are the only two words I can persuade my lips, tongue, and teeth to form.

"Our young miss Muriel," Apple answers.

"But...but..."

211

"Before you make it a hat trick of 'but's, I'll fill you in. First, though, take the triangle out, pop it in your pocket with the others. No way I'm having its loss on my conscience if you get knifed and robbed again." She chuckles.

I reach down, pluck the triangle from where it sits in the middle of where the cross's arms meet. I put the piece in my jacket pocket.

Getting heavy in there now. And it's a good feeling.

I hand the trinket box back. "You should have this. It's more of a girly item, you know?"

She scoffs. "Yeah, 'cause I'm a big Christian girl, right?"

"Well, no, but you can still appreciate its beauty, can't you?"

She sobers a little. One corner of her mouth lifts. She nods and takes the trinket box, places it at the bottom of her purse.

"So come on, spill already," I say, as the bus lurches around a corner. Looking out the window quickly, I see that the fog is thickening again. Judging by what Apple said about the neighbourhood Hell's Kitchen is in, we should be back to pea soup any minute now.

"You were right a minute ago," Apple says, "when you asked

if you missed something. That's exactly what happened." She pulls out her pack of smokes, lights up, opens her mouth to continue. But before she can say another word, a prim-looking young woman two seats down looks over our way, coughs exaggeratedly and waves smoke away from her face.

Apple doesn't miss a beat. She takes careful aim at the woman's head, flicks the lit cigarette into her poofy coiffure. The woman yelps in surprise, bats at her head till the cigarette drops to the floor. She stomps on it, gets up, and moves several seats away from us. Sits down again, and glares daggers our way, her nostrils flaring, threatening to unleash the cleansing fire of Righteousness upon us.

Apple ignores Dragon Lady, dips back into her pack, lights up another smoke, turns back to me. "When you spotted Salinger and went over to talk to him, Muriel immediately grilled us all, testing us to see if we were the real thing. Like Portnoy, she'd been reading about and researching her piece of the puzzle for as long as she could remember. She knew someday someone would come for it, and she just had to be doubly, triply, no-doubt-left-in-her-mind *sure* that she was releasing it to the right people.

212

"I showed her the books and PigBoy told her about his sister, and that seemed to clinch it for her. She was still pretty reluctant to hand it over, but she did after saying a quiet prayer over it and kissing the box gently.

"And that was that. I figured something funky was up with you over on the pew with your gun against some guy's head, so I told the fellas that no matter what, we're not giving up, we're not letting this out of our grip—not when we're this close. That was the closest I've ever come to a pep talk in my entire life."

Apple smiles and nods, flicks ash to the bus floor. She turns to dragon lady, brings her hand up in front of her, takes aim with her cigarette at the woman's head again, closes one eye as if lining her shot up, then puts the cigarette back between her lips, and laughs.

The woman flares her nostrils again, looks out the window, nose high in the air, eyebrows arched in indignance. It's a good view up her nostrils, and we agree that she could use a good chimney sweep.

"Saloon door," Tom says.

"What's that, big guy?" I ask.

"Saloon door," he says again, and points at the obvious globs of snot up Dragon Lady's nose. "Won't go back up, won't never come out. Saloon door." He breathes in and out of his nose quickly to illustrate his point.

We bust out laughing.

"Good one, Tommy," says PigBoy.

The bus stops and Dragon Lady gets up from her seat. She passes us, nose still sky-high, and when she gets just about to where Tom's sitting, he starts with the quick breathing in and out.

I just about fall out of my seat.

Our laughter subsides, the bus stops at the end of its line, and we and the remaining passengers disembark.

The bus blasts black smoke out of its tailpipe as it trundles away, rocking back and forth from the potholes in the cobblestone.

"What now?" I ask Apple.

"Trolley, chum," she says. "Should be here any minute. It's a dedicated vehicle. Goes only to and from The Kitchen." We cross the street and walk with the other five people that got off the bus to a trolley sign posted kitty-corner to where we were dropped off. Written in red ink on the small white sign is a thin circle with little devil horns and a goatee.

"Okay, but shouldn't we check out the fourth riddle to be sure that Portnoy's guess was right?" I say. "I mean, he's been on track up to now, but he *did* try to murder us all, so…" I spread my hands out. "You know?"

"You're right," Apple says, brings out the second book, flips to the back. "Here it is: Steaks of the Damned. Hidden under clothes. Slick in a bloodbath."

213

Below the scrawled writing are scribblings of chains, what looks like the barrel of an old-style machine gun, and a roughly sketched turn-of-the-century hat. I think of Salinger's fedora and hope to hell that he's got no more part to play in this.

A thin film of sweat breaks out on my forehead, regardless.

"Well, the bloodbath part sounds especially encouraging," I say. "Any early ideas about the rest of it?"

"I can see where Portnoy would infer The Kitchen from it, for sure, considering the 'Steak of the Damned' bit," Apple says. "But other than that…" She shrugs. "Guess we'll have to see what we see when we get there, hope that big murdering bugger was right."

I nod, quite accustomed by now to flying by the seat of my prophetic pants.

I glance around at the houses here. Same shape as in the other places we've seen, only slightly more…taken care of, I guess you'd say. It's tough to put a finger on, but it's as if no one had ever lived in any of these houses. They look like models, or like a new neighbourhood often does when it's just been erected. Not a shingle out of place.

THE DISTANCE TRAVELLED

"Fog isn't so thick here," says Apple, "but the trolley ride to The Kitchen is really something else. It's like you're floating into another world. You can't see a single thing out the window. Nothing but white, and it always seems to be pressing against the trolley, like it's trying to get in. Never fails to creep me out." Apple shivers. "But hey, a gig's a gig, you know? And they sure pay better than Jimmy Crack Corn's Corn and Other Nibbly Bits."

"That shitty little shop still around?" I ask.

"Yeah, but under new management. They made me sing the company song every day before I stocked the shelves with cans of corn, corn, and more corn. I never did figure out what the 'other nibbly bits' were."

Apple shrugs, squints through the light fog. "Usually a trolley about every ten minutes, so we shouldn't have long to wait now."

Looking around at the houses again, I notice there are no lights on in any of them, and there's only the one street lamp above the trolley stop. "Not much for wasting electricity out here, are they?" I say.

214

"Everyone's probably at The Kitchen," Apple says. "It's a serious attraction for miles around."

"What's so special about it, besides the good food? Is there an amusement park inside it or something?"

"Nope, just good eats and *damn* fine entertainment," Apple says, winks at me.

Through the fog hovering about three feet off the ground, I see twin beams pierce the darkness.

"Thar she blows," PigBoy says. "I sure as hell hope once we get this fourth piece, something directs us to the fifth one, 'cause if not, I'm gonna shoot this place up—fuck the consequences." He lifts a hand, taps his jacket where his sawed-off rests inside.

We know PigBoy well enough by now not to even bother commenting on this idiotic remark.

I glance over at Tom as the trolley's headlights get brighter. I'll be damned if he hasn't gotten almost another foot taller. Got to be nearing twelve feet.

"Tom," I say. His eyes track me slowly. He seems to be swaying ever so slightly where he stands. "You're *sure* you can do this? You look a bit unsteady on your feet, big guy. You know?"

"No pai—"

"Don't even say it, Tom. Come on. You have to be feeling *some*thing. How can it not hurt? You're *stretching* inside and out."

Tom frowns, concentrating hard. He looks down at the ground, pinches his thin rodent lips tight, looks back up at me. "Honest, Stu. More honest than daylight is long. No pain. We're friends. No pain…" he says, shaking his head from side to side. Again, he tries on a smile, but there's too much gums, and his face muscles seem tight, stretching his face, like pigskin across a drum.

"There's still time to go home, Tom," I say.

Tom shakes his head faster. "For Gus. Seein' it through. I want to and I'm gonna. Gonna go for my friend."

A tear drops from one eyelid; Apple moves to comfort him, strokes the fur on his arm, presses it to her cheek. She tells him that it's going to be alright. Tom nods and says, "I know. I know."

When it comes free of the heavier fog farther down the line, the lights from the trolley blast us in the face like the sun coming out from behind a cloud. I shield my eyes with one arm, take a step back. The trolley does a slow loop on its track, using the entire width of the intersection to make the turn, comes back around in front of us.

The front doors open, four or five greys get out sluggishly, stumble past us in a daze, staring at the cobblestones. There's another door about mid-way through the trolley. It spews out several greys onto the street, but also a few more colourful characters. Young people, a few teenagers—Mexican jumping beans bouncing around once their feet hit the street. They laugh and punch each other in the shoulder. An old guy wearing a banana-yellow suit follows them out, waving his cane around and calling them 'shitfuckers.'

"Poor old bastard," I say. "Little punks probably stole his dentures or something."

The old banana picks up his pace, trying to corral one of the group's stragglers. Before he can snag the kid, though, he trips, falls to the stones. The kid bops around, just out of arm's reach, laughs hysterically.

"GODDAMN SHITFUCKERS!" the old guy roars, slumped against the street-side wall of a red brick house.

The kids disappear around a corner; the old man lifts himself to his feet with his cane. Cursing quietly to himself, he carries on down the street, lashes out at a garbage can near the curb—which, apparently, is also a 'goddamn shitfucker.'

Beating on old men in the street is exactly the kind of crap I used to do back on Upside. Only I would have probably stomped the old fuck into the ground, like our Alex in Kubrick's *A Clockwork Orange*. Soon as he hit the ground, I'd've had my boot shoved up his ass.

THE DISTANCE TRAVELLED

What a prick I was.

Am.

Some days I actually fool myself into believing that I don't deserve to be here. That all that crap I did was just having a little fun, and that the little girl I creamed, well, that just wasn't my fault. A complete accident, so why should I be punished?

But I know in my heart that I'm a selfish, hateful little shit. I deserve to be here just as much as anyone else. Maybe more so.

"Onward, me droogies," I say, snapping out of another of my pitiful reveries. "Let's go see what's cookin' in The Kitchen."

We board the trolley, along with the other five greys. It *pings* loudly twice.

And once again, we float away into the fog.

27

 see nothing more for another ten full minutes. There is only white outside. Occasionally, a small patch of darkness swirls by, but is quickly eclipsed by the thickest fog I've ever seen. It's like we're floating through a massive, puffy cloud. And Apple's right—it *does* seem as though it's trying to get in.

A shudder runs through me; when it hits my scalp, I close my eyes for a few seconds, re-open them to see that there's a red tinge to the fog now.

"Almost there, boys," Apple says, pulls out a compact, powders her cheeks and forehead.

The red in the fog slowly takes over the white. Then, like the curtains having been flung wide, the swirling soup vanishes, we break out of it, and there is only the insistent red pulse from the neon sign screaming the name of the most famous restaurant in the entire underworld:

HELL'S KITCHEN
Really, *Really* Hot Food!

I blink my eyes several times, trying to wash them of red, but it's impossible. The sign is so pervasive, nothing is left untouched by the broiling crimson hue.

The building itself is a giant cube, like a squat, evil Costco.

THE DISTANCE TRAVELLED

The trolley makes its loop, turns and slows to a stop in front of the building.

We wait for the greys to get off, then disembark after them.

These nothing-people—non-entities that could have been mistaken for coma victims had they not blinked every once in a while—suddenly turn into wild, excited children. On the bus, they were all bald heads, greying hair, sad, dead-dog looks in their eyes, but once they set foot on this section of red soil, they're jumping around like little kids, ooing and ahing and yelping and hopping and skipping and high-fiving and pointing at the roof, way up at the roof, where I follow their waggling little fingers and see—

"Sweet fancy Moses," I say, completely agog.

Squatting on the roof of Hell's Kitchen is a super-colossal inflatable Satan, strapped down with giant steel cables.

It's the classic representation of The Big Red Fella that you see everywhere—great black twisting horns, pointy goatee, flaming eyes, beet-red skin, pointy tail, pitchfork in one hand, and...

Oh.

A hand puppet on the other.

I tap Apple on the shoulder. "What the fuck is that?" I say, point to it.

"That's Satan," she says, looks at me funny. "What did you *think* it was?"

"Hey, thanks for the clarification, but I knew that. I meant, what the fuck is that bloody great...*thing* on his left hand?"

"Oh, that. That's Yoniga."

Tom looks up and smiles at the giant green shrunken head attached to Satan's hand. "Yoniga," he says, as though tasting a fine gourmet dish.

"Sounds like a kitchen appliance," I say.

PigBoy says, "Looks fucking *pissed off,* whatever it is, dude. Check it out."

Yoniga's lips are pulled back into a snarl, a double row of sharp teeth exposed. He's got an über-tight black ponytail, and his skin is stretched across his face like a fat thigh in spandex.

"That's one *ugly* motherfucker," PigBoy adds.

"Helps him cope," Apple says, lights a smoke, tosses me one. We walk toward the blazing red cube.

"Come again?"

"Yoniga helps The Big Red Fella cope. Gives him someone to talk to. At least that's the story."

"Story from where?" I say.

There's a gaggle of midgets hanging out in front of the main double-door entrance. They're playing hacky sack with a rotting baby pig's head. Other people stand around smoking, drinking, chewing on thick, burnt steaks. There are a few picnic tables scattered about.

"Story from The Kitchen," Apple says. "Not exactly the font of wisdom, I know, but why lie about something as fucked up as that?"

Fair enough.

We dodge the nearly fleshless baby pig's head as it arcs over us, push through the double doors.

Inside, it smells like a slaughterhouse. I inhale deeply, nearly choke on the fumes.

"Artificial," Apple says. "Just like the meat. Cooked up by hapless, Alzheimer-ridden scientists. But god*damn* if it doesn't taste good. Not exactly like the real thing—though I've nearly forgotten what that tastes like—but close enough that you eventually get used to all the other weird chemical aftertastes."

The interior of the place is pretty much like any Mickey D's back on Upside, except for the garish red furniture…and red plastic seats and red-painted walls and red floor and the staff's red uniforms and the shitty red abstract art hanging from red ropes in the red ceiling.

219

"Bit obvious, this, isn't it?" I say.

"Yeah, pretty touristy," Apple replies, "but it brings in the business. This is the place everyone wants to go when they first get to Hell. Except people like you, Stu—people who live in their own little worlds." She smiles, nudges me. But I don't feel like being nudged.

All this red—granted, it's at least different *shades* of red—is making me want to murder. Everything's too loud; there are too many people, too many voices all chattering at once.

"You get used to it after a while," Apple says.

But it sure as shit isn't something I'd *want* to get used to.

"How's the coffee here?" I ask, trying to take my mind off the colour scheme—or, rather, lack thereof. We spot an empty table, head toward it.

"Shit," Apple says. "Pure and utter. Thick as engine oil and twice as slick. But it's piping hot, boy, let me tell you that."

She manages to squeeze the slightest smile out of me. "Well, I'll have to get me a cup when I go up to order."

"They don't have any at the counter; you have to get it from the machine." She points to a decrepit black and brown coffee machine crammed into a corner a few feet away. People buy stuff from the surrounding candy and chip machines, but no one goes near the coffee machine.

I dig in my pocket for some change, walk over to where it sits forlornly in the corner, find a loonie, pop it in. A crumpled cup drops down, black sludge dribbles into it, and the machine chugs to a stop.

Lovely.

I walk back to the table, sit down, sip gingerly at the steaming liquid.

Tom wrenches himself into two of the four plastic non-adjustable seats at the table, sucking in his gut to make the fit. He lets his stomach expand again. The plastic table holds, but by the sounds of the creaking metal screws it's fastened together with, it doesn't hold by much.

Looking around the place, I see that the other difference from your average Mickey D's is the stage tucked into the far corner of the room. A divider wall separates the counter area from the stage and the extra seating in this part of the restaurant.

"That where you do your thing?" PigBoy asks Apple, nodding his head in the stage's general direction.

Just then, a portly man with all the sex appeal of a glistening slug approaches the table, leans on it, says in a helium-high voice through a mouthful of something brown and rancid-smelling, "Performin' tonight, honey?"

"Nah, Gerald," Apple says, moves her head as far away from his mouth as she can. "Here on pleasure, not business." She tries on a smile, but it doesn't stay on her face long.

"*Damn*," Gerald says, and lets out a long, lumpy fart, full of crisp little *brrrrap*s and round-shaped *fwuh-fwuh-fwuh-fwuh*s.

"Charming," Tom says, and it's such a non-Tom thing to say that I burst out laughing.

Gerald looks at me, clearly annoyed, then looks back to Apple. "Well, I'll see you around, darlin'," he says, and waddles back into the crowd.

"Are all your friends here that pleasant?" I ask.

"You wanna try the food, or what?" she says, ignoring my remark. She gets up from the table, heads toward the counter.

I get up after her, catch up. Turning around, I say, "Back in a sec; I'll grab you boys something, too, okay?"

Tom and PigBoy nod distractedly, their attention now focussed on the stage. Before I can see what they're looking at, I'm out of range, having now caught up to Apple.

We find a relatively short line, discuss our choices from the pathetically clichéd menu, which features, for instance, the Hell

In a Handbasket (combo deal where you get a bit of everything on the menu); the Hell's Half-Acre (giant slab of pseudo-meat with your choice of toppings); the Apocalypse Deluxe (four horseman-shaped pieces of battered mock-chicken with your choice of dipping sauce); Johnny Pentagram's Goat's Head Soup; and the Gehenna Greasy Spoon Special.

All combos are priced at $6.66.

How utterly clever.

There's an ad near the cash counter for the 'toy of the week.' It's a Yoniga head, whose teeth chatter when you wind it up.

Which reminds me—

"So what about this Yoniga head, Apple? What did you mean about it helping The Big Red Fella cope? Cope with what?"

"Stress," she says. "You don't think being the ruler of the most formidable realm in existence would be just a touch intense?"

I look around the room. The hacky-sacking midgets have moved indoors and are currently engaged in a scholarly game of Marco Polo, only they've incorporated the rapidly dissolving baby pig's head into it, 'Marco' throwing it at the 'Polo's as hard as he can when they call out.

Most formidable realm? I think it could be said that we've strayed a bit from our roots.

221

"There're a lot of decisions to be made," Apple continues. "Hell doesn't run itself, and I imagine it'd be hard enough running a country, but can you imagine having to keep tabs on the daily business of a whole plane of existence? As cruel as he is, you gotta admit that The Big Red Fella probably has a damn fine work ethic."

"Okay, I'll give you that. So what you're saying, then, is that talking to this little hand puppet calms him down, keeps him from blowing his top, losing his mind completely?"

"Something like that," Apple says. "I mean, everyone needs someone to talk to, right? And maybe TBRF doesn't feel he can be straight with anyone around him. Probably because they're so terrified of him and will do and say whatever they think he wants them to. So where do you go to get some straight answers about yourself? Where do you go to let it all out? Some people have loved ones; Satan has a shrunken-headed hand puppet. It all comes out in the wash."

"Yoniga was Dr. J. Taniguchi's idea."

"Who?"

"TBRF's therapist. Quite well-respected."

"Oh, naturally," I say.

"Not many therapists still practising down here," Apple says.

THE DISTANCE TRAVELLED

"A little too draining a profession, if you follow. And apparently Taniguchi's the cream of the crop, so TBRF hired him on as his exclusive shrink. Real tall fella. Wears a fedora. Nice, long, charcoal-grey trench coat. A right snappy dresser. And I should think so, considering who he works for."

As we move closer to the front of the line, she squints at the lit-up menu behind and above the counter. "You decided what you want yet?"

"Yeah, probably the Apocalypse Deluxe. I gotta see what those little horsemen look like. I mean, do they leave in the chicken bones for Death? And what about Famine? Isn't it a little hypocritical of him to allow his image to be used as a food item? Pestilence and War are alright, though, I suppose."

Apple looks at me sideways. "You know, you analyze things way too much. You should just enjoy stuff. Kick back and chill a little."

"Sure, easy for you to say. You're not the one mysterious ancient prophecies are being written about."

"This is true," she says. We're just about up to the counter when she adds, "So what do you think—couple of Hell In a Handbaskets for the other strapping young lads?"

"Sounds good to me."

222

The guy ahead of us—a rail-thin soggy-looking young man—picks up his tray, moves to the left. We step up to the counter. I look at the petite woman in the all-red outfit, a sizzling orange "HK" emblazoned on her breast pocket. Her nametag underneath reads, "Olivia."

"Hi, Olivia," I say, smiling. "Could I please get one Apocalypse Deluxe, two Hell In a—"

That's when my eyes settle on the chain around her neck. I follow the chain down to her shirt.

There's a triangular lump under it.

She smiles at me, tilts her head, awaiting the rest of my order. "Is there something wrong, sir?"

"Uh…shit. Um, this might sound a little odd, but could I see the rest of your necklace, please?"

She looks down at herself. "Why?"

"It's a long story, but I assure you, it's quite important."

Apple leans in close to my ear. "What are you *doing*?" she whispers.

I lean over, whisper back, "I think she has the fourth piece. Around her neck!"

Apple looks back to Olivia's chest. Her eyes widen. "No way."

"I know," I say. "Too easy."

"What are you guys talking about?" Olivia says, interrupting us. "*What* seems too easy, and why aren't you ordering food? This *is* a restaurant, you know. And there are other people in line, so—"

"Look, um, tell you what," I say. "You show me that necklace and we'll get out of the way. We won't even hold you up further by ordering."

"Oh, Jesus Christ, fine. Here. Here's the fucking necklace," she says and pulls it out of her shirt in a huff.

And there it is. The fourth piece. Hanging from a chain around this tiny girl's neck.

I feel such an attraction to it, I nearly reach over the counter to try to rip it right off her. But I stay my hand, clench it into a fist and force myself to keep it at my side.

"Okay...thanks," I say, my voice fluttery. I grab Apple by the arm, drag her away, through the lines and back toward our table. When we're clear of the lines, she whispers harshly in my ear, "What's *wrong* with you!? The piece was *right there*. Why didn't you take it!?"

"How do you propose I do that? Just reach over and grab it from her?"

"Yes!"

"No way. It could turn ugly real fast. Tiny as she is, Olivia's down here for a reason, too, and we'd be foolish to underestimate her—especially this close to finishing the puzzle. We need backup. We'll get Tom and PigBoy first."

223

She wrenches her arm free of my grip, stops dead in the middle of the restaurant. "Fuck that! We need to *get* that piece and get *moving*, Stu!"

And before I can stop her, she's marching back to the counter, pushing people aside.

I'm torn: Go back and get the boys, or try to stop her on my own, knowing she can kick my ass into next week without breaking a sweat?

So—as happens most times when I can't make a choice—I do nothing, just stand there weighing options, rendering myself completely useless.

Apple reaches the counter, puts the palms of her hands on it, leans forward. Standing on my tippytoes and looking around Apple's slight frame, I see Olivia clutching her chest where the triangle is. She does not look happy.

Finally making up my mind, I turn to go back to the table, get the guys, when Apple bellows, "I don't fucking CARE if it's an heirloom! You're giving it to me or I'm ripping off your head to get it!"

Wonderful. Here we go.

Looking around the people in line, trying to get a decent view of what's going on, I see that Apple has Olivia by the collar with both hands, has pulled her forward over the counter, and is grabbing at her chest madly, trying to rip the chain from the poor girl's neck.

"Give it here!" Apple roars in the smaller girl's face.

This is not the Apple I know. The Apple I know would have devised some creative plan to get the piece. I've no idea what's gotten into her.

Finally able to look away from the struggle, I actually get my feet moving in the opposite direction, toward the table where Tom and PigBoy wait. When I get past the divider wall, I see that they, along with several other tables, are standing, coming around the wall to see what all the commotion's about.

I nearly run smack into big Tom as he lurches around the wall. "She's okay? Okay? My girl, my girl is…?" Tom bends down, puts his hands on his knees, seems to be choking on the words.

"She's okay, Tom, don't worry. But we've got to—"

More screaming comes from the counter area, smacking sounds, flesh on flesh. People have formed a semi-circle to get a good look at the action. Of course, they're rooting for their favourite instead of trying to break it up. Not that I could expect much different, considering the venue.

224

"Come on," I say, head toward the counter.

Before we take more than three steps, there's a triumphant, "*Ha!*" and a pale, thin, black-clad arm shoots up out of the crowd. It's holding the fourth triangle. The crowd parts a little, and I see Olivia sitting slumped against the bottom part of the counter at Apple's feet. Her face is beaten and bruised; blood runs from both her nostrils.

We've just about reached them when I bump hard into a tall Asian man wearing a fedora and a long, grey trench coat. He drops the briefcase he's carrying. I mutter an apology.

The man says nothing, just picks up his briefcase and melts into the crowd.

A distinct feeling of urgency comes over me then, and I take larger strides to get to the girls, to the fourth triangle.

"Apple!" I shout, only a few feet from her now. She spins around, grins, holding the triangle aloft. She takes a step toward me…and I see it a split second before it happens.

One of the hacky-sacking midgets barrels through the crowd, utter glee on his face, his eyes fixed on the triangle. He runs head-long into Apple, taking her out at the knees. She yelps, falls sideways against a few of the people forming the loose semi-circle, drops the triangle to the floor.

The midget grabs it up, streaks away, heads right toward Tom, PigBoy, and me. I snatch at him, but he's too quick, squirts out of my arms. PigBoy gets a handful of collar, but nothing more. Then Tom brings down a mighty mitt. The midget sees it coming, and tosses the triangle high into the air, away from us, into the crowd, just as Tom's hand grasps his little head.

Tom, distracted by the triangle's arc of descent, lets the little bugger's head go. The midget kicks Tom in the shin, dives back into the growing crowd.

People can sense when shit is getting seriously out of control. They lock onto that, feed off it. That whole mob mentality thing is the farthest thing from bullshit. And it's twice as bad in Hell.

Someone catches the triangle, yells, "Hot potato!" and tosses it back up into the air. Someone else catches it, tosses it up again. Everyone's laughing and jostling each other, whooping and hollering, and it's a complete fucking zoo.

I put my head in my hands in disbelief that shit can get this retarded in what's supposed to be the darkest domain in creation.

When I raise my head again, out of the corner of my eye, I see the guy I bumped into. I notice him because he's the only person, besides us, not jumping around like a lunatic.

The triangle goes up, comes down, goes up, comes down. The Asian man in the fedora watches this for a moment, then very calmly sets his briefcase down on the ground, bends over, opens it up, gets down on one knee, and starts assembling what looks to be some sort of firearm.

I nudge PigBoy. "Hey, check it out."

PigBoy turns, looks, whistles low. "Goddamn."

The man finishes putting together a Thompson submachine gun. He points the weapon in the general direction of the crowd, and opens fire.

Bodies crumple everywhere. Blood shoots into the air from head wounds, splatters the floor from gut shots. The guy hoses the crowd like he's watering his lawn.

Apple instinctively ducks, hides next to Olivia, tucks herself as far under the counter's lip as she'll go.

PigBoy, Tom, and I have no need to hide, as we're apparently of no interest to the guy.

He runs out of ammo, slots another box clip in, and keeps spraying until every last person in the counter area is down, including the staff. A wisp of smoke rises from the barrel of his gun when he's done.

THE DISTANCE TRAVELLED

Blood paints the floor.

He stands expressionless, pointing the gun at no one.

People moan and curse about the pain. Those less seriously injured sit up and look at the gunman, shake their heads, make comments about only wanting to have some fun for chrissakes.

Scanning the carpet of bodies, I see the fourth triangle resting on the floor between two fat bikers.

"Can't fucking stand that shit," the Asian guy finally says.

Apple peeks out from under the counter's lip. Her brow is furrowed deep. "Taniguchi?"

"My friends call me Dr. J.," he says, lowering the Tommy. "Might wanna pick up your little triangle thingy before people heal enough to move around again."

Apple spots the triangle between the bikers, who still lie motionless. One of them twitches, but a decent-sized chunk of his head is missing, so it'll be a while yet before he even understands that he's *capable* of movement.

Apple picks her way over the bodies, accidentally stepping on various body parts, eliciting more complaints and grumbling. When she reaches the triangle, she bends down, picks it up, wipes it on her jeans, and puts it in her purse, which she'd somehow managed to keep on her shoulder throughout the whole ordeal.

The fourth piece securely in our possession, I feel the need for courtesy. "Uh...thanks," I say, nod my head in Taniguchi's direction.

"You're quite welcome," he says, bends down on one knee again, dismantles the Tommy, packs it back up in his briefcase, stands to his full height again, adjusts the brim of his fedora. "It amazes me the level of immaturity down here. In all my years as a therapist, it wasn't until I was sent here that I lost hope. I thought of all the places a person could straighten themselves out good and proper, it would be here. Because if you're here, it's because you've not adjusted particularly well to what your society deemed necessary of you. Why people don't want to change that is frankly beyond me. They choose instead to give up, to slip further into the darkness."

He sighs, hefts his briefcase, turns to go, sees that Tom's expression is still one of shock and incomprehension. He reads the look, says, "My big friend: I have no therapist to turn to. I listen to the Prince of Darkness whine and pule all day, every day. As I'm sure you know, he is obsessed with conquering Upside, reclaiming what he says is rightfully his. It's the same centuries-old story, and I'm sick of it. Yoniga helped—for a while—but he's assimilated the character into his own psyche now, given him his own needs and desires, troubles and concerns. And I now have to counsel them *both*. Mercifully, though, he hasn't shown up for his last few appointments, so I've strafed fewer public eating establishments than usual lately."

Taniguchi hangs his head for a moment, then looks up again, meets all our gazes, says, "Some people have therapy; I have my good friend Tommy." He pats his briefcase, turns on his heel, and walks out the double-doors. When he reaches the loop, he puts his briefcase down in the dirt, and waits patiently for the trolley to arrive.

Apple slips and slides over to us, arterial spray-patterns arced across her body. She hands the fourth piece over to me; I put the blood-slathered triangle in my pocket, pat it down, making sure it's in there securely.

We look from one to another searching for words, but there just aren't any.

"Well," I finally say, "that shitty coffee went right through me. I'm off to the loo. Be back shortly. If some of the kitchen staff heals before I return, grab me that Apocalypse Deluxe, will ya, Apple? We'll figure out what to do about finding the final piece of the puzzle when I get back. If the directions appear magically in the sky or something, be sure to come down and let me know, okay?"

I smirk as I turn away, scan for the washroom sign, spot it, head in that direction.

At the end of a long, dank, poorly lit, smelly hallway, two small neon signs pulse:

DEMONS

DEMONESSES

Again with the tourist-class originality.

Shaking my head, I push through the DEMONS door, switch on the light. Of the two long, fluorescent bulbs in the low ceiling, one of them pops and goes out, the other flickers erratically.

The place is grotty, with brown streaks on the walls, cracked mirrors, and smashed soap dispensers barely clinging to the tiles. Yellow water flows in a steady rivulet from the toilet in one of the stalls, dribbles down a drain hole in the middle of the room.

I move toward the urinal, unzip—

—and hear quiet singing coming from one of the stalls behind me.

28

he voice is familiar.

   Though I can't quite place it, I know I've heard it before—and recently, too. The song itself is unknown to me, though its cadence reminds me of a religious hymn.

I finish at the urinal, zip up, and walk toward the sinks to wash my hands.

I turn on one of the stained taps. Even though it's the 'hot' tap, no hot water comes out. It's cold—and I don't mean just tepid; it's *iceberg* cold. I'm only able to leave my hand under it for a few seconds at a time.

I dry my hands on my jeans as I take a few steps toward the singing stall, my booted footsteps echoing loudly in the small washroom. When I'm nearly to the door of the stall, the singing abruptly stops.

I'm silent, waiting for it to start up again, or for whomever's inside to come out.

The steady dripping of water replaces the singing.

I take a step back, look under the stall door, notice there're no feet visible, but this is clearly where the thin dribble of water going down the centre drain hole is coming from.

"Hello?" I say. "Are you alright in there?"

Nothing, except the steady *drip-drip* of water hitting something plastic.

I push the stall door. It gives way, swings open.

The Distance Travelled

And there's Cloud Guy, squatting on top of the toilet seat. His black dress shoes are positioned on either side of the seat, knees up to his chin, umbrella still in hand, forming a semi-circle of black vinyl close to his head.

A broken water pipe above the stall drips onto his umbrella, runs down the side of it, falls to the floor.

There's a big, lumpy cloth bag beside him, next to the toilet.

"Cloud Guy," I say. His crisp black suit is now rumpled, damp-looking, seeming to hang off his frame.

He just stares at me with watery eyes.

"What are you doing in here?" I say. "Why aren't you following the cloud around?"

"The cloud…" he says, his voice small, brittle as bird bones. "The cloud is…no longer functional."

I wait for him to say something else, but he just leaves his mouth hanging open. Licks his lips, looks back up at me.

"Do you remember me? From the gas station?" I ask. "From Gus's library steps? From the city streets a little while ago?" For some reason I cannot understand, I feel it very important that he remember me. It disturbed me the last time we met that he didn't.

"Yes," he says. "Yes, of course I remember you. Sometimes I do forget things, though. Sometimes quite important things, unfortunately. But you…you I remember."

He offers me a smile. His eyes soften, bushy eyebrows lifting a little. I hadn't noticed it before, having not had the calmness of moment to take note, but I'd originally thought him middle-aged; it's clear now that he must be in at least his late 70s.

I return his smile, ask, "What happened to the cloud, then? What do you mean it's no longer functional?"

"It fell to the street. Puffed and chugged trying to right itself before it fell, but it was no use. I think it ran out of rain. Ran out of something, anyway.

"When it hit the street, I went over to it, picked through its parts, rummaged around until I found its engine. It was charred black and still smoking. Dry as a bone."

"Did it ever take you somewhere you'd never been?" I ask.

"Yes, it did," he says, looks around him. "It brought me to this bathroom stall." He grins a little. "I scooped up all the broken bits of the cloud, put them in this bag," —with his free hand, he motions toward the cloth bag beside the toilet— "intent on rebuilding it, if I could. You see, I'm an inventor of sorts. I build things, create things, love to dissect their inner workings, come up with new ways for them to run. Smoother, more efficient. But I also love an old derelict. And some things should just be left to run their course, you know?

"This cloud, though—this cloud was the only machine of its kind in all of creation. As far as I know. I could very well be forgetting something, but I believe I only made one of these."

"You...wait a second, *you* made the cloud?" I say.

"I'm relatively certain, yes." Cloud Guy frowns, scratches his temple. With the other hand, he twirls his umbrella one full rotation; water flicks from its edges. "And sometimes I like to come back to something I've created and left to its own devices. I wait until it runs itself down, then I pick up the pieces, take it home, decide whether or not to rebuild it.

"I have this nagging feeling that I've created other things that need looking in on, but I am old and easily confused these days. And I always feel that I should be doing *more* than I do. Do you ever have that feeling?"

I think about it. "No," I say, after a moment's reflection. "I think I do enough. I think I do more than a lot of people. Maybe that's giving myself more credit than I deserve, but that's how I feel. I could be a far worse person than I am." And I'm unaware of where these words are coming from, because I've never really thought this way before. "I could choose to be a complete and utter piece of shit—because I know I have that in me. It would be the easiest thing to just give in to it. But I don't. I make the conscious decision to be better than I am."

231

Cloud Guy nods, but acts like what I've just said has worn him out completely. His eyelids droop, and he wavers on the toilet seat, shifting his weight from one foot to the other.

"I think," he says, "that I have forgotten so many things—so many incredibly important things—and I have no way of retrieving those memories. They only come back to me in quick flashes. Sometimes so quick that I can't quite latch onto them, and they drift away again. I am a sad old man, and have been forgotten by others as much as I have forgotten about them. I think it is what I deserve. And it is what *they* deserve, too. But," he says, brightening ever so slightly, sliding his tired eyes upward at the sound of the dripping pipe hitting his umbrella, "I remember you." His eyes come back down to meet mine. "And only the moment is important, because so much of life is made up of just such moments. If we can stay *in* those moments, understand their meanings, then we can perhaps prolong them, learn from them, and carry something forward *out* of them."

Cloud Guy's eyes flare open momentarily.

"Ah!" he says, groaning as he leans his free hand against the stall door, moves his feet off the toilet, stands upright, still holding the umbrella over his head. "That reminds me of something that perhaps you can help me with." He reaches down, opens up the big cloth bag with the cloud parts in it, pokes around inside. "I may be an old fool who's lost most of his memory, but there is a piece in this cloud that I'm quite certain I did not build into it."

He rummages around some more, finally brings out a rusted square. I remember the centrepiece of the drawing of the puzzle in the first book, and nearly fall over where I stand.

"Here it is," he says, turns it this way and that in the dim light. "It fits nowhere into the workings of this machine, so I can't for the life of me figure out how it could have gotten in there. Am I missing something? It's been bothering me ever since I found it."

Without a word, I reach into my pocket, pull out the other four pieces of the puzzle, spread them out in both my hands, and say, "I think, sir, that square might be the centrepiece to this puzzle I've been building."

My whole body shakes, my voice trembles, and sweat beads on my forehead.

Cloud Guy looks confused, picks up one of the pieces of the puzzle in my hands. He slots the wide end of one of the triangles into an edge of the square.

232

It fits perfectly, clicks securely into place.

My stomach turns over. The room spins, and I have to hold onto the stall door to keep myself from falling over.

Cloud Guy says, "Quite interesting." He takes the two pieces apart, and the room returns to its normal upright position. I frown, fill my lungs with air, puff my cheeks out, and exhale slowly, steadily.

"It would appear our meeting was more than mere coincidence, then, eh?" he says, smiles, places the two pieces back with the three others in my hands. I coil my fingers around them tightly, place the whole lot in my jacket pocket, and leave my hand inside, not wanting to let go, wanting to feel all five pieces against my skin for fear they'll disappear.

I look up at Cloud Guy, the weight of the situation crushing me, pushing me to move on, to get back upstairs, to find Barnes's place, to get the girl back.

To end the journey.

"Why did you come down here after your cloud crashed?" I ask, and for some reason, start to cry.

"Because," he says, "the cloud went down just outside this restaurant, and I'm a believer in fate, to a certain extent, so I thought that maybe it had led me here for a reason. So I came inside, looked around the place until my feet led me down here. I heard the dripping and knew I'd found it. I needed to find a place where I could use my umbrella. Can you understand that? I'm sorry if I'm not being very clear."

"Yes," I say, the tears streaming now, dripping from my chin. "I think I can."

We just look at each other for a few seconds, me crying, wiping my eyes, while he simply nods.

I feel the need stronger now than ever to be on my way. I put my hand out for Cloud Guy to shake. He does so, his grip firm, strong.

We exchange a final smile, then I back away, wiping my sleeve one more time across my eyes.

I raise a hand in farewell, leave him standing in the bathroom stall, umbrella overhead, the harsh lights flickering, revealing and then hiding him in turn.

I flick the light switch on my way out, leaving him in complete darkness.

Just as I found him.

«« —»»

At the end of the squalid little hallway, barely illuminated by the flashing neon washroom signs, is a rusted old payphone. I walk over to it, pick up the receiver, drop a quarter in the slot.

The dial tone hums in my ear.

I reach into my jeans pocket, pull out my notepad, reread the only thing written there:

SEEN GOD?
WE WANT TO KNOW!
(All calls are private and confidential)
1-800-SEEN-GOD

I dial the number.

Back up the stairs, feeling drained, feeling completely out of sorts. But still ready to go, ready to burn, ready to fucking rip it up, get to the end of this thing.

I push through the door leading back out into the main dining area. A few blood-spattered customers have gotten back up and are trying their luck at walking. For some, though, their heads are still too damaged to have grown back the parts of the brain that handle that task, and so are bumping into walls, knocking other people over, and just generally making nuisances of themselves.

I head toward our table, come out on the other side of the divider wall—

—and see Tom collapsed on the floor, his eyes rolled back in his head.

I rush over. Apple and PigBoy are kneeled at his side.

"What the fuck *happened*!?" I say when I reach them.

Apple is in tears, holding Tom's head in her lap. She strokes his forehead, her tears dripping onto the fur of his face.

PigBoy says, "We were just talking, watching the show up on the stage."

I remember that Taniguchi hadn't gone over to spray his death shower at the performers on this side of the divider wall.

"Angels," Apple says through her blubbering. "There were…angels on the stage. Dancing, singing religious hymns or something. Tom just kept saying 'lovely, so lovely,' and smiling and smiling and smiling.

"Then he just...." Apple's voice fades out and she stares blankly at nothing.

PigBoy finishes for her, saying, "Then he just looked straight up at the ceiling and fell over out of his chair. Hit his head pretty hard on the floor."

I look down and there's a fairly wide stream of blood coming from under Tom's head.

"Tom," I say, feeling my own tears coming. It can't end now. He can't leave us yet. We're on the last leg. So fucking close.

"Tom, can you hear me?" I put my hands on his cheeks, feel the face muscles stretch. He smiles. His eyes roll back down, search for me, find me, and focus.

"Lovely," he says. "So, so lovely, Stu. You gotta see 'em."

"Yeah, big guy, I know, I missed the show. I wish I'd been around for it. But someone I met in the washroom sidetracked me. It's a long story, but *I've got the fifth piece of the puzzle.* We just have to go to Barnes's now, get PigBoy's sister out of there and—"

"Too big," Tom says. "Just got too darned big." His thin lips curl into a small smile. His eyes don't share it.

"Yeah, Tom, I know, but we just gotta get you up and on your feet again, then—"

236

"Time," Tom says. His body kicks. Apple cries out, holds his head closer, strokes his cheeks. "Time is fun," our friend says. "Have it. Okay, Stu? And you promise me for my girl, you'll do that, right? Promise me for my girl that she'll—" His body kicks again, and it's the hardest thing I've ever had to watch in my entire life. "—always be safe with you around instead of me. Instead of my love, Stu, she—"

Tom's body bucks again. His face scrunches up, he cries out, tears spring from his eyes, and he looks up at Apple, his mouth open, trying to speak. A trickle of blood seeps from one corner of his mouth.

"Come on, Tom China, don't talk about this shit, don't you *dare* fucking talk about it!" I scream at him. "Just a little bit farther now and—"

But he doesn't hear a word I'm saying. "—instead of my love, she gets yours," he says, and raises a giant hand to Apple's face. Places it there, then lets it drop slowly to his side.

His eyelids droop and he struggles to keep them open. "So lovely," he says. "My lovely girl, like the angels in the show. Tom's girl is just like that…"

"Tom, come on, Tom, please don't do this, sit up, sit up," and the words stream from my mouth, "sit up and we'll go catch the trolley, we'll wait for the trolley and it'll be fun because please, Tom, please, please, sit up," and I'm pushing under him, trying to lift his back up, "come on now, Tom, let's—"

His eyes focus on me again, and he says, "No pain. No pain, Stu. It's okay. Remember? No pain." His eyelids start closing again; his body bucks once more.

I stop pushing on his back, blink a few times. I put my hands in one of his. Apple puts hers in his other one.

"That's right, Tom," I say. My body shakes and I want nothing more than to destroy everything around me.

This is not fair.

None of this is fair.

"No pain," I say, nodding, crying so hard my throat is stripped raw.

Tom's eyes close completely.

His body does not move.

Apple stops crying, hitches in a final sob, and just stares down at the body with wide, unblinking eyes.

PigBoy doesn't even look, just stares out the window, expressionless.

I stand up slowly, feel to make sure the five pieces of this fucking piece of shit puzzle are still in my pocket, and walk out of Hell's Kitchen.

Angry at PigBoy for asking me to help him get his sister back.

Angry at Oliver for his shit-fucking prophecy.

But most of all, angry at Cloud Guy.

For forgetting about us.

30

he trolley ride back to the city is in the heaviest
silence I've ever experienced. No one wants to
speak. No one wants to say a thing.

Apple is basically gone—PigBoy and I had to
maneuver her onto the trolley because she wouldn't
respond to anything we said.

I'm far past believing that this is worth the cost. Unless
PigBoy's sister is destined to grow up to be another Mother
Theresa, these scales are unbalanced in a distinctly obscene way.

I no longer care about being taken seriously, being in control,
being entrusted with leadership, or about being in charge of my
own destiny. All that matters now is seeing this through to its con-
clusion. There simply *is* nothing else.

And so I speak:

"So it looks like I might get to see my Camino again, huh?"

PigBoy nods, says, "I know how to get to Barnes's place
from the end of the subway line out near your place. Dante and
his pals always blindfolded me when we got near the house itself,
but they never bothered until we were nearly to the house's gate.
I think there's some kind of code to get in, but they never let me
see it—I guess in case I went around blabbing."

I have my arm around Apple. She's dead quiet. Not a peep
out of her. Hell, she barely blinks now.

We say nothing more for the rest of the fog-filled trolley ride.

Once off the trolley, we make our way to the closest subway

stop in this part of the city. I half expect to find Salinger there with his goons. If I did, I've no doubt in my mind that I'd just give up the ghost. Apple might try to convince me differently—and if she brought Tom China into the conversation, she just might succeed—but my first inclination would be to lay down arms and call it a day.

Life can beat you down pretty hard, but Death's blows are twice as heavy and truer by far.

But Salinger's goons aren't waiting at the subway entrance. We board the train, and it's an uneventful trip back out to the sticks.

The stuttering ticket-taker tells us to enjoy our stay in the "c-c-country," and we ascend the stairs that we descended what feels like a hundred and fifty years ago.

"Unreal," I say, as we take the top step of the staircase that leads back out in the stifling, raw heat of the day. "It's still fucking here."

My Camino sits exactly where I parked it. Only the hubcaps have been stolen.

"God," I say, feeling the tiniest bit of a boost from this completely unexpected bit of good fortune, "works in hilarious ways."

《《——》》

The Camino roars along the lakeshore again, this time heading in the opposite direction of the gas station, my house, and the flame pit.

The black rock on our right slowly gives way to grey, which soon turns to a deep, dark blue. The reflection of the lake glistens off it, hypnotizing.

The road, still of red dirt, is less pitted and I'm able to increase my speed. PigBoy tells me to turn left or right when we hit intersections. It's a good thing, too, because they all look the same to me.

We're silent for awhile: PigBoy just watching the different-coloured rock walls go by; me just listening to the familiar crunch of the gravel under my wheels; and Apple just staring out the window, not focussing on anything. She hasn't said a word since Tom died, and it doesn't look like she'll be ready to anytime soon.

PigBoy breaks the silence: "What do you think they're doing to her, Stu? I mean, what do you think they took her for in the first place?"

"Dunno," I say. "You never saw her any of the times you were with them, and they didn't mention her?"

"No. Not even once. There were times when I thought maybe I had everything wrong, that they didn't even take her in the first place, that she's at home right now, sitting on the floor cross-legged, watching her favourite TV shows, laughing, giggling behind her hand, embarrassed by her braces...."

"She used to sit on my lap when she was smaller and sing little songs—songs she'd learned at school, songs my grandparents had taught her. That always made me smile. Her voice always cracked on the higher notes and that would set us both laughing.

"She'd better be alright, Stu," he says, looks at me hard. "She just better fucking be alright."

"Well," I say, "our only hope is that this little Oliver prick actually had his visions straight. I mean, I know it'd be *way* too coincidental for it not to have a lot of truth to it, considering we've made it this far based on his riddles, but in any unfinished bit of business, there's always—*always*—room for error. And maybe his visions were all dead on...up until the very end. Maybe his prophetic little neurons misfired, his wires got crossed, and now we're on our way to Barnes's to rescue a blue-footed boobie instead of your sister."

That gets a little smile out of him. Gets one out of me, too.

"Nah," he says, "I think the prophecy is true and my sister will be at Barnes's house. But just because we get there and have the pieces of the puzzle doesn't mean we know what the fuck to do with them, you know?"

This is true.

Keeping my eyes on the road, I pull the puzzle pieces out of my jacket pocket, hand them to PigBoy, say, "Well, put them together and let's see what happens."

He takes the pieces, slots the triangles into the appropriate square edges, so that it looks like the drawing in the book. He slots the last one in.

And nothing happens.

"So, uh...what's it supposed to do?" PigBoy says.

"Not sure. Neither of the books said jack about this part of it, did they?"

"Don't think so, no."

"Apple," I say, turning my head to project my voice into the backseat, "you remember there being anything about how this doodad's supposed to work?"

Silence.

THE DISTANCE TRAVELLED

"Apple?"

She's a vegetable. Completely retreated inside herself. Which is wonderful news, considering we're down to three people now, and we're just getting to the hard part.

"Well," I say, "I guess we're back to flying by the seat of our pants again. Maybe there're some kind of magic words we're supposed to speak when we get to Barnes, and once we say them, he vanishes in a lovely little white puff of smoke."

"Yeah," says PigBoy, "I'm sure it'll be just that easy— assuming we even had magic words to speak."

I'm quiet again, then, just thinking things over. Trying to psych myself up for this battle we're going into with big fat fucking blinders on.

About ten minutes later, the dark blue of the rock wall tapers in closer to us, forms a short, narrow tunnel, then the walls suddenly spread wide and we shoot out into a sea of green grass.

I slam on the brakes, shocked. PigBoy braces himself against the dash. We screech to a halt, the only sound his raspy breathing and the Camino's rumble.

Grass. Green fucking grass. A whole bloody field of it.

Impossible.

"I'd forgotten about this," PigBoy says.

I turn my head, see the grass all around us reflected in his glasses.

242

I roll down my window, breathe in the air. It's so fresh I nearly choke on it. I roll the window back up, trying to wrap my head around the idea of *green grass*. I haven't seen anything even remotely resembling it in over thirty years.

"This is near Barnes's house," PigBoy continues. "House— yeah, right, who am I kidding? Mansion is more like it. Fucking place is gargantuan."

"It's close to here, you're sure?" I get a knot in my gut just thinking of going anywhere *near* Barnes, never mind venturing into his *house*.

"I'm sure, yeah." PigBoy looks out the windshield, shakes his head, the green from the vast field of long grass ahead shifting shades in the wind: light green to dark and back again in endless waves. "How we gonna do this, Stu?" he says.

I lean back, ask Apple for a cigarette, hoping against hope that the familiar habit will trigger something.

She doesn't move.

I reach back, fumble with her purse, find her smokes, pull them out, pop one from the pack, and return it.

I light the smoke using the car's lighter.

"Where is the place, exactly?" I ask PigBoy around the cigarette, squinting as I take an eye toke. "Down and to the right, beyond that hill, or straight ahead into the valley?"

"Straight ahead," PigBoy mutters. "Not far."

Looking out the windows on both sides of the car, the walls seem to have completely disappeared. Looking behind me, though, I see the place we've just come from, the tapered blue rock walls not much farther apart than the width of the Camino. Looking a bit closer, neck straining, I see that the ends of the walls aren't cleanly sheared off, but look to've been broken off, a messy zigzag pattern from top to bottom...or as near to the top as I can make out. The ceiling here is far higher than in the area we just came through.

It's like an extension. As though Barnes—or someone, anyway—built a wing onto this reach of Hell.

I wonder if The Big Red Fella even *knows* about this.

Smoke curls up through my vision. I nearly catch another eye toke, but manage to shut my lid in time. Viewing the scene with only one eye somehow loosens the knot in my stomach. I shut both eyes, then, and try to imagine PigBoy's sister safe and away from this place. Nothing she could have done in her ten years Upside would justify a life down here. Especially a life with Barnes.

243

As I open my eyes, I think of The Big Red Fella, wonder briefly again if he knows about any of this. For some reason, I think he has an obligation to make sure things like this don't happen—King of the Underworld or no. Gods, *any* gods, have a duty to protect their kingdom, to see that it's run properly and in accordance with the rules they themselves set.

Even chaos needs some sort of structure to keep it running smoothly.

"So, how we gonna do it?" PigBoy asks again, still looking straight ahead.

I puff on my smoke for a little while before answering, just savouring the rumble of the Camino. "I don't know," I say, stub the cigarette out in the ashtray, watch the final curl of smoke coil up and around the rearview mirror before dissipating. The knot in my stomach returns, all theological musings lost to the impending sense of dread.

"I have no fucking idea."

here's this sort of preternatural calm that sets in just before a soldier goes to battle. I don't think it makes him a better soldier, but it makes him more aware of his surroundings. Whether he has the presence of mind to react to this gift is something else entirely. As the Camino rumbles down into the valley, belching black smoke in its wake, I grip the steering wheel tightly and hope to be privy to this sense of calm.

My knot tries to come back, but I concentrate on the view through the cracked windshield. Then the mansion appears in the crack—set low in the valley, all turrets and extended gables, green shutters against red brick walls—the grounds of the place easily the size of a football field. An enormous, black, spiked gate protects the mansion—and yes, 'mansion' is by far a more appropriate term than 'house.'

As the road dips toward the entrance, I make out a key-code box, just like PigBoy said there might be.

Wonderful. Another hurdle we've no means of getting over. But maybe there's a number in one of Oliver's books—somewhere in all that apparently mindless scribbling—that we can try. Worth a shot, anyway.

I bring the Camino to a stop just in front of the gate, cut the engine.

"So, wanna be the first one to guess?" I ask PigBoy, grin a little, trying to lighten the mood.

The Distance Travelled

"Four, fifty-one, ninety-two, seventeen," he says, deadpan.

I frown, turn to look at him, and see it plain as day in his eyes. I sigh.

Then his fist slams into my head and smashes it through my window.

246

other*fucker*," I say when I regain consciousness.

I'm lying on a couch in a small, undecorated room. I sit up slowly, head throbbing, nebulae exploding behind my eyes.

All lies. I can't fucking believe it.

Everything.

A set-up.

Naturally, my first instinct is to get the hell out of here, try to figure things out from a safer distance. I stand up groggily, move to the door: locked. I turn around, spot the window, walk over to it, find that it's not only locked, but nailed shut.

Perfect.

I glance around, see a barstool in one corner of the tiny room, put two and two together, march over, grab it, and throw it through the window. Glass shatters; the stool bounces around on the lawn outside. I bunch my jacket's sleeve down to cover my hand, chip away at the remaining glass at the bottom of the window.

Then, with one leg out the window, the door behind me flings wide on its hinges. A very large gun is raised into view, attached to a very large arm, which, in turn, is attached to a very large man with long dreadlocks and a punk-as-fuck Sid Vicious sneer.

"Barnes," I whisper, just before the gun explodes and the bullet rips through my rib cage. My body slams into the window frame; the bright, flaring pain sends me dribbling down the wall like molasses.

"Stand up," Barnes barks.

I stand up slowly, one hand pressed against my shiny new bullet wound.

He raises his cannon again and ventilates my left thigh. I howl in pain. Then the cannon takes a chunk out of my other leg. Unable to stand, I collapse to the floor.

"You're gonna take us up into that hole," Barnes grates.

I roll over on my back, trying to stem the flow of blood from my three gunshot wounds, and look up into his snarling face. It's the first time I've seen him this close-up. He's actually kinda handsome.

"What hole?" I ask.

He levels the gun at my face.

"The fucking pig hole, retard."

The bullet holes are healing; I feel the skin contracting, sealing still-smoking bits of lead into my body. The pain is pretty intense, but I struggle to stand. I gain my feet, fall again, land on my ass, and decide to settle for the floor view of the cannon.

"You're gonna fulfill Oliver's prophecy, lead us up into Upside."

"What are you talking about, Barnes?" I say, trying to buy time so I can piece this shit together. "Look, can you at least help me up, so I can stand like a man and talk to you face-to-face?"

Barnes grins.

Uh-oh.

248

He quickly reloads his gun, squats on his haunches, takes aim at my chest, and pulls the trigger five times in rapid succession, blowing me across the room and against the wall.

Using the wall for support, I stand up, my chest feeling like a thousand red-hot pokers are pistoning in and out of it. I open my mouth to speak, choke on blood, spit it out, wipe it off with a sleeve, try again—more blood, more wiping. Third attempt, I manage to croak out my appreciation: "Thanks."

Then PigBoy and Dante walk into the room—Apple in tow.

"Apple, are you okay?" I say. "Have they hurt you? Are you—"

PigBoy cuts me off. "You're a gullible son of a bitch, you know that?"

Dante reaches into Apple's black purse, idly flips through the three books he finds there.

Three books.

Holy Mother of God. What the fuck?

Dante grins at me. "Oh, oh, kill my daddy for me," he says, mocking his earlier request. "You bought the whole fucking thing, you dumbass."

My mind reels and spins. I feel sick to my stomach.

"What the hell are you all *talking* about!?" I yell, my frustration boiling over.

PigBoy very calmly takes the third book from Dante's hands, walks over to me, opens the book up, leafs through it casually, holds it so I can see the pages as they flip by. "There are three books, Stu," he says. "*Three* books to Oliver's prophecies." He grins at me, his mouth nothing but teeth.

I try to concentrate, piece it together in my head, but the pain from the eight hunks of lead embedded deep in my body is too much. I can't grasp any concepts, can't staple them together to come up with anything that makes sense.

I watch as he shows me the pages to the third book. I see the puzzle, but it's been folded up into a pyramid. That math class flash I had earlier when I first saw the image comes back to me, and it makes sense. The original image was a net of this image. You fold up the tips of the triangles and it forms a closed pyramid.

He continues flipping the pages, and when he gets near the end, I see an image of someone half-in, half-out of a hole, arms to his sides, pulling himself up through it. There are grain sacks in the background, and a half-drawn pig snout off to one side.

I look at the face of the man coming up through the hole— and it's me.

"So you see," PigBoy continues, "it would seem you're destined to lead the Hordes of Hell into Upside, Stu. And we couldn't very well just tell you that, now could we? Not with you being such a fucking pansy. You'd never have signed on willingly, and we couldn't have forced you to do it, since the only real threat we'd have was killing you, which, of course, we couldn't do if we wanted the prophecy fulfilled. QED."

He closes the book and walks back to stand beside Dante and Apple.

"But where's the third book from? I don't understand how—"

"Apple," PigBoy says. Just the one word.

I look at her. Her face is like cookie dough. Pale, sagging. Defeated doesn't even begin to describe her expression.

I just stand there, looking confused.

"Lemme give ya the Scooby Doo run-down, okay?" PigBoy says, "And let's get this goddamn show on the road already. Now listen up, 'cause I'm only saying this shit once:

"Me and my boys were just shooting by in our buggy when we saw these pigs dropping out of the ceiling, falling into the flame pit. We stopped, checked it out, came back home, told Dad—"

"He's *your* father, too?" I ask.

"Yeah, we're all one big happy fucking family, now shut up and listen:

"Came home, told dad. Dad says well, holy shit, there's a way into Upside, a way to rule again. The Big Red Fella will crap his drawers when he hears the news, so let's look into this, pronto. We looked into it, did some reading, found out about this Oliver kid's prophecy. Tracked down a list of people who had copies of the books. Gus was one of them, him and his secret little library. But not so secret once you start waving wads of cash in people's faces.

"So we paid a little visit to young Miss Appleton here, told her about the hole, the prophecy, the whole thing, and said that if she helped us get at those three books, we'd give her anything she wanted. First words out of her mouth were all about her boyfriend, Tom, and how he was dying and shit, and how if we could somehow help him, cure him even, then she'd give us the books, help dupe you dumb fuckers into embarking on this journey. We told her The Big Red Fella's got several HellRats on staff and that some of them had the same disease her Tom has, and we could cure it in no time—if she helped us out.

"So she sold you all down the river for her boyfriend—who's dead as Elvis now anyway." PigBoy laughs loud and hard, actually goes so far as to slap his thigh.

"Thing is, and even she didn't know this till now: There never *was* any cure. It was a flaming pile of bullshit."

I look over at Apple. Her sagging features sag even more at PigBoy's words. Her legs give out from under her. She crumples, curls up into a ball, and cries quietly, shaking her head from side-to-side gently.

PigBoy chuckles some more, turns back to me. "So we checked out these books, saw that you were the one who had to make it happen. Figured we'd get the ball rollin', you know? Miss Appleton here, she gave us the third book, but kept the first two on the shelf—and clumsy old Tom just made my 'finding' it all the more believable.

"Doing our homework, finding out how you mashed that little girl into the road Upside, we cooked up the little sister drama and voila, motherfucker—here you are, all five pieces in your little pocket and under my daddy's gun to do precisely as we say."

Questions scramble around in my mind like headless chickens. Dead, but unaware of it. I latch onto one, trying to poke a hole in this, wishing desperately for something that makes it all untrue.

"But what about Salinger coming after us, finding us at the church and—"

"Set-up," PigBoy says. "We had to make you believe the authorities were after you, or you might get suspicious."

"But Muriel—"

"Set-up," PigBoy says again. "We got to her first, threatened her with the destruction of her precious little church and everyone in it, unless she went along."

"What about me beaning you with the drill, knocking you out of the buggy—"

"If you'd missed, I'd've just acted like I lost my balance and fallen out of the buggy."

I cast my eyes down, searching, searching.

"But when Apple attacked Salinger—"

"Set," PigBoy says, takes a step closer, mere inches from my face. "Up."

I close my eyes, lower my head.

"Yeah, and we would have gotten away with it, too, if it weren't for you meddling kids!" Dante says, busts out laughing.

All I can think is how badly I want to die. I want Barnes to blow my stupid fucking head right off my shoulders. But I know that no matter what happens, he won't do that. He *can't* do that. I have to do this now. I have to go through with it. There's no choice. I'm crippled, hobbled. I can stand, but only just. There's no way I could escape. I wouldn't get any farther than the front gate before they caught up to me—assuming that I could even come up with some distraction to give me enough time to get *that* far.

251

It's done.

I'm fucked.

Portnoy Spavin's words float back to me, through time, through memory: "I can't let it happen! You'll destroy everything!"

He was trying to stop this from happening. He knew all along what the full prophecy was.

PigBoy turns to Apple. "Get up, girly," he says. "We don't need you any more. Get the fuck out."

Apple picks herself slowly off the floor, hitching in sobs. She doesn't bother to wipe the tears from her eyes. She shuffles toward the door, puts a trembling hand on the knob, turns around, looks at me, searches my face for something. Compassion. Forgiveness. Understanding. Anger. Hate. Disgust. Anything.

I give her nothing.

I just continue to stare at her, nothing-faced, until she drops her eyes, pulls the door open, and walks through, closes it behind her softly.

Her footsteps fade.

And finally disappear.

Tom will haunt you, I think. *Tom China will haunt you and you'll never be free of him.*

As I stand there swaying, a sort of glee builds up in me. I feel disconnected, punchy, as though I've pulled my brainstem out, unplugged myself.

A thought pops into my head. Something that doesn't add up.

"How do you know that you guys can't just go up that hole yourselves? Fuck the prophecy," I say. "Piss on it. Why not just head on up there yourselves? If I can go through, why not you? Did one of you try and fail or something? Is that what prompted you to go digging around in the first place, trying to find information on the hole?"

Barnes and PigBoy glance at each other quickly. Something passes between them. Then Barnes says, "We're not going to tell you that."

"Why not?"

"It's too embarrassing," says PigBoy. Another furtive glance at Pops.

"What do you mean 'embarrassing'?"

"Too many questions!" barks Barnes.

"Fuckin' A," says Dante.

"Tell me or I won't help you," I say. After all, what do I have to lose? If I hold all the cards, then it's up to me when I decide to play them, right?

Barnes and PigBoy exchange one more quick glance, nod to each other, then a goodly portion of the left side of my face gets blasted out the back of my head.

he next thing I see is the interior of a car. A view from the backseat.

I look around out of my one good eye.

It's *my* car. They've kidnapped me using my own fucking car.

PigBoy and Barnes are in the front seat. No one beside me back here. Guess Dante decided to round up the boys and go out pigging again.

Red walls streak by as we head toward the hole—

—and that's when it hits me in a sudden flash of insight: the answer to the question I asked just before lead carved a tunnel through my skull.

Red walls.

Red Fella.

Holy fuck.

"The Big Red Fella's the one that failed at getting through the hole, isn't he?" I sit up painfully, my mouth having healed just enough for me to form words. Garbled-sounding, like I have rocks in my cheeks.

I stare cyclopean at Barnes, trying to gauge his reaction. His face goes ashen in the rearview mirror. The kind of look you might get if someone had asked you if you'd shit yourself, and you had.

He turns around, dreads whipping, says, "Sit back and shut your hole," then faces front again, motionless except for tiny corrections in the course of the Camino as we speed along the lakeshore.

I smile and sit back slowly.

Satan, God of Darkness, Emperor of Evil, Lord of the Flies, and all manner of other neato epithets, is dead. Must be, or else why the touchiness?

It's tough to suppress a giggle.

"How'd he go, Barnes?" I say, taunting him. "Messy, was it?"

"Shut up. Just shut up, alright?"

Barnes has a lump in his throat. I hear it in his voice, wavering and cracking.

I decide to press this button for all I'm worth, start thinking up great questions to ask that'll get Barnes to absolutely blow his top, maybe empty his gun into me again, give me sweet oblivion—at least for a little while.

But then the sight of my house going by distracts me.

I see the sheet metal still half-pinned up, the bottom curled in from where the Boo Berry-eating pig blew through.

I think of my cupboards full of Irish Cream, and wish Barnes would just stop the car, let me out, so I can go brew up a pot, unwind, watch some TV. Forget about everything.

254

I sniff, wipe the single tear of remembrance from my single eye, and say, "How do you propose to get through, anyway, Barnes? You think hanging off my legs as I jump through is gonna do it? How do you know you still won't die once the portal senses your non-prophetic, evil little head?"

"Well, that's a chance I'm willing to take, Stuart," Barnes says.

My house fades away behind us, and I ask, "Why didn't The Big Red Fella make *you* go, Barnes? Why'd he risk it himself?"

Barnes turns around. Tears actually glisten on his eyelids. "I tried to make him let me go in his place, but he wouldn't have it. He insisted on being the one to go through. He was sure it was his ticket back Upstairs. And I don't just mean Upside, you know? I mean Up*stairs*. I tried to reason with him, but he was adamant. And then even before half of his body was up the hole—"

Barnes chokes back tears, hitches in a sob.

"—he just imploded. Folded in on himself and winked out like a tiny, tiny Christmas light."

Was this Barnes saying this? Torture-you-till-you-shit-yourself Barnes? Stretch-you-till-you-feel-your-eyeballs-being-dragged-down-to-your-balls Barnes? Holy crap.

He turns away, unable to go on. I fully expect him to put the back of his hand to his forehead and faint.

"Jesus, Barnes. What's with all the waterworks? You're acting like you two were lovers or something," I say.

He says nothing, but weeps a little bit heavier at my words.

Good Lord. They *were* lovers.

I wonder distractedly how Yoniga felt about the arrangement.

"So, anyway," I say, shaking my head quickly, intent on breaking the surrealism of the moment, and eager to just get this shit over with, "if you're willing to take the chance, then fine, let's get to it. No point wasting time, you know? Bring on the fucking Apocalypse."

Barnes nods slowly, head lowered. He wipes his leather jacket's sleeve across his eyes and sniffles again.

It's getting hard to talk now; my face is starting to heal around my mouth, bunching up the flayed muscles in reparation. Part of my blasted eye is reforming, too. Trickles of colour seep into my brain.

I feel sleep tugging at my eyelid, so I close it, feel muscles and flesh bend and pull together on the other side of my face.

I am blessedly unconscious for the rest of the ride to the hole.

ext thing I'm aware of, someone's slapping my face hard. I look around me. We're up on the ledge of the flame-pit, the pig hole somewhere just above our heads. Barnes's handsome face swims into focus, hands me the puzzle, the triangles folded up to form the pyramid depicted in the third book. I take it in my morning hands, barely able to keep hold of the thing.

I place it in my jacket pocket.

"Right, now get the fuck up," Barnes says, yanks me to my feet. He and PigBoy each take an arm and a leg, lift me up high, get their grubby mitts far enough under my ass to shove me though the hole. Once Barnes has a relatively firm hold on my butt cheeks, PigBoy stands to the side of his father, trying to hold me vertical so I fit through.

"Stop squirming!" Barnes shouts at me, one hand slipping and glancing off my balls as he holds me up with just one of his massive hands. He fiddles around in his coat pocket for a second, then I feel both hands return. I glance down quickly and see that Barnes now has two giant guns—as well as my ass—in his hands.

"Jesus Christ, Barnes!" I yell, closing my one-and-a-half eyes tight, waiting for the blast that will flense my scrotum from my torso. "Put down the guns!"

"Fuck it," he says, grunting. He squats low, tells PigBoy to grab me under the arms and hold tight, then counts, "One, two—THREE!" They both heave and fling me upward. I don't even have time to soundly curse them out before my head pops out into Upside. I *do*, however, have just enough time to lash out once more with one of my legs.

I boot PigBoy squarely in the chest, send him flailing over the edge and down. There's a slight *woof* from below as his body is engulfed in flame.

And I couldn't be more pleased with my effort.

Popping into Upside, both my head and arms completely through—fulfilling to a 'T' young Oliver's ultimate vision of me—I open my eyes…and see that my sudden arrival has garnered the attention of about twenty distinctly unhappy-looking pot-bellied pigs. Some snuffle, some just narrow their beady eyes at me. But in either case, the message is the same: Get out of our barn before we crush your skull.

And these pigs are BIG. They can do it.

"Keep *pushing!*" I roar down into the hole, sweat exploding from every pore I have. "*Push, goddamnit! PUUUUUSH!*"

At my bellowing, the pigs take their cue and rush me. Just then, though, Barnes gives one final push, and all but my legs below the knees come through. I feel something drag on me, hands wrap tightly around my feet, something solid, metal, digging into my anklebones. But I can't think about it anymore.

258

I scramble for purchase in the muddy ground around me, trying to pull myself up. As I lean over, groaning at the added weight beneath me, the first pig butts heads with me, knocking me to one side, blood cascading down the side of my face. More hooves scramble at me, teeth sink in, snuffling and squealing—a blurry montage of angry pink balloons.

"Fucking hell!" I roar, the familiar curse words giving me the last bit of strength I need to pull myself completely out of the hole.

Then, the balloons pop.

All around me, sprays of pink, sliced flesh, and gouts of dark red blood erupt. Pained squeals, the roaring of a man, and the firing of that man's weapons envelop my senses. I cover my head with my hands, face in mud and pig shit.

When the firing, yelling, squealing, snuffling, and squirming has finally stopped, all twenty-odd pigs lay silent—and the torso of a very angry, dreadlocked monster of a man pokes out of the earth, smoking guns at the end of his thigh-thick arms.

Pig crap smothering my nose, I watch his huge barrel-chest expand and contract like bellows—breathing not out of need for oxygen, but out of sheer *anger*.

Bracing himself, palms down in the mud and shit, Barnes

turns himself around to face me. Tears stream down his cheeks; bits of mottled pig flesh and splashes of blood spatter his chest and face. Some of it drips from the ends of his dreads.

I squint at Barnes, only able to see out of one eye again, an errant hoof or tooth having sliced the other, half-formed one.

"You killed my boy," Barnes says.

I simply nod. It's all I can do.

I know he's going to shoot me in the face again. Only this time, I'm Upside. Bullets kill people up here.

I smile, close my eyes, blood pounding in my ears, and simply wait for the cannon's final skull-shattering report.

It's then that I hear the distinct shuttling of a shotgun shell behind me. I turn my head to see the pig farmer, come to finally catch whoever's been stealing his pigs all this time. His shotgun is aimed at Barnes's head.

I just lay there and look at the farmer, barely propped up on one quivering elbow.

That's when the finished puzzle drops out of my pocket into the mud and shit, jostled out by my rubbery elbow. When it hits the ground, it lights up from the inside, an orange glow seeping out from the sides of the folded-up triangles.

It floats into the air, opening up slowly like a blossoming flower, filling the entire barn with its glow.

Barnes's guns explode.

The farmer's shotgun erupts, scattering shrapnel through the air.

Barnes's bullets turn my throat into a quick-spray clump of blood and gristle.

The farmer's shot wrenches Barnes's head from his shoulders, splatters it across a grain sack behind him. He crumples forward and leaks life into the mud and shit, guns limp, spent, short squiggles of smoke rising from the barrels.

I do pretty much the same, only in a more comfortable position, lying on my side.

As darkness creeps into my peripheral vision, swallowing the brilliant orange light with every passing second, I see the opened puzzle hovering over Barnes's headless corpse. It settles down into the stump of his neck, there's a blinding white flash, and just before the encroaching black swallows everything, I hear the farmer above and behind me mutter, "Fucking hell."

Bastard stole my line.

261

EPILOGUE

t's not so bad here.

Nicer house. Moderate temperature, too. No need for air conditioners; no need for heaters. I don't even have to go out and get food and coffee anymore. I wake up and my cupboards and fridge are replenished, like in a video game when you hit Reset.

The only thing that's disconcerting is the utter blackness outside my kitchen window. It's not even a nighttime kind of blackness, you know? Just emptiness, as if nothing exists outside these walls.

And maybe nothing does.

Maybe this is limbo, or purgatory. I've no clue, but it's not Heaven, I know that. I'm sure a guy would *know* when he was in heaven…wouldn't he?

Ah, hell, whatever. There're no airborne pigs sitting at my kitchen table eating my Boo Berry, so it's definitely a step up.

I just wish I knew the answers to some questions. For instance, I wonder if Barnes is still stuck in that hole, his headless corpse acting as some kind of cosmic stopper, the fireworks from that pyramid puzzle sort of gluing him in, forever preventing the hordes of Hell from invading the land of the living. Was that the point of Oliver's prophecy? If so, then it's a damn good thing Portnoy didn't stop us, after all. The poor fella just misunderstood, same as PigBoy and Barnes.

Everyone thought the third book showed me leading the

charge for Hell on Earth, but it looks like Oliver's vision wasn't as clear as it might have been. Sure, he drew me coming out of that hole, and sure enough I popped straight up through it. But then, so did Barnes, and he wasn't in the book. Neither was the farmer that blew his giant head clean across the barn. So maybe even Oliver didn't know. Maybe he thought he *was* prophesying the end of the natural world.

But someone else just had other designs.

Cloud Guy comes to mind, but I'm not sure if he had the mental faculties left to do something so cunning. But maybe he did—set the whole thing in motion, then just forgot about it, like he's done with so many other things.

Was I right in calling the phone number in my jeans pocket? Did I really see who I think I saw?

I was perfectly content before to think that no one ran the show, that maybe The Big Red fella just snatched the bad guys when they died, and J. C. took the good ones Upstairs. But after all that's happened—and after having been placed here instead of back at my old address down under—I'm inclined to think that there must be some sort of governing body or bodies. So it logically follows that there's a Rulebook.

264

I wonder sometimes who wrote it, and I wonder if their name is on the cover.

But then, I pour myself another cup of Irish Cream, let the steam rise up my nostrils, and it all fades away. The questions, the confusion, all of it—gone. I'm lost in the void outside again.

Maybe that's what the nothingness is for.

I set my coffee down next to the sink on the kitchen counter, walk past the table, past the fridge, over to the front door.

Because I have to know.

I put my hand on the cold doorknob. Twist it, pull the door open.

Stare out into the black.

My stomach clenches, my eyes water. There's not even a porch to step out onto. Nothing to ease me into it—just an immediate drop into nothingness.

I poke my foot out in front of me, dip it down, like I'm testing the temperature of a pool. My boot meets solid ground.

Smooth. Slippery. Like black ice.

I take a step out, eyes shut tight, still holding onto the doorframe with one hand. I don't drop and spin to my death. I don't vanish in a theatrical puff of smoke. I just stand, and look out into the complete absence of light.

One more step. My hand falls away from the door. Another

step, then another. Five steps, ten steps, then I look behind me, see the soft glow of the kitchen light filtering out into the darkness, watch it get swallowed, sucked down and away.

Fifteen, twenty steps, and it gets colder the farther I go. Thirty steps and my house is half the size, and dwindling.

At forty steps, I stop, stand in the cold, shivering.

One thought: *How easy would it be to just keep walking?*

And my feet want to do it. My body urges me on, welcomes the cold after thirty years of withering, bone-baking heat.

Very easy, I think, and shiver again.

But then I think of Tom China. My friend, dead, disappeared. I think of what he used to say: "Time is fun. Have it."

And I don't see Tom's ghost hovering in front of me, don't hear his voice echoing in my head. I hear the thought like it's my own, said in my own voice.

I turn around, look at my small, dimly lit house in the distance. I think of my coffee on the kitchen counter. The feel of the mug, warm between my hands.

And that's all it takes.

I walk back. Forty steps.

Moving through the front door, I close it behind me. Walk past the fridge, past the table, back to the counter.

I pick the mug up between my hands, smile, close my eyes, relax, and let the Irish Cream work its magic.

Steam from my coffee swirls through my mind, and I wonder: Is it the journey that really counts, not the destination? Is that all the explanation I need? Is the distance travelled enough?

I didn't used to think so, but now I might.

I miss Gus and Tom and wish they were here with me. I even miss Apple, because she did what she did out of love.

And there's something to be said for that.

I put one hand on the cold windowpane, set my coffee down, put the other hand next to it.

Nothing. I feel nothing.

Just the inky dark and the distance travelled.

photo courtesy of Sandra Kasturi

Brett Alexander Savory is the Bram Stoker Award-winning Editor-in-Chief of *ChiZine: Treatments of Light and Shade in Words*, is a Developmental Editor at Scholastic Canada, has had over 40 stories published, written two novels—*In and Down* and *The Distance Travelled*—and writes for *Rue Morgue Magazine*.

In the works are a third novel, *Running Beneath the Skin*, and a dark comic book series with artist Homeros Gilani. A benefit anthology he co-edited with M. W. Anderson called *The Last Pentacle of the Sun: Writings in Support of the West Memphis Three* was released in 2004 through Arsenal Pulp Press.

When he's not writing, reading, or editing, he plays drums for the southern-tinged hard rock band The Diablo Red, whose debut album, *Rojos*, was released in late 2005. He can be reached through his website:

http://brettsavory.com